BENEATH A STORMY SKY

ANNEMARIE BREAR

ALSO BY ANNEMARIE BREAR

<u>Historical</u>

Kitty McKenzie

Kitty McKenzie's Land

Southern Sons

To Gain What's Lost

Isabelle's Choice

Nicola's Virtue

Aurora's Pride

Grace's Courage

Eden's Conflict

Catrina's Return

Where Rainbow's End

Broken Hero

The Promise of Tomorrow

The Slum Angel

The Market Stall Girl

The Tobacconist's Wife

Marsh Saga series

Millie

Christmas at the Chateau

Prue

Cece

<u>Contemporary</u>

Long Distance Love

Hooked on You

Where Dragonflies Hover (Dual Timeline)

Short Stories

A New Dawn

Art of Desire

What He Taught Her

BENEATH A STORMY SKY

AnneMarie Brear

To all those pioneer women

CHAPTER 1

Off the southern coast of West Australia, December 1879.

LOUISA BRACED herself against the cabin wall as the ship swayed and groaned under the onslaught of the storm. The sewing needle pricked her finger and she cursed softly, sucking the blood away. The tiny room was lit by one single lantern which swung dangerously on the hook by the bed. Rain pitted against the small window. She stared at the wind tossed waves in the moonlight.

Her stomach rebelled at the rough motion, her Christmas dinner sitting heavy. She fought against being sick, not wanting to bring up the wonderful roast chicken and vegetables the cook had served them hours before. After a long voyage across the immense span of the South Atlantic and Indian oceans, it had been exciting to make port at Fremantle on the western side of Australia a few days ago. The ship had taken on fresh food and water for the last part of the voyage. She and the other passengers had disembarked and strolled around the town for the day, buying fruit and shopping for items they'd run out of on the long journey from England.

Louisa's first experience of Australia spurred her imagination. The sunshine, the rustic buildings, the strange gangly trees called eucalyptus and her first site of native aboriginals were all fascinating. She asked her brother David so many questions, but despite the books they had read about the country before leaving England, they still did not know enough.

Some of the local people had done their best to answer what they could as they toured the wide dirt streets of Fremantle. David insisted on buying them tea and cakes and they'd savoured every mouthful. Regretfully, Louisa had left the township and boarded the cramped ship with her head full of information. She was eager to arrive in Sydney and begin their new life.

A knock on her cabin door brought her head up and she put her sewing aside. Although dressed in her nightgown and robe, she knew it would only be her brother knocking. 'Come in.'

David entered, dwarfing the space which was meant for only one person. He held onto the door as the ship tilted alarmingly. 'You need to get dressed. Quick as you can.' His pale face showed a mixture of worry and fear.

'Why?' Even as she asked, she was pulling a dark blue skirt and bodice out of the narrow wardrobe built at the end of her equally narrow bed.

'I've just come from the saloon where Captain Tanner and his First Mate were talking to Mr Hammersmith. Captain Tanner wants everyone ready in case we have to abandon ship.'

Her hands stilled in mid-air, then she grabbed onto the bed as the ship tossed to the other side. The lantern swung against the wall with a crack. 'Abandon ship? Surely not?'

David spread his legs apart to keep upright. 'We're taking on water, apparently. The storm doesn't look like it's going to ease any time soon and Captain Tanner wants us all to be prepared.'

'Nothing will come of it, will it? I mean, we had a storm off the coast of Africa and weathered it just fine.' She found under-garments, stockings and shoes while stumbling around like someone drunk.

'This storm is worse than the previous one we had, and it's blowing us towards land. Captain Tanner believes if we do ride out the storm, we can limp into Albany and make repairs.' David looked over his shoulder as one of the passengers ran past him.

'Albany?' Louisa asked, a tremor in her voice.

'A small coastal town a couple of days' sail from here. The captain says it has a good harbour. We just have to make it there.' David ran his hand through his brown hair. He looked tired, strained. 'I'll leave you to dress and come back for you in five minutes. Please hurry.'

She nodded and stood staring at the door long after he closed it. Abandon ship? It seemed a little dramatic, surely? Glancing out of the window, the rain still lashed down and the waves took the ship up high before crashing it back into the grey swirling water. She banged her hip trying to dress, then was sent flying across the floor as she tried to slip on her shoes. She'd be black and blue at this rate.

Grabbing her shawl, she picked up a small framed photo of her parents, a lasting memory of their dear faces before they'd died. She stuffed the frame in the deep pocket of her skirt, then impulsively, she opened her trunk and took out the velvet pouch that held the few jewels she owned. The pouch went into her pocket as well.

The ship tilted again, and she fell against the wardrobe. Her books and sewing fell to the floor and she feared the lantern would be flung from its hook and catch fire.

'Louisa!' David opened the door and was now wearing his coat. He grabbed her arm to steady her. 'Here. Take this.' He thrust a wad of money into her hands. 'I have half and I want you to take half.'

'But why?'

'Just take it, please.'

She looked into his green eyes so like her own. Words stuck in her throat as the ship's timbers crunched and groaned. She took the money with shaking hands, not liking David's urgency.

'Excuse me, sir.' A young boy, one of the passengers, tugged on David's arm. 'Can you help me, please? My mother has fallen, and I can't get her up.'

David nodded, then turned back to Louisa. 'Stay here until I come back for you.'

She sat on the bed, scared. The wad of money went into her pocket and retrieving her sewing, she quickly broke the thread attached to the flower she was embroidering on a handkerchief. Sitting in a narrow cabin which swayed and pitched like a drunken man walking down stairs, Louisa rethreaded her needle and quickly sewed her skirt pocket closed. Usually her stiches were small and neat, but the hurry was too great to worry about that now. Satisfied she'd sewn the pocket closed well enough that nothing would fall out, she opened the cabin door and looked for David.

Passengers' calls were louder in the corridor and people rushed about knocking into her with their cases and belongings.

'Louisa!' David turned the corner of the corridor and gripped her arm. 'Let's go. We have to get on deck and find a spot on the shore boat.'

She nodded following his back as he pushed forward through the crowd and up the steep stairs to the deck. Rain hit her face, making her shiver. It was so cold out in the night air. The ship carried a small boat to ferry passengers to shore, but it wasn't large enough to carry everyone off the ship at once. Passengers were queuing up for a place inside it, but the crew kept pushing them back.

Louisa clung to the wet railing as a wave soared over the bow and washed over them. In moments she was drenched and cold.

'Hold on to me!' David shouted above the roar of the wind and rain. The storm was much worse than she had realised. The small window in her cabin had given her a glimpse, but the wildness and ferocity was real and frightening. The weak moonlight which disappeared behind scudding clouds made the scene before her even more terrifying.

She grasped David's belt, the deck slippery and unstable beneath her feet. The ship's timbers groaned in protest as it was lifted high on the swell and then plunged back down again. Something cracked above their heads and David pulled her down to her knees as a spar broke free and the wind hurled it like a weapon onto the decks.

A woman screamed as a wave gathered in height, its white froth looked menacing. It rose above them like a living demon and smashed onto the ship. It ripped a woman out of her husband's arms and into the wild black sea. Sailors worked fast, trying to launch the boat, but the rigging snagged. When a huge wave tipped the ship sideways, the rigging snapped like a cracked whip, releasing the shore boat over the side. The force took three sailors with it, crashing into the sea. Shouts and yells were drowned out by the boom of the wind.

David pushed her behind a stack of cargo and held onto the ropes securing it. 'The shore boat is gone.'

'Is there another one?' She wiped water from her face, peering at him in the dimness.

'I don't think so.' Rain plastered his hair to his scalp.

She fought back a gulp of fear, concentrating on David's face. As she went to speak the ship tilted alarmingly sending everyone skidding to the left.

Louisa screamed as she slid along the deck and smashed against the rail.

David grabbed her, the ocean rising up just a few feet from where they lay. 'We are listing badly. That cargo is straining its ropes. We've got to get off the ship. It's going down.'

Expecting the ship to right itself, Louisa's eyes grew wide with panic as it stayed on its side and water rushed down into the decks below.

'Come on!' he yelled in her ear, scrambling along the rail. 'Hurry!'

The noise of the ship breaking apart seemed incredible, unbelievable. People screamed, the wind roared, the waves crashed on them and timbers squealed in protest. Lanterns had gone out, pitching them all in darkness.

David threw an empty crate over the rail. 'We are going to jump in and swim to the crate. It will keep us afloat.'

Nodding, she held fast to his wet coat.

He stared into her eyes and in the murky light she gulped at his serious expression. 'You go first and swim as fast as you can to the crate. Don't stop, just get to the crate. Understand?'

'Yes.'

'I'll be right behind you. Now go.'

Terrified, she looked at the angry black ocean wreaking havoc on the ship and passengers. The wind whipped her wet hair into her eyes as she climbed over the railing. Waves rose up to meet her and she shrieked as her foot slipped.

'Go Louisa!'

'I can't do it!' she called back to him. She'd never been so frightened in her life.

He grabbed her arms to steady her. 'Look at me. Do you trust me to keep you safe?'

'Yes.'

'Jump. Now.'

She leapt into the back abyss as he told her to for trusting David was easy. She'd done it all her life. Her big brother was the best of men in her eyes. She had accompanied him to the other side of the world to build a farm because he said they would have a better life in a new country where hundreds of acres were available and cheap to buy, not like England where only the rich held land.

She hit the churning water hard and went under a long way. The cold made her gasp and choke. Fighting the dark gloomy depths, her dress making her heavy in the water, she swam her way up to the surface. Sucking in air, a wave smacked her in the face. She coughed on the salty water, kicking to keep afloat. Her shoes had come off and she'd lost her shawl. The crate bobbed a few yards away. She swam fast, concentrating on reaching the crate. Many times, she had raced David in the river near their old home. She was a good swimmer and never more thankful for the skill than now. The waves rose her up high. With a lunge, she reached the crate and held on to it like she was never going to let it go.

Triumphant, she looked up at David and waved to him. Her eyes, grown accustomed to the dim shadowy light, saw him wave to her. He shouted something through cupped hands, but the wind took it and she couldn't hear him. Suddenly, one of the ship's masts broke. The sound was similar to cannon fire she'd heard in a park one time. With a suspended breath, she watched the massive beam fall and strike David down onto the deck. He was gone from sight instantly.

She screamed his name. Rain lashed her face, blinding her. A wave took her up and away from the ship. She choked on water calling for David. The salty sea water burned her nose and throat. She tried to swim back, but the waves took her away. She kicked violently, hindered by her skirts, her body tired. She strained to see her brother in the darkness. Had he survived?

Not finished with them yet, the storm twisted the ship apart like a child's toy. The noise of the timbers as they cracked and splinted hurting her ears. She fought against the swell, torn between hanging on to the crate or letting go and swimming back to the sinking ship to search for David. Chaos reigned. People flung themselves overboard. Women cried, men yelled, babies were held aloft as though they were offerings to appease some sort of evil water god.

Drenched and swamped by wild waves, she watched in a daze as the ship listed even further, then quickly sank, taking with it the brother she loved.

CHAPTER 2

Through the black angry night, Louisa held on to the side of the wooden crate. Wind-whipped waves washed over her relentlessly as she bobbed on the enormous swell. The taste of salt filled her mouth and stung her nose and eyes.

Silence reigned now. The cries from the other passengers had long since died away. The creaks and groans of the sailing ship had gone when the broken vessel slipped beneath the thrashing ocean. The storm still raged on, turning the sea into a frenzied foaming pool of hidden depths and unseen terrors.

The weight of her dress and petticoats pulled her down, limiting her ability to kick out and swim as she'd been taught in the river near where she grew up back home in England. She clung to the crate, staring into the dark, trying to make out shapes. Tiredness made her weak. Her cold fingers were numb and stiff from holding onto the crate.

'Is anyone out there!' Her voice seemed small and insignificant.

Tears wouldn't fall. The enormity of the situation hadn't fully registered, yet.

She thrust her hand under the water and felt her skirt pocket. Relief flooded through her. The items were still in there. She thanked the fates for having asked the village seamstress to make deep pockets. Her mother had laughed at her, saying no one needed pockets in skirts, an apron, yes, but not in a day dress. What would she ever need to put in there?

Now Louisa knew.

Shaking the image of her mother from her mind, she fought back a wail of despair. She'd lost her parents and now David. Her heart twisted in an agony of pain. She gasped. Water filled her mouth, choking her. Her grip slipped from the crate and she went under. For a moment she drifted down. The world was silent, dark. Nothing mattered under the water. She could join David…

However, the need for air overrode everything else. Kicking hard, hands scrambling to hold onto something, anything, she broke the surface. Spluttering, her lungs fit to burst she sucked in air. She grabbed the crate again and pulled it tight to her chest, heaving.

'Help!' she called out into the blackness. Surely, someone had survived the shipwreck? She couldn't be the only one left?

'Help!'

The only answer was the storm's wind song.

On the voyage, she'd heard the sailors joke about never learning to swim. How they lived their lives on the water yet never went in it unless they were strapped by rope tied to the ship. Louisa genuinely believed that she and David were the only two people on board who could swim. But David couldn't swim if he'd been knocked unconscious. With the mast hitting him, he'd likely have died before he went into the water.

As the storm headed to the east, Louisa became exhausted and was so cold her teeth chattered. The night sky grew lighter. On the horizon, below the angry clouds, a thin line of bluish purple appeared. She stared at it, her eyes heavy with the strain. Dawn was breaking. The giant waves also seemed to tire and settle into a less chaotic rhythm. The swell lessened and rocked her gently.

Something bumped into her from behind, making her jump. Spinning about, she pushed away a canvas deckchair, wishing it was another human. With the light turning from grey to pink, she could make out more floating debris from the ship. Kicking her legs, she pushed through the water, concentrating on finding someone alive. Perhaps people were clinging to life as she was, but had simply coasted away from her in the night?

For what seemed hours she pushed through the wreckage, but no one clung to boards or crates as she did.

The sun rose in a clear blue sky as though she had imagined the whole storm. She laid her head on the crate and drifted, not caring what happened to her.

When the sun blazed directly above her head, the wind picked up again, bringing with it a scattering of high flat clouds that raced across the sky. The sea rose and fell, gathering strength. In the sunlight that dazzled off the water, she stared at the dark line on the horizon, which had sprung from nowhere.

Land?

A roar came to her over the water. She glanced around, not knowing what was happening. The wind gathered pace, topping the waves with white. She was carried forwards, the roar louder now, like thunder. When a large wave rose her up high, she could clearly see huge waves smashing onto a golden sandy beach. Then she realised the noise was the surf and she was heading for it!

The top of her head burned from the sun's heat. Salt dried on her face, crusting on her lips and eyelashes. Her throat raged with thirst. However, what concerned her most was surviving the crash of the waves as they took her closer to the rocks near the beach. In the haze of the blistering sunshine, she gazed at the land and the line of trees and scrub coming closer. She'd never manage to get to shore while holding on to the crate, it would smash on impact and she risked being injured by it.

Reluctantly, she stiffly let go of the crate on the crest of a wave. It was flung away and she rode the wave forward in a rush of sand-churned foaming water. She was flipped suddenly, somersaulting under the water. Her dress came over her head, smothering and disorientating her. She swallowed seawater and grits of sand. Panicking, needing air, she scrambled up, her knees scrapping along the beach.

Louisa landed with a thump, as though the sea was done with her and spat her out. She lay for a moment, gathering her breath back, her cheek pressed into the cool wet sand. Ripples of tiny waves ran up to her, tickled her feet then receded shyly. Dazed, she realised she'd lost one stocking.

She reached to feel for the package in her pocket and sighed in relief that amazingly the sewing had held, and everything was still secure. Sitting up, feeling as though she'd been beaten by a hundred hands, she took in her surroundings. Ignoring the sea, for she'd had enough of that, she turned her attention to the trees hugging the shoreline. Hues of greens and greys went for as far as she could see. Along the beach, some of the ships' debris littered the sand.

On shaky legs, holding her wet skirts high so she wouldn't trip, she walked amongst the deposits. Every now and then she'd stare out at the ocean, desperate for someone to wave, shout for help. The only sound was the waves rolling onto the sandy beach, which stretched for miles, and the cry of a sea bird.

The sun blasted down on her like a furnace. She needed shade. Climbing up the beach to the trees, Louisa sighed in relief at the immediate effect of being out of the sun. She sat on the grass, then laid back. Sticks and spiky grass pricked her back, but she was too weary to move. Finally, she was on land. Safe. Tiredness pulled at her bones. Above her the trees swayed in the breeze. Her sore body relaxed, and she closed her eyes.

When she woke, a small brown face peered over her. Louisa yelped and scurried a few feet away, her heart in her throat. She glanced about, expecting to see native warriors thrusting spears at her, but there was no one, only a young girl.

The girl, an aborigine with large brown eyes, quietly studied Louisa. Then she smiled, showing bright white teeth. She wore no clothes, except for a flap of woven leaves over her private area. She pointed to her chest. 'Akala.'

'Akala…' Louisa whispered and then pointed to her own chest. 'Louisa.'

'Loo… sa.' Content, the girl beckoned Louisa to follow and walked out of the trees and onto the beach.

Louisa hesitated. She'd read about the native people, some were hostile, others friendly. Perhaps this girl's tribe would help her find the nearest township? Or they could kill her…

She swallowed nervously, her throat sore and dry. She needed water. Seeing as she had little choice but to follow the girl, she got to her feet, shaking the sand out of her damp skirts. Her hair fell in untidy salty strands around her shoulders. Her toes stuck out of her one remaining stocking and she pulled it off and flung it aside. She looked a fright and hunger clawed at her belly.

Standing at the tree line, Louisa gave a long lingering look at the ocean. The wind had dropped as the sun began to set. More wreckage had washed ashore but no bodies. No one had survived the disaster. David and all their hopes and dreams had gone down with the ship. She was alone.

'Loo… sa.' Akala gestured for her to go with her as she headed along a track through the bushes.

Heart heavy, she turned her back on the sea as Akala took her hand and lead her away.

Today was the first day in her new life. What would it bring, and did she even care?

* * *

LOUISA SAT in the dirt by the fire, watching the small kangaroo carcass smoulder on the flames. It had been thrown on the glowing coals, fur and all. The stench of burning fur filled her nose and made her stomach churn. Yet, she was so hungry, she'd eat anything at the moment.

Akala had led her to a camp a few hundred yards inland from the beach. Only one woman greeted them, Akala's mother, or so Louisa thought her to be. Her name was Kiah and she accepted Louisa without barely a glance. She wore only a cloth about her hips, her breasts bare.

'You eatem,' Kiah instructed, once the kangaroo had been thoroughly cooked and blackened.

Louisa needed no second bidding and took the offered piece of meat Kiah had hacked off the carcass with a sharpened tip of a broken spear. She struggled to chew the tough meat but washing it down with sips of water from a bark bowl Akala gave her helped.

'You live here?' Louisa asked Akala between mouthfuls.

'About. Whitefellas chase. We hide.'

'White people chase you?' Louisa gasped. 'Why?'

'Mission school.' Akala shuddered. 'I no go to Mission school. Whitefella hit.'

'Whitefella no take me.' Kiah threw a bone into the fire.

Louisa stared at Kiah. 'Why would white men take you?'

Kiah glanced at Akala and away, her movements jerky. 'Makum his woman.' She glared at Louisa. 'We hide. Abim.'

'Abim?'

'Abim. We em…ghosts.' Akala grinned as though it was a huge joke, but Louisa saw the watchful glint in Kiah's eyes.

Astounded, Louisa was unable to comment. They spent the evening sitting and eating until Louisa was too full too move. Warily, she expected more natives to join them, but no one else came as thousands of stars sprinkled a navy sky. She felt somewhat relaxed with the girl and woman, but knew she'd feel differently should a group of warriors arrive.

'Whitefellas,' Kiah said, pointing back towards the beach, then spoke in her own language for some time.

'I don't understand,' Louisa said, glancing from one to the other.

'Whitefellas feed sharks.' Akala spoke solemnly.

Louisa shuddered. She hated to think that David and her fellow passengers were a meal for the sharks.

Akala and Kiah talked in their language to each other and then to Louisa, but she couldn't understand them. There was a lot of pointing back to the beach and she assumed they were talking about the shipwreck.

Louisa stared into the flames. Thinking of David would begin her grieving and she couldn't do that yet. She needed her strength to find the nearest town. Then what? Return to England? She had no family or home there. She had no family or home here either.

Tears pricked behind her eyes and she rubbed a hand over her face. The future seemed as desolate as the country she'd washed upon. Weary, she curled up into a ball and fell asleep.

The next morning, she woke alone. The fire just a mound of winking embers. Beside her head was a bark bowl of water and in the middle of that was placed a hunk of meat. Why had they placed the meat in the water? She ate the lump of kangaroo, but didn't drink the water, and waited for Akala and her mother to come back from wherever it was they went.

The heat grew intense and Louisa moved further into the shade of the trees. She sat and watched the different coloured birds hopping from branch to branch, kinds she'd never seen before. Their calls were sharp, piercing the air. Small lizards darted in the coarse grass, beady eyes watching until they scurried away into the undergrowth. She pulled leaves off the trees, screwing them up to release the eucalyptus aroma. She'd read about these trees back home. Some people thought the extracted eucalyptus oil could be used in medicinal ways.

With the sun high and hot, Louisa grew bored of waiting and headed back to the beach. The roar of the surf guided her long before she saw the ocean.

High tide had shifted the ship's wreckage further up the beach. Louisa walked amongst ripped sails, broken crates, rigging and jagged planks.

She gazed out past the breaking waves to the calm expanse of ocean beyond. Nothing. Sea birds swooping and diving was the only form of life out there.

The blazing heat burned her skin. Her face felt hot and dirty. Impulsively, she splashed into the shallows, the water cold on her legs, not caring that her dress and petticoat soon became saturated. She sat in the water, watching it ebb and flow around her. She washed her hands, running the wet sand through her fingers.

Finally, boredom won again and wondering if Akala and Kiah were back, she left the beach and headed back along the track.

The camp was deserted. Frowning, Louisa looked around for any indication that the natives had returned, but the site appeared exactly as she left it. She was thirsty, but the discarded wooden water bowls were empty.

'Akala!' she called loudly, scaring the birds from the trees. A flock of parrots flew above her head screeching, the sound piercing.

Thinking perhaps they were out hunting, she added little sticks and leaves to the fire's embers in readiness of what they brought back. It took little time to encourage the cinders to become flames, dried eucalyptus leaves combusted like gunfire but died out just as quickly. Persevering, soon the fire grew, and Louisa searched the area for bigger pieces of wood. The blaze added to the heat of the day. She wiped the sweat from her face. She needed a drink. Her head throbbed.

Dusk turned the sky a pinky-orange and the bird calls

quietened. Louisa became worried. What if the two natives didn't return? What if white men had found them and taken them? Her panic grew. She couldn't think what to do.

The snap of a twig made her jerk around in alarm. Akala and her mother walked through the scrub, full of smiles and expressive hand signals as they gabbled in their language. Kiah held up a dead lizard, at least three feet long and threw it on the fire.

Relieved, Louisa smiled and nodded, grateful they had returned. She'd never dined on lizard before, or seen one so large, but her stomach growled with hunger and she knew she'd eat it.

Akala tapped Louisa on the shoulder, indicating for her to follow. Picking up her skirts, she hurried after the girl, who was light and quick on her feet.

Within a short distance of the camp, Akala stopped by a small stream, well hidden in the thick of trees and scrub. The trickling water headed towards the sea. Akala filled the bowls she carried with fresh water and gave them to Louisa to hold. 'Water. Akuna.'

'I didn't know this was here,' she said to Akala, who replied in her own language with lots of hand gestures.

Louisa drank thirstily. 'This water is good.' She smiled at Akala. All this time fresh water had been close by and she'd not known. She felt foolish.

'Akuna.' The girl pointed to the water. 'Akuna. Water.'

'Water is akuna?' Louisa asked.

Akala bent, refilled the bowl and held it out. 'Water. Akuna.'

'Why do you put the meat in the water for me?'

Akala peered at the ground and pointed to the ants crawling over the sandy soil.

'Ants?' Louisa's eyes widened in realisation. 'The water stops the ants from getting to the meat. I understand now.'

Back at the camp, Kiah had removed the lizard from the coals and was ripping the flesh off it before placing it on flat pieces of bark which served as plates.

17

They ate as darkness descended and Louisa wondered what the next day would bring. She pulled a small twig out of her hair. She needed to get to a township.

She drew houses and stick figures in the dirt next to the fire. 'Town. People.'

Akala shuffled closer and peered at the drawings before talking to her mother.

Kiah shook her head. 'Whitefellas. No good.'

'I need to be with my own people.' Tears of frustration built hot behind Louisa's lashes. 'Kiah?'

'Whitefellas. No good.' Kiah walked away.

Upset, Louisa stared into the flames. It was obvious Kiah had come into contact with white settlers. Akala, if she was her daughter, had been taught a little English in a missionary school. Had they hurt Kiah or her people? Were settlers close by? How would she find them?

Akala touched her arm and spoke in her language.

Louisa shook her head. 'I don't understand. English.'

'Whitefellas commem. No take.'

'I go to whitefellas. They are my people,' Louisa said trying to make her comprehend how important it was for her.

'No whitefellas.' Akala shook her head.

Louisa turned away in disappointment and wished she was miles away from the little camp. She ignored Akala and once more curled up into a ball and waited for sleep.

The following morning, Louisa woke alone again. No food had been left for her but knowing where the stream was she went there to drink her fill. Thunder rumbled overhead. Dark clouds covered the rising sun and wind rustled the trees. The birds were quiet today.

Returning to the fire, she threw sticks and broken thin branches on it to keep it going. Looking at her hands, with broken nails and ground-in grime, misery filled her. Her dress was torn in many places, her petticoat underneath no longer brilliant white.

She looked around at the bushland surrounding her. Ants scurried over the sandy soil, the gangling eucalyptus trees swayed in the wind, dried leaves and twigs littered the ground between long weedy clumps of grass the colour of wheat. None of it was like the countryside back home, which was green and lush. Here everything she'd seen so far was dry, brown and harsh.

Sighing, she walked to the beach. The rumble of the waves carried on the wind, and as she stood on the edge of the sand, she gazed at the shipwreck's debris. There seemed more of it than before.

Intrigued, she strolled amongst it. Ignoring the ropes, broken timbers and torn sails, she picked up a small wooden box a hand span wide. She was dismayed to find it locked. She took it further up the beach to the path and left it there before returning to the wreckage. A hundred yards along the water line she found a bottle of wine, the cork firmly in place. It took some effort to get the cork out, and when it finally popped, she grinned with triumph.

The red wine, drunk straight from the bottle, tasted like nectar from the gods. Determined to save some for later when she ate whatever animal Kiah brought back from her hunt, she replaced the cork and set the bottle next to the little wooden box.

She continued scouting among the debris, finding a man's boot. Her heart stopped, for it looked similar to the ones David used to wear. The boot joined the box and bottle.

It started to rain lightly, but she ignored it. The bottom of her skirts were wet anyway, so it didn't matter. Besides, it was cooling on her sunburnt face and arms.

Further down the beach, an object caught her eye. Still in the surf and half buried in the sand she found a round leather portmanteau. She dragged it out and up the beach away from the waves. Sitting on the sand, she pulled the leather straps through the shiny buckles and opened the case. Her shoulders slumped in disappointment as she took out the wet men's clothing, consisting of two white shirts and a brown pair of trousers, long johns, four pairs of woollen socks, a black neck tie and a small wallet of shaving equipment with the initials W.W. on it. At the very bottom of the bag was a thin leather pouch and inside it held a wad of wet money. When counted it added up to one hundred pounds. Heart thumping, Louisa glanced about the deserted beach, feeling like a thief. Quickly she replaced all the items and carried the heavy bag up to the path to join the other booty.

'Loo… sa.'

She jumped as Akala seemed to appear out of nowhere. The girl was like a living ghost. 'You're back then.'

Akala squatted down beside the haul Louisa had collected and fingered through it. She shook the bottle of wine, but Louisa took it off her.

'Wine.' She popped the cork and gave the bottle for the girl to sip. 'Wine.'

Akala sipped and then immediately spat it out. She gave the bottle back to Louisa, shaking her head and pulling funny faces.

Chuckling, Louisa corked the bottle and then gathered up her finds.

Akala took the little box and the boot, jabbering away in her own language as the rain increased, soaking them through.

Back at the camp, the fire was out. Kiah sat under a tree working on a piece of bark that she was making into a vessel of some kind. Next to her was a flat stone with tendrils of smoke escaping from under it. From time to time, Kiah lifted it and fed bits of grass and twigs to the embers she'd saved from the fire pit. The embers lay in a hollowed out hole, and the flat stone kept out the rain.

Dumping her items down, Louisa sat beside Kiah and watched her work. She'd seen the other woman carrying a pouch made of thin paper-like bark, which inside held sharpened stones, spear tips and dried meat.

Kiah work quietly and efficiently. She spoke to Akala, glancing at the items Louisa brought back. Akala said something and the woman nodded.

Lightning sheeted the sky as Akala put the boot on and hobbled about in the rain, making them laugh.

Pausing in her work, Kiah picked up the wine and uncorked it. She drank a bit of it. 'Whitefella drink.' She gave it back to Louisa.

The rain eased a little after a while. Louisa had no idea of time, but as darkness threw deepening shadows, she fell asleep against the tree trunk, hungry, damp and chilled.

She woke during the night to find Kiah gone and Akala staring into the darkness. 'Akala?'

'Kiah gone. I stay Loo… sa.'

'Gone where?' She rubbed the sleep from her eyes.

'Walkabout.'

'Walkabout?' Louisa was none the wiser. 'When does she come back?'

'Long time.' Akala shrugged her shoulders.

'And she's left you?'

'Loo… sa here.'

'Yes, but I need to find a town, my people.'

'Whitefellas no good.'

Thirsty, Louisa sipped from the water bowl. The rain had stopped, and the night was filled with the humming noises of insects and the odd snap of a twig from an unknown creature. She was annoyed Kiah had left, leaving her with Akala, who wasn't her responsibility. 'Can you take me to a town, Akala?'

The girl shook her head. 'No Mission school.'

'No, not school. You won't have to go back to school. Just show me where there are people.'

'Whitefellas no good.' The girl curled up on a sheet of tree bark and went to sleep.

Louisa shivered as a light cool breeze blew in from the ocean. Huddling against the trunk, she thought of her family's cottage back in England, of her parents and of David. No. Shaking her head, she wiped them from her mind. It hurt too much to think of them. She had to remain focused on surviving, especially without Kiah.

CHAPTER 3

*S*oft white clouds drifted across the sky, but the hot sun shone between them as Louisa walked down the beach to the water's edge. She scanned the empty horizon, willing a ship to come into sight.

It'd been ten days since the shipwreck. She'd counted the days and drank the rest of the red wine on New Year's Eve. The first day of eighteen hundred and eighty had dawned just the same as the other days since the ship went down. A day when she prayed she would be rescued, but nobody came for her.

Ten long days living with a native. Akala refused to take her to the nearest settlement, and not knowing in what direction a town might be, or how far, Louisa could not consider going alone. To become lost out there in the inhospitable bushland would lead to certain death.

So the camp and the beach were her home… for now.

Sighing, she turned her attention to the ship's debris washed along the beach shoreline. More broken parts of the ship and other items arrived every day and Louisa had built quite a collection.

She walked amongst it, seeing what else had been brought in

with the high tide during the night. Abruptly she stopped. She stared at the body lying on the sand, tangled in ropes.

Hurrying towards it, heart in her throat, she prayed it wasn't David. She skidded to a halt a few feet from the body. It was a man. Not David though, for the worn clothes were that of one of the sailors.

Tentatively, she rolled him over and gasped at the distorted and bloated face. She didn't know him well. He had simply been one of the sailors she smiled and said good morning or good night to as she walked the decks and he went about his work. Still, the shock was real. He'd been someone living with her on that ship. He could have been one of the passengers she dined with every day, or he could have been her brother…

'Loo… sa?'

She turned and looked sadly at Akala. 'We need to bury this man.' She didn't even know his name.

Akala shook her head and ran off down the beach.

Sighing, Louisa tucked up her skirts and began the difficult task of dragging the sailor free of the encroaching water as the tide turned.

It took longer than she thought, and the body was heavier than she expected. Dragging him up the beach to the beginning of the grass exhausted her. She had no energy, and since Kiah left days ago, very little food to keep her going.

Still, she had to bury the man. She couldn't live with herself if she simply left him to rot in the sun.

Akala had gone to the far end of the beach to scramble about the rocks jutting out into the sea.

Using a piece of broken plank from the wreckage, Louisa dug a sandy hollow between tufts of long coarse grass. Blisters formed on her hands and she had the odd splinter by the time she'd finished the shallow hole. It wasn't as deep as normal graves, but she was spent. She rolled the sailor into the hole, shuddering at the feel and smell of him. On her knees, she scooped the sand over him until he was covered. She stuck the broken piece of wood at the top of the grave as a marker.

When the task was finished she walked down to the water and washed her hands and the sweat from her face. She had buried a person. Goosebumps rose on her skin. She shivered, even though the sun beat down.

That man had been someone's son, or brother, or maybe even father. He'd died alone at sea and was now buried in a sandy grave on a deserted beach. She thought of David, part of her wishing it had been him she'd buried for at least then he'd be with her. Instead he was at the bottom of the ocean…

Akala joined her, and grinning, she opened her pouch to show Louisa the oysters she'd pried off the rocks.

'Shall we have them now?' Louisa walked with her back up to the dry sand where they sat, and using a spear tip, struggled to open the oyster shells. Louisa had never opened one before and watched Akala. Eventually, her hands sore and stinging from all the work they'd done, she got one open and tipped it into her mouth. The salty juices ran down her chin and she sighed in pleasure at the chance to eat something different than the dried pieces of meat left from Kiah's last hunt.

The wind picked up and in the distance darker clouds built. Akala strolled down to the debris and sorted through the ripped sails and tangled rigging.

'What are you doing?' Louisa asked her.

'Whitefella humpy.' Akala pulled the ropes free of the timbers.

'Humpy? What is that?'

Akala screwed up her face in thought, then drew in the sand a house type shape.

'A tent?' Louisa looked at the wreckage about them. 'You want to build a tent?'

'Humpy.' Akala shrugged and dragged the torn sails up the path.

Enthused by the idea. Louisa gathered more rope and sails. Why hadn't she thought to do that before?

Back at the camp she stretched out the torn sails, pulling the rope through the holes. 'We can tie it up in the tree.' She pointed to a branch above her head.

Akala gabbled in her language and then shimmied up the trunk as easily as a monkey. Lying flat on the branch she waited for Louisa to throw the rope and she wrapped it around the branch several times before tying it off. The sail flapped in the breeze.

'We need to tie it to this tree now.' Louisa pulled the ropes to lift the sail horizontal. 'This tree, Akala.'

The girl climbed again and repeated the process.

'Well done!' Louisa smiled. They had a cover over them to keep out most of the rain, which meant the fire would stay lit.

'Let us go and see what else we can use.' Louisa set off back down the path, but Akala stayed behind and added sticks to the fire's embers.

On the beach once more, Louisa made an effort to think of uses for everything she saw. Wooden planks were pulled up to be stacked on the beach. On her fifth journey of taking timber to the path Akala was waiting for her.

'Look.' Louisa pointed to the wood. 'We can use this to make a floor under the sail. We can sleep on it. Help me take it to the campsite.'

Akala remained silent and instead turned away and walked down to the rock pools.

Sighing in frustration, Louisa began the exhausting task of taking the planks to the camp. Under the sail, she laid each one side by side, making a floor of sorts. Her efforts were paid off when she stepped across it and felt an instant sense of pride and achievement. She had a roof and a floor.

Spurred on, she returned to the beach and combed through

the debris. High tide washed some items further up the sand. She kept walking, going further than she'd done before.

At either end of the beach, clumps of rocks jetted out into the ocean. The western end was where Akala found the oysters, but Louisa ventured towards the eastern side, which was further away. Here amongst the rock pools, she found a pig-skin ball that one of the children had been playing with on deck. The sight of it brought tears hot and stinging behind her eyes. She blinked them away. The wind whipped her hair about her face and she angrily pushed it away. The shipwreck had been unjust. To kill innocent people, little children and babies. How had she survived and no one else did? Was it because she could swim? Because David had thrown the crate and told her to hold on to it? How had she been the only one to escape with her life?

She grabbed the ball, tucking it under her arm and she scoured the other pools. She saw lots of crabs darting away. She needed a spear. Crabs could be dinner. Jumping from rock to rock, she paused when she saw something red snagged on a rock a few feet away. Clambering down to a lower level, she tugged at the material and when it came free, she saw the pretty printed pattern woven on it. A shawl. A woman's shawl. She'd not seen any of the women wearing it on the ship. It must have come from a broken trunk.

Louisa crossed the rest of the flat rocks, bringing her over to the next beach along. She peered at shoreline. Wreckage was scattered there too.

Slowly, she headed down off the rocks and across the sand. She could no longer see Akala, the girl was too far away.

Louisa's steps slowed as she saw them. Bodies. Bloated, half submerged in the sand, thrown up by the high tide. Two women, three men and two children, one only a baby.

Dropping onto her knees, she stared at them. Sickened and sad.

Seven bodies to bury. She closed her eyes, exhausted.

* * *

Louisa finished washing the men's clothes she'd found in the portmanteau and hung them up on the rope strung between two trees on the other side of the camp. She had plans to wear the shirt and trousers for the ease of movement in the bush. Sand and salt water had ruined her dress and petticoat which were now full of rips and close to threadbare. The European clothing wasn't practical in the Australian bushland. Hunting with Akala the first time had proven difficult. Her skirts snagged on bushes making so much noise the animals were scared off before Akala could get close enough to strike.

For weeks they'd been living off crabs, oysters, grubs and small lizards. Louisa had lost so much weight that her skirt and petticoats fell off her hips. At least with the man's trousers she'd be able to belt them up. Akala although knowledgeable on the ways to hunt, was only a young girl, and her strength to throw the spear and capture an animal wasn't equal to Kiah. Many days would go by without them having meat to eat. But the fat white grubs dug up out of the dirt were plentiful and although Louisa couldn't enjoy the taste of them, she was so hungry she ate without complaint.

Heading down the path towards the beach, Louisa looked for Akala, who'd gone from the camp some time ago. Louisa expected it was so she didn't have to help with washing the clothes and other chores around the camp. The shelter meant a great deal to Louisa, for it resembled something close to civilisation. She had a timber plank floor and a sail roof and when it rained they were dry, and the fire remained lit.

On the beach, a stiff breeze blew her tangled hair like a flag behind her. Slightly tensed, she scanned the area hoping not to see a body washed ashore. Finally, she spotted Akala in the rock pools on the western side, the girl's favourite spot. She wandered down towards her, noticing more debris washed ashore. She'd come back to that later as she'd noticed with surprise Akala sweeping the larger rock pools with something like a net.

'What do you have there?' she asked, stepping up onto the slippery rocks. The tide had not been out long, and everything was shiny and wet. 'Was that washed ashore last night?'

Akala held up the net which was torn and only a yard square. 'DjilDjit.'

'DjilDjit?'

The girl pointed into the pool and made a movement with her hand like a fish swimming. 'DjilDjit.'

Louisa peered closely at the water and then saw the little fish swimming. 'Oh, I see! Fish!' Louisa understood and learned another word.

Nodding, Akala grinned. 'Fish.'

'How do we get them?'

The girl jumped into the rock pool, the water coming up to her thighs. 'Loo… sa.' She indicated for Louisa to join her.

Sighing that she'd be wet again, Louisa bunched up her skirts and climbed into the cold water. 'I need to be nearly naked as you are. It would make life easier.'

With Akala on one end of the net and Louisa on the other, they walked slowly together with the net stretched out between them towards the other end of the pool.

Frustratingly, the fish escaped by swimming under the net and around their legs.

'I don't think this will work.' Louisa frowned, trying and failing to think of a better way.

Akala knelt in the water, where it rose just below her chin. Doing the same, Louisa gasped as the cold water touched her chest. On their knees they shuffled forward, with the net lower in the water. In a quick movement, Akala scooped up the bottom of the net and lifted it high up, forcing Louisa to do the same at her end. Two small fish jumped and flapped caught in the net. Akala tossed them onto the rocks and grinned at Louisa.

'We must do it again!' Louisa grinned.

Fuelled by their success, they dropped to their knees again. The water was churned up, making it difficult to see the fish and three more attempts resulted in no fish, but then they had two successful catches, and Louisa climbed out of the pool. In all they had seven fish.

'My knees hurt.' She lifted her skirts and stared in dismay at the grazed scratches on both knees. However, they would eat well today.

'Knee.' Akala patted her own. 'Knee.'

'Yes. They are your knees.'

Akala laughed, gathered up the fish in the net and then they walked back along the beach.

Louisa stepped amongst the flotsam washed up in the latest high tide and squealed. 'Akala, look. A deckchair.'

She opened out the collapsed canvas deckchair and sat it upright on the sand. 'I'll have a chair to sit in now, or even sleep in. No more hard floor!' She was giddy with delight.

Akala sank her bottom into it and spoke rapidly in her own language, but Louisa didn't care about making her translate to English this time. She was too excited to have found the deckchair. She carried it up the beach and along the path to the campsite where she set it up next to the fire in pride of place. She sat on it and sighed at the sheer pleasure of having something soft give beneath her, something that shaped to her body.

She watched Akala cook the fish and her mouth watered. 'I'll fetch us some water.'

Flipping the fish over on the hot stone at the edge of the coals, Akala nodded and sang a song in her own language.

Collecting the water bowls, Louisa headed for the stream. Living with a native made her more aware of the landscape around her. She knew to tread carefully, to not make unnecessary noise by placing her feet on cleared dirt, not on twigs and dry grass that could snap and rustle, which could scare of a potential meal. She no longer simply looked at the trees around her but noticed each individual trunk, the branches. A lizard might be perched on one, blending in with the background, and once seen it was another potential meal. Also, by identifying the shape of the trees, she reduced the risk of getting lost. Akala had shown her the wild fruits and berries that were safe to eat and the ones that would make them sick. Her eyes now found the tracks left by small animals, the droppings of kangaroos and wallabies.

At the stream she filled the bowls from a tiny waterfall that fell over a clump of rocks near the bank. Akala told her this running water was clear and fresh. They must never drink from stale stagnant ponds.

When the last bowl was full, Louisa stood and froze. Across the bank stood three native warriors. All three wore white face paint, their naked brown bodies glistening in the sun. A shiver of fear ran down her back. She couldn't move. One of the men spoke and pointed his spear at her. Louisa thought her knees would give way, but she kept staring at him, her heart pounding.

Another warrior spoke, and the three men crossed the stream.

Louisa squealed. Dropping the bowls, she ran as fast as she could, holding her skirts high. She crashed through bushes and dodged around trees fully expecting to feel the sharp pain of a spear in her back. Stumbling into camp, she ran to Akala who stood, short spear in hand.

'Whitefellas?' Akala's eyes were wide in her dark face.

'No. Natives. Warriors.' Terrified, Louisa picked up a stick from beside the fire. It was a pathetic defence weapon, but there was nothing else.

The three men walked from out of the trees. The eldest warrior spoke in their language to Akala and she replied. The conversation went on for some time and then suddenly the men walked away, disappearing into the trees like smoke.

Shaking, Louisa lowered the stick. 'What did they say?'

Akala knelt by the fire and rescued the burnt fish, which had dried and curled. 'Askem why I stay wit whitefella.'

'Whitefella?' Louisa frowned not understanding.

'Whitefella Loo… sa.'

'You mean me?'

On a flat piece of paperbark, Akala laid out the fish and gave half to Louisa. The girl was calm, her initial fear gone.

'Are they coming back?'

Akala shrugged.

'Akala!' She yelled, frustrated and scared. 'Do we need to hide or run? Will they come back and kill us?'

'My tribe.'

'Your tribe?' Louisa frowned. 'They are your people? Then why aren't you with them?'

Akala shrugged. 'Loo… sa good whitefella.'

'You told them I was a good person, yes?' Trying to breath steadily, her gaze darted about the trees. At any moment would a spear fly through the air and pierce her body? Would they take her hostage?

The girl ate her fish, pulling out the little bones and tossing them in the fire. She spoke in her language and Louisa wanted to slap her.

'English, girl! Are we safe?' Tears clouded her vision. She was more scared now than she had been when the ship sank. The thought of wild men attacking and killing her made her legs shake and heart pound. She'd heard tales on the journey over about settlers and Aborigines fighting each other, but she'd never thought something like that would involve her. She couldn't fight them. She didn't own a gun or even a knife. With all her heart she wished David was alive and with her now.

'No takkem Loo… sa.' Akala's stare was honest and reassuring. 'Not like whitefella. No kill.'

Slowly, Louisa lowered herself down onto the deck chair, feeling as brittle as the dry leaves underfoot. The encounter had shaken her badly. For so long she had thought it was just her and the girl on the stretch of beach. The campsite had become a haven of sorts. They had food and shelter and she had expected nothing more until perhaps, a ship sailed by and rescued her. But to find that warriors, men with spears, roamed the area gave her such a shock, had ripped apart the isolation, the security in knowing she was safe.

As the shadows lengthened and the sun slipped beyond the horizon, Louisa remained in the deckchair, watchful. She ate a little of the fish but found the overcooked dried flesh tasteless. Her eyes grew heavy. She dreamed of home, of the cottage she lived in with her parents and David, of the lush green fields they farmed and the warm kitchen where her mother cooked delicious meat stews and light fluffy cakes.

Something touched her face and she opened her eyes with a jerk. A strange brown face was inches from hers. She screamed.

The warrior jumped back, the whites of his eyes showing, his spear raised.

Coming out of the shelter, Akala spoke in their language and the native stepped further back, closer to the other two men.

'What are they doing back here?' Louisa scrambled out of the deckchair. 'Why did they come back? Will they kill us?'

One of the men wore cut-off trousers and crouched to inspect the items Louisa had brought from the wreckage. He picked up the boot and put it down again. Next, he pulled the trousers and shirt from where they hung drying. He looked at Louisa. 'Trade.'

She stared at him, not expecting him to know or speak English. That he did lessened her fear somewhat, made him less of a savage, but only slightly.

He held up a short-handled axe. 'Trade.'

Louisa glanced at the axe. It wasn't native made but came from an English house. The axe would be useful, but she really wanted to wear the trousers when hunting. Her skirt wouldn't last much longer. 'No.' Her voice sounded high to her ears.

The man raised his chin. 'Trade.'

'No.'

He spoke to Akala, who murmured something back to him. He seemed satisfied by the answer as he dropped the trousers onto the ground. He stared at Louisa and touched his chest. 'Djarrahly.'

Did the men want to be friends? Could they be trusted?

Akala stepped forward. 'His name Djarrahly.'

'Djarrahly.' Louisa repeated without great success. 'My name is Louisa.'

'Loo… sa.' He nodded. 'Boss fella name me Jarrah.'

Akala looked at Louisa. 'Jarrah. Whitefellas name.'

'I can call him Jarrah?'

The girl nodded.

On silent feet the three men walked away back into the trees and out of sight.

Letting out a sigh of relief, Louisa felt light headed. She needed to eat. 'What did they say to you before, Akala?'

'Askem whitefella treat me good.' Akala added more sticks to the fire. 'Yesem, Loo... sa good whitefella.'

She hid a smile at being called a whitefella. Obviously, the natives didn't have a word for woman. She was tired and hungry, but she wouldn't sleep not after the encounter with the warriors. The flames glowed red and orange as the darkness descended. Louisa yawned.

'Jarrah work for whitefella, Akala's father, boss fella,' Akala said watching the sticks catch alight.

'Your father?' She processed the simple words. 'Jarrah worked for your father, who is a white man?'

'Father dead. Kiah…' Akala struggled to find the words, so mimed the act of laughing.

'Your father died and Kiah laughed about it?'

'He bad whitefella.'

'Oh.' She didn't know what to say to that. After weeks of

living with the girl she still knew so little about her. However, she now understood that Akala was a product of a white man and Kiah. 'Jarrah is a good man?'

Shadows from the fire flittered across the girl's face. 'Jarrah good warrior.'

That wasn't what she meant but let the matter drop. The girl didn't understand the difference between being a decent man and a fighting warrior. Perhaps in their world it was the same thing. She carried the deckchair under the sail shelter and sat down. Hunger made her stomach growl and Akala grinned at her.

Although she tried to stay awake, her eyelids grew heavy. Akala climbed onto her lap, squishing in beside her on the narrow deckchair. Louisa wanted to scold her, worried the precious chair might break, but she was too tired to speak.

When they woke the following morning, a dead kangaroo lay beside the fire. The man's trousers were gone.

Excited, Akala built up the embers and threw the animal on the fire. The smell of burning fur stung Louisa's nose, annoying her further. She'd wanted those trousers. The kangaroo wasn't a worthwhile swap to her, when she and Akala could get fish and oysters.

Still, by the time she was chewing on the cooked meat, her mood had changed, and she devoured each mouthful until she thought she'd burst.

After they'd eaten, Louisa and Akala walked down to the beach. The tide was high, swallowing much of the beach and all the rock pools. A cool breeze kept the heat from being too intense.

Akala pointed out to the waves where a pod of dolphins leaped through the surf as though racing each other.

Louisa watched them, counting at least eight, when suddenly an object further out to sea caught her attention. She squinted in the sunshine, placing a hand above her eyes to see better. Her heart stopped. A boat!

'A boat! Akala, a boat!' She jumped up and down, waving her hands. 'Over here!' She yelled as loudly as she could over the noise of the crashing waves. 'Here! I'm here!'

The boat continued on.

'Whitefellas.' Akala sounded unimpressed. She turned and walked back up the path.

Louisa kept waving. She stripped off her petticoat and waved that too. She continued to yell until her voice gave out. She ran up and down the narrow strip of sand available, wishing the tide was out so she could go further down the beach. Could she swim out to the boat? She took a step into the water, the coldness tingling her toes. Despite being a good swimmer, she'd never make it that far.

She sobbed as the boat sailed further away, heading east.

'Please come back,' she whispered, her throat sore.

Dejected and heartbroken, she watched the boat until she could no longer see it.

CHAPTER 4

*L*ouisa dug in the wet ground at the base of a tree, looking for white witchetty grubs to eat. Her dress was filthy, her hands caked in mud. Akala was up in another tree picking native berries. Since the sighting of the boat two days ago, Louisa had felt miserable. She couldn't shake it. Nothing Akala said or did could raise a smile. Even when the girl disappeared for hours yesterday, Louisa hadn't cared.

It had rained for two days straight making the camp conditions unbearable. The sail had to be constantly retied as the weight of the water loosened the ropes, the campfire smouldered because the wood was wet. The waves crashed over the rook pools so they couldn't fish. They'd not eaten since gorging on the kangaroo and Louisa had little energy or inclination to do anything but sit in the deckchair and watch the rain, fondling the small bag of jewels, the small portrait and money still stitched in her pocket. She wanted to see the damage done to her parents' small portrait but to unstitch the pocket would leave the money and jewels at risk of getting lost.

However, this morning Akala had pulled her up and dragged her out of camp to find food.

Sitting back on her heels, she gave up trying to find the grubs, not caring in the slightest. A twig snapped behind her and she spun around. Jarrah stood a few feet away. He wore the trousers.

'What do you want?' she barked, angry and not caring if he killed her with the spear he held. What did she have to live for? Existing in the middle of nowhere with no prospect of being found? She wished she'd gone to the bottom of the ocean with David.

'Whitefella commem.'

She sighed and stood as Akala slithered down the tree like a snake. She showed her pouch full of berries to Jarrah.

Louisa walked away from them back towards the camp.

'No, Loo… sa.' Akala ran beside her. 'We go. Jarrah go to whitefella. Takkem Loo… sa.'

She paused and looked at her. 'What are you talking about?'

'I takkem Boss Loo… sa to whitefella.' Jarrah's eyes never blinked.

'I askem Jarrah.' Akala smiled shyly.

Rooted to the spot, Louisa glanced between them both. 'He will take me to where white people are?'

Akala nodded, puffing up her chest. 'Loo… sa takkem Akala.'

A glimmer of hope unfurled inside her chest. 'Yes, I'll take you with me.'

Jarrah strode past talking to Akala in their language and the girl followed him like a devoted puppy.

'Wait!' Louisa stumbled after them. 'I need to get my things.'

Jarrah frowned but stopped and waited as Louisa hurried to the shelter. She opened the portmanteau and stuffed in the items she'd collected, then closed up the deckchair.

Jarrah continued to frown. 'Heavy, Boss Loo… sa. No takkem.'

She lifted her chin determinedly. 'I can't leave them behind.' If they broke her back she didn't care. These items represented the ship, the people on it, and David.

Jarrah shrugged and walked away.

'Loo… sa.' Akala indicated for her to come and, after a last look at the shelter, Louisa joined her and they set off behind Jarrah.

After a while Louisa's hands hurt, then blistered from carrying the deckchair and case. She lumbered on always several yards behind Akala and Jarrah. No one spoke. The bushland became a blur never changing as the sun soared above their heads. Through gaps in the trees, Louisa saw the ocean and understood they were heading east. Sweat dripped down her face and she used her forearm to wipe it away.

A few hours before sunset, Jarrah stopped in a clearing over-looking the ocean. He swept his hand over the dirt to clear a space for a fire while Akala gathered wood.

Feeling as though she couldn't take another step, Louisa dropped the case and deckchair. Tiredly she opened the chair and flopped into it. Every part of her body ached. Her bare feet were cut in places and throbbing. 'How far must we walk?'

Jarrah looked at her, his infantile fire growing with every twig he placed on it. 'Bo.'

'Bo?'

'Longem way.'

'A long way?'

'Bokitja. A longem way.' He nodded then quietly walked into the trees.

Louisa was too tired to ask more questions and was in awe of Akala and Jarrah for not seeming to be worn-out in the slightest. But then they were clever and didn't carry anything but a spear, nor were they wearing hindering skirts.

Jarrah came back a short time later carrying a lizard which he threw on the fire. He also had lengths of stringy bark which he entwined together to make a rope. As the lizard sizzled on the embers, he tied half of the rope to the handle of the portmanteau. He slung it over his back to show Louisa his intentions.

'Oh yes, that is such a good idea.' She smiled in gratitude.

Having the case slung over her back she'd have her hands free for the deckchair.

They ate the lizard as night fell and Louisa was asleep soon after, despite her throbbing feet and aching arms.

Loud bird calls woke her early the next morning, and it took effort to open her eyes and get out of the deckchair. Her body protested every movement she made.

Jarrah sat by the fire roasting two small birds. 'Morning, Boss Loo... sa.' He broke apart the bird with his fingers and gave her a leg.

'Good morning.' She found it weird to be with this strange man and away from the little camp by the beach. She ate quickly, ravenous. 'Do you work for a white man?' she asked him, as Akala stirred and stretched.

'Some.' He shrugged. 'Trade wit whitefella. Jarrah work... trade whitefella.' He touched the trousers he wore. 'Boss fella... clothes.'

'Jarrah wants whitefella clothes... to be whitefella.' Akala giggled.

Jarrah preened. 'Jarrah whitefella.'

Akala laughed and ate some bird.

Before long they were on the move again just as the sun rose above the trees. Already the growing heat of the day warmed them. Jarrah tied more rope to the collapsed deckchair and slung it over his shoulder. Louisa did the same with the portmanteau, deeply appreciative that Jarrah had taken some of the weight from her.

They walked through bushland and scrub, always heading east with the ocean on their right. When they sun was high at midday they stopped to rest in the shade and all three slept for a while. Again, it was hard for Louisa to wake up and start walking once more. Her bare feet hurt from cuts and scratches, but after weeks of wearing no shoes they were hardening up.

She made no complaint when they walked until nearly dark

even though the rope had cut into her shoulders and she felt her back was on fire from the case constantly rubbing against her. Another fire was lit, but she was asleep before any food was hunted and cooked.

The next morning brought another hot day. Louisa ploughed on, placing one sore foot before the other, not noticing nor caring about her surroundings. She kept her gaze on Jarrah's dark back as he led the way. Sweat dripped down her face, into her eyes, soaking her clothes to her back.

Eventually, Jarrah turned inland, and Louisa no longer saw glimpses of the ocean between trees.

By mid-morning they'd reached a river, flowing fast. Jarrah spoke quickly to Akala, who nodded and turned to Louisa.

'We crossem river.'

'We do?' Louisa stared at the flowing water. 'It's running fast.'

Jarrah placed the deckchair high above his head and stepped into the shallows. He waded across, the water reaching his chest. After placing the deckchair on the opposite bank, he returned for the portmanteau and repeated the process.

When he returned once more, he hitched Akala on his back and smiled his big white toothed smile at Louisa in encouragement.

Lifting her tattered skirts up high, Louisa walked into the water beside them. The coldness made her shiver, even though her skin was hot and sweaty. Stones and pebbles crippled her. She stumbled and wobbled, gasping as the water rose higher around her waist. The pull of the current tugged her sideways. Curling her toes into the sand, she edged her way towards the opposite bank.

'There aren't any crocodiles in this river, is there?' she murmured, the sudden thought of them lurking in the depths chilled her.

Akala laughed, her skinny arms wrapped around Jarrah's neck. 'No croc, Loo…sa.'

With the water nearly to her chin, Louisa concentrated on staying close to Jarrah and getting across. The wet weight of her clothes made the task more exhausting, but finally the water lowered as they reached the other side.

Akala slipped from Jarrah's back and Louisa flopped onto the grass to catch her breath. Hunger gripped her belly.

Jarrah gave her a strip of toughened meat and she chewed it slowly. It tasted like leather and gave her no pleasure, but it was better than nothing. With reluctance she got to her feet, slipped the case rope over her aching shoulder and followed the two natives into the bushland.

Just after midday, Louisa felt so tired she doubted she could take another step. 'Can we rest soon?'

Jarrah pointed to a hill in the distance. 'Whitefella.'

Each step became slower as Louisa walked head down but determined to not give in to the temptation to fall to the ground and sleep.

They walked over a rise and suddenly before them lay a scattering of buildings sweeping down to a wide open bay with ships riding at anchor.

'Whitefella.' Jarrah pointed, smiling at Louisa. 'Jarrah good. Yes?'

'Yes. Very good.' Louisa nodded, tears in her eyes. She'd done it. She'd made it to civilisation. Happiness flooded her like a breaking dam. She blinked to clear her vision and followed him down towards the town hugging the shoreline.

They soon walked along a dirt path, which turned into a rutted cart track. She could see a horse in a field, more timber buildings, a cottage with a tiny garden out the front, then finally people. A woman crossed the road, a man pushed a wheelbarrow. Two young boys were rolling a hoop. Several men were hammering new shingles on a roof of a two storey building. The noise sounded strange after so long listening to only nature. Yet, it was all normal things. Her world. The one she belonged to.

Suddenly nervous, Louisa's steps faltered as an old woman stared at her as they neared her garden gate. She looked at the woman who, stooped and grey, opened her gate and took a step closer.

'Nay lass, what's ever happened to you?' The old woman peered at her, taking in Louisa's bare dusty feet, her torn dress and ragged hair. The woman's gaze darted to Jarrah and back again. 'Are you in trouble? Have these savages hurt you?'

'I...' Emotion caught in her throat. For the first time since losing David, since fighting for her life since the shipwreck, someone had shown her compassion and it tore at her fragile heart.

The woman moved aside. 'Want to come in? Perhaps a cup of tea?'

Tea? To have a cup of tea...

'Yes...' Louisa nodded, desperately wanting to do something ordinary, to taste something ordinary. She took another step, but Jarrah and Akala stayed where they were.

'No blacks in my house.' The old woman shook her head.

Louisa faltered. 'But they are good people.'

'They can wait out here.' The woman's expression was full of disdain.

Louisa looked at Akala, the girl's eyes were huge in her thin face. The child needed to eat as much as she did, and Jarrah had saved her. It was impossible to go inside and drink tea while they stood outside.

'Are you coming in or not?'

'No, thank you.' Louisa turned away and headed down the street, this time Jarrah and Akala followed her.

The road led them down to the bay. Nestled between large hills, the township was a mixture of timber and stone buildings. Her mind was in a whirl as she forgot the woman and absorbed the sounds of a new town.

Louisa was conscious of the stares, the pitying looks from

people as she neared the busier streets in the centre of the bustling town. Subdued, Akala walked so close to her she kept tripping on Louisa's skirt. Jarrah kept his head high, but his eyes missed nothing as they glanced from side to side.

Two women stopped talking and openly gasped at the sight of Louisa, their eyes wide and mouths open. Children pointed, and a shopkeeper paused in his window cleaning.

A man dressed in white moleskin trousers, riding boots and a blue shirt left a group of men he was chatting to and crossed the road to her. 'Miss? Can I be of assistance?'

Heart thumping, feeling as though she was an exhibit at a show, Louisa swayed, her emotions fluttering through her like a trapped bird in a cage. She could take no more. 'My name is Louisa…' She licked her dry lips. 'Louisa Reynolds. I was on the *Blue Tulip.* It went down.'

'Yes, we know. Two survivors were found weeks ago. We sent boats out looking, searching for miles out to sea. We had black trackers along the coast.'

'I was on the coast.'

'Well, obviously they didn't go as far as where you were.'

'They were only two other survivors?' Hope for David flared within her chest. 'Who? Where are they? My brother—'

He raised his hand to stop her, his tone gentle. 'A man called Paul Phelps and a woman called Lucy Pittman. They are the only ones who survived, and now you.'

The names meant nothing to her. She needed to hear the name David Reynolds. The blow was too much. David really was dead. Her knees buckled, and she sank into blackness.

CHAPTER 5

*L*ouisa woke in a bed. The sheets white and clean, the room sparse and hot. She wore a linen shift and the sun peeked through a gap in the curtains. Was it morning or afternoon? She moved her bandaged feet and they throbbed in response. Turning her head, she looked out of the open door, but could see nothing much of the next room. However, someone was singing softly.

Louisa could recall little of how she got here. A man with dark blue eyes, Akala calling her name, the sensation of being lifted and carried. Lots of voices all talking at once, confusing her until she no longer cared what happened. Then a cool cloth on her head, a sip of water and the softness of a mattress. She remembered nothing more after that.

The singing stopped, replaced by the squeak of a door and the sound of plates being stacked. Louisa knew how to listen properly. Weeks of tracking food with Akala had taught her to listen effectively.

She frowned as she heard voices, one male, one female. She stiffened warily as two people entered the room. A man with long grey whiskers and a short black coat. He carried a medical bag. The woman was short and round with a tight smile and an inquisitive stare.

'You are awake I see,' the man said. 'I'm Doctor Jamieson. This is Mrs Casey, my housekeeper. How do you feel, Miss Reynolds?'

'I don't really know,' she whispered, her throat dry.

Mrs Casey rushed forward and from the bedside table poured her a glass of water from a brown earthenware jug. 'Have a sip. We'll have you right as rain in no time. Won't we, doctor?' She spoke with a Scottish accent.

The water tasted warm, but it eased her throat. 'Thank you.'

'From what I can gather you've had quite an ordeal?' Doctor Jamieson felt her forehead for her temperature. 'Mrs Casey has washed and changed you while you slept, for there was no waking you. Fifteen hours you've slept for, but you obviously needed it. Apart from bruises and scratches and being under-nourished, you seem fine. Unless you have something you wish to tell me, some injury or condition I am not aware of?' He raised his grey eyebrows, they were nearly as bushy as his long side-whiskers.

'No, there is nothing.'

'Good. Well, you can stay here for a day or so and then we'll get you booked into a hotel. I have alerted the authorities in Perth of your survival. No doubt correspondence will be arriving shortly. An investigation has begun on the sinking. The other two survivors have already been taken to Perth for interviews. Did you have insurance?'

'I'm not sure. My brother, David, handled everything.' She thought of the money sewn in her pocket and panicked. 'My skirt!'

'Do not worry. It's all here, even the deckchair though I fail to understand why you'd want it.' Mrs Casey reached under the bed and pulled out the portmanteau and opened it. She took out the small wooden box and opened it. Inside were the wads of money, both hers and the one she'd found, plus the little leather pouch holding her few precious pieces of jewellery. 'The painting didn't survive, I'm afraid.' Mrs Casey handed Louisa the small portrait of her parents, but their dear faces had been washed away after been emerged in so much water for weeks.

Louisa felt a surge of despair rise in her chest. It was as though she had lost them all over again. She closed her eyes, fighting grief. She mustn't break down in front of these people.

'Mrs Casey is most trustworthy, Miss Reynolds. All your belongings are safe.' Doctor Jamieson pulled at his coat sleeves. 'I'd best be off. Calls to make.'

Once he had left Mrs Casey replaced the portmanteau under the bed. 'He's a good man. Much in demand in Albany. Not enough doctors here. Now, what would you like to eat?'

'Anything at all.' Her throat was full of unshed tears. She doubted she could eat a mouthful. Besides, after all the things she'd eaten in the bush she no longer had preferences.

'That's what I like to hear. I've a beef stew for later, but how about a nice bowl of porridge? We have honey too. And I baked fresh bread this morning.'

'Is it morning?' Louisa had no idea of the time, or even what day it was.

The housekeeper chuckled. 'Oh, bless you, yes. Just gone nine o'clock.'

'And day?'

'Twentieth day of February, eighteen hundred and eighty.'

She blinked in amazement. 'February? I didn't think I'd been out there for so long. I tried to keep track of the days.' She frowned, wondering when she had started to go wrong, but it was too difficult to work out. Obviously at some point she had forgot to cross off the days she'd marked on a tree trunk.

So much time had gone by. David had been dead for months...

'I'm sure it was difficult for you. The *Blue Tulip* went down last December, didn't it?'

47

'Christmas night.'

'Shame. All those people lost.' The older woman opened the curtain and sunlight flooded the already warm room. 'I'll make you up a tray. I'll be as quick as I can.'

With Mrs Casey humming in the kitchen, Louisa lay in the bed and glanced around the room which held only the one window. Suddenly a head popped up at the glass and stared into the room.

'Akala!' Flinging back the bed covers, Louisa gently tiptoed to the window, her feet and legs protesting at the pain of walking. Louisa winced as she slid the window up and it squeaked.

'Loo… sa.' Akala grinned. 'We go now?'

'No. I need to stay here.'

The joy left the girl's face. 'I stay with Loo... sa?'

'I don't know.' Louisa glanced at the doorway. Mrs Casey stood there holding a tray full of food.

'Ahh, the young native girl has returned.' The housekeeper put the tray on the wooden chair by the bed.

'Akala saved me, Mrs Casey. I owe her a great deal for she has kept me alive all this time.'

'Where are her tribe? Won't they be wondering where she is?'

'Her mother went walkabout, left her. She has no one, only me.'

'No one? She doesn't look more than ten years old! She must have some family members.'

'Well if she does, I don't know where they are, and they don't seem eager to find her. Jarrah, the native man who led us here might know more.'

'Jarrah? I've not seen a native man poking about, but then they come and go as sneakily as snakes. They steal from houses and then disappear like ghosts in the night.'

'Jarrah was very good to me.' Louisa defended the native who had led her safely out of the bush.

'Well, anyway, that may as be, but he isn't welcome to hang

about here. It'll be hard enough to hide the girl from the doctor.' Mrs Casey frowned. 'The doctor won't want her in the house. He's a good man, compassionate, but…' The older woman tapped her chin. 'The girl could sleep in the laundry. Doctor Jamieson never goes in there. I'll make a bed up on the floor.'

'Thank you so much.'

'Hop into bed and eat your breakfast.' Mrs Casey then looked at Akala. 'Girl, go around to the back of the house.'

Akala hesitated.

Louisa smiled her encouragement. 'You'll be fine. Go. I'll come out and see you as soon as I'm dressed.'

'She'll be all right as long as she doesn't make any trouble,' Mrs Casey said as she helped Louisa settle into the bed and gave her the tray. 'I'll teach her a few things to give her something to do until you're well enough to sort yourself out.'

'I do appreciate your help.'

Left alone, Louisa gazed at the porridge with its big dollop of honey on top. Her mouth watered. Proper food. The first spoonful was savoured on her tongue like some precious nectar, then she ate quickly, enjoying the sweet taste of the honey. She was full before the bowl was empty and felt bad she couldn't finish every drop. It seemed so wasteful. She drank her milky sweet tea, believing it to be the best cup of tea she'd ever had in her life.

'How are you getting on?' Mrs Casey asked, coming into the bedroom. 'Are you ready for a proper bath and a good wash?'

'Yes, that would be wonderful.' She touched her matted hair that felt like straw.

'Good. I've got the tin bath ready in the kitchen and the doors are locked. No one will come in.' She took the tray, looking at the porridge left in the bowl. 'You managed a decent amount. Doctor will be pleased. After your bath, I'll make you some toast.'

'My clothes…' Louisa mentioned following her into the kitchen.

Mrs Casey added another kettle full of hot water to the half-filled bath. 'I'm sorry, my dear, but the clothes you arrived in fell apart in the wash tub. I scrubbed them a bit too hard I'm afraid. I do apologise.'

Louisa tenderly removed the bandages on her feet. 'I have nothing to wear then.'

'Not true.' The housekeeper lifted a brown serge skirt and a brown bodice. Beneath those were a cream corset, linen shift, bloomers and a petticoat. 'They were my sister's. She was about your height, though you are much thinner. I can adjust the skirt band. I'm afraid I don't have a bustle. Neither she or I follow the latest fashions.'

'She won't mind I'm wearing her clothes?'

'She died last year. I've not been able to give away her things yet.' Sadness echoed her words. 'You don't mind wearing them, do you?'

'No, not at all.' What choice did she have? She was reduced to wearing a dead woman's clothes, at least for now.

'Once you're back on your feet properly, you can go shopping. Misses Thirsk have a very good shop on York Street and will fit you out with everything you need, or Miss Vincent, but she's a bit pricey, as she thinks she's in Paris, not Albany.'

Louisa stripped off the nightgown and eased into the water. 'Is Akala settled?'

'She is, yes. I've got her unravelling wool for me. She's sitting on her mattress doing that and eating oat cakes.' Mrs Casey poured warm water over Louisa's head and using a lavender smelling soap started to wash the sand and dirt from her hair. 'What will you do with her though? She can't stay in a hotel with you.'

'I'm not sure. I've not thought about it yet. As I said, I'm all she has.'

'She can stay with me until the doctor finds out. You need to make some plans, my dear. Will you stay in Albany?'

'I've not thought. It's all very hard to comprehend. I kept believing that my brother was alive, somewhere, washed up on another beach… Silly of me really to think that.'

'It's not silly at all. Why wouldn't you hope your dear brother was alive? You've been through a terrible ordeal.' Mrs Casey rinsed the soapy suds from Louisa's hair. 'The sun has bleached the ends of your hair yellow.'

Louisa gave a small smile. 'I wouldn't know. I've not seen myself in a mirror since I was on the ship. I dread to see what I look like now.'

'The ends are as dry as straw. They need cutting off.' Mrs Casey lifted up the jug for another rinse. 'Once your hair is dried, I'm imagining it'll be a variety of shades of brown and blonde. Very unusual.' She leaned forward to peer at Louisa's face. 'The freckles will fade in time though. Rub some lemon on them.'

Hours later, Louisa sat in a rocking chair on the veranda of the doctor's cottage. She felt decent and civilised once more. The brown skirt and bodice were too large for her, but she didn't care. To be wearing fresh underclothes, stockings and low-heeled black ankle boots felt wonderful. Her hair washed and dried was rolled into a tight bun at the back of her neck, secured in a fine net and held in place with shell combs.

At her feet, Akala sat shelling peas, though she ate more than what went into the bowl, having got the taste for this new vegetable she'd never eaten before. Mrs Casey had gone to the shops and the doctor was still out making calls, so Louisa relaxed and watched the comings and goings of the street.

It felt strange to be amongst people again. The feeling of being alone and lost was stronger here than when she was in the bush with Akala. She felt out of place, a stranger but not a stranger. She belonged to no one and no one belonged to her.

She turned to speak to Akala, but the girl ran from sight in the blink of an eye. The garden gate screeched as it was opened, drawing Louisa's attention. Doctor Jamieson walked down the path and Louisa realised why Akala had gone.

'How are you feeling, Miss Reynolds? I must say you look one hundred percent better than when I left.' The doctor sat on the wooden bench near the front door. He fanned his face with his black hat.

'I am feeling a lot better, thank you.'

'A bath and decent clothes, and good food, will go far for a person's general well-being.'

'I appreciate your help and generosity, doctor, especially allowing me to stay here another night.'

'You are welcome. That room is kept for patients, and luckily, we have it spare. Mrs Casey does enjoy having someone to take care of besides me.'

'She is a kind lady.'

He placed his hat on his knee. 'I've taken the liberty to enquire about renting a room for you at one of the hotels. The best one in town. I hope you don't mind?'

'Oh, you have? No, I don't mind, not at all. I know no one nor nothing about this town, so your advice and acquaintance is of great benefit to me.'

'If I may extend that advice, I would suggest putting your money into the bank. Mrs Casey washed your clothes and noticed the sewn pocket. Naturally she told me. It is a good amount that you have, plus the jewels, not that I've seen them.'

She smoothed the material of her skirt. Talking about money was new to her. 'My brother and I were travelling to Sydney to buy land for farming.'

'What will you do now then?'

'I don't know. To return to England is a choice, but I have no close family left there, no home.'

'Where in England do you come from?'

'Near York in Yorkshire.'

'Indeed!' He smiled widely. 'I have been to York.'

'You have?' This news made her happy. That someone had visited the city she knew so well.

'My wife and I went there not long after we were married.'

'Your wife?'

'My late wife. Sadly, she died in childbirth having our son. A long time ago. Over thirty years now.'

'How sad.'

He sighed. 'I couldn't stay in our house without her, so I thought to travel. I ended up here ten years ago, and here I'll stay. Albany is in a beautiful part of the world. I like it here. Maybe you will too?'

'Or I could continue on to New South Wales, to Sydney.'

'To do what?'

'All I know is farming.' She shrugged. 'I have no other skills. I was to keep the house for my brother once we bought our farm in Sydney.'

He patted her hand like a grandfather would. 'There is no rush in making your decision yet. Take some time to think it through. At least in Albany you now know me and Mrs Casey.' He smiled, his grey eyes kind.

'Yes, and that is more than I would have in Sydney. Besides, the thought of going aboard another ship fills me with dread.' She shivered despite the heat.

'A natural thing to feel. A few weeks at the hotel will give you plenty of time to make up your mind. Perhaps you could find a position with a family and be a nanny or governess? Such places are greatly valued out here where females are in short supply. Who knows you may even marry.' Doctor Jamieson rose as the gate squealed again.

Mrs Casey hurried down the path, her basket overloaded with fresh produce. 'Oh, you are back, Doctor. Come away in and I'll make some tea. Miss Reynolds you must be parched as a desert.'

With a smile, Louisa picked up the bowl of shelled peas and followed the doctor and housekeeper inside, her mind a flurry of thoughts about the future. Could she stay here in Albany? And if she did, what would she do?

* * *

A WEEK LATER, Louisa was strolling the streets, her arms full of parcels. She'd been shopping all morning and was ready to return to the hotel. Akala had stayed at the doctor's cottage, for she wasn't allowed in the hotel. Mrs Casey assured Louisa that Akala could help her in the kitchen.

A few people walking past nodded to her, and she smiled back. No doubt she was talk of the town. The shops weren't plentiful, but they met her needs. It wasn't until she moved to the hotel that she realised just how little she owned. She needed a whole new wardrobe of clothes and underclothes, a hairbrush and combs, stockings and shoes, handkerchiefs, nightgowns, hats, gloves and a parasol to ward off the worst of the midday sun.

Having money of her own was a novelty as back in England she'd only received a few shillings from her father to spend on trinkets or books in the village shops. However, she was a sensible Yorkshirewoman and knew how to spend wisely.

She opened an account at the Union Bank and deposited the money David had given her and the money she found in the portmanteau. She felt a calming sense of security in having that money. A niggling amount of guilt played on her mind at the money belonging to an unknown man with the initials W.W. but he was dead and didn't need it. That find could set her up in a new life, she was a woman alone, and she needed all the help she could get.

The pouch of jewels also went into a deposit box except for one necklace that her father had given her on her eighteenth birthday. He'd gone to Whitby on business and bought her a necklace with a small pendant of the famous Whitby black jet.

She had fastened the necklace around her neck as a sort of talisman. Wearing the necklace made her feel closer to her father.

Before leaving Doctor Jamieson's cottage and moving to the hotel, the local magistrate had visited and spoken to her about the shipwreck. He'd mention sending her to Perth, but she'd shaken her head, refusing the idea. The thought of getting on another boat frightened her, and the doctor had said it was unwise in her current state of fragile health to travel so far. Thankfully the matter was dropped, the magistrate took her statement and left her in peace. She had no wish to go to Perth, or even to Sydney just yet. She just needed time to adjust to all that had happened to her.

Earlier she had walked down to the harbour and stared out over the bay which she now knew to be called King George's Sound. The water held an array of boats and ships and, as she wandered along the shoreline, she'd stopped to watch fishermen and whalers bringing in their catch. Seabirds had swooped and cried on the breeze matching the calls of the seamen working on the docks.

She walked past a group of men leaning against a wall and who eyed her appreciatively and made some comments she couldn't quite hear. She quickened her steps as one of them laughed. She'd heard conversation in the hotel's dining room about layabout men, usually former convicts, who didn't want to find work and instead hung around the town causing havoc.

'Miss Reynolds?'

She turned at the sound of her name, surprised that someone even knew it. She stared at the stranger until he took his hat off and she recognised his dark blue eyes. He was the one who spoke to her when she first arrived in town.

'Do you remember me?' he asked, his voice deep, the corner of his eyes crinkling in the sunlight. His thick brown hair lay flat from wearing his hat and he pushed his fingers through it.

'I do, yes.' She smiled warmly, liking the look of him. 'I must thank you for helping me, Mr?'

'Munro. Connor Munro.' He shook her hand, returning her smile.

'You remembered my name.'

'Normally, a new person entering the town causes a sensation and has everyone speaking about it for weeks. The shipwreck was big news, too. However, you are the talk of the town at the moment because you, a woman, survived not only the ship going down but also lived with the black fellas for months.'

'Oh, I see.' She didn't like the thought of everyone talking about her.

'No harm is meant by the gossip though.' He put his hat back on for the sun was burning harshly today. 'You are recovered from your ordeal? I must say you look much improved than the last time I saw you.'

She blushed, embarrassed by the state she was in when she walked into town. 'Yes, thank you, I'm much better. Doctor Jamieson and Mrs Casey took good care of me.'

'She's my aunt, you know.'

'Oh really? She never said.' How odd that the housekeeper wouldn't have mentioned such a thing.

'No, she doesn't speak of our connection. Her brother married my mother and we fell out many years ago.' He shrugged, showing that it was so long ago, or it didn't matter to him, she didn't know which.

'That's a shame.' She enjoyed looking at him. He was a tall handsome man. He wore white moleskin trousers and a dark red shirt. She liked his eyes, the blue were the colour of the sea and expressive.

'So, what are your plans now?' he asked, his stare intent.

She juggled the parcels in her arms into a more comfortable position. 'I don't know. Everything is different now. My brother and I were meant to buy a farm in Sydney.'

'You can farm here, can't you?'

She frowned. 'On my own?'

'Why not?' He said it as though such a thing was an everyday occurrence.

'I wouldn't know where to begin, not without David.'

He waved to someone walking down the street, leading their horse, and then turned back to her. 'You could start with something small, perhaps? A little holding on the edge of town. Raise some chickens, have a cow, vegetables.'

'I suppose I could of course.' She liked the thought of such an enterprise. A home of her own. 'I shall give it some serious thought.'

Another man, much older than Mr Munro came out of the tobacconist shop next to where they stood. 'Ho there, Connor. I'm that pleased to see you while in town.'

Munro patted him on the back, declaring the ease they had with each other. 'Good to see you, George. Sorry to have missed you last week, but I had trouble on the north boundary. Sheep rustlers I suspect.'

'Pesky devils. Need hanging.'

'Agreed.' Munro indicated to Louisa. 'Let me introduce you to Miss Reynolds. Miss Reynolds this is Mr George Henderson, my neighbour and good friend.'

'Ah, the shipwreck girl?' Mr Henderson took his hat off with a flourish, showing a shock of white hair. He shook her hand vigorously. 'Delighted to meet you. What a time you've had, my dear. Shall we all go to luncheon?'

'Oh, er...' Stumped at the sudden invitation, Louisa looked from one to the other.

Munro grinned. 'Albany is very relaxed, Miss Reynolds. There is a class society here, naturally, but the rules are bent rather a lot.'

'And Connor and I would enjoy the chance to dine with a

beautiful young woman such as yourself.' George bowed like a gallant knight, his eyes twinkly with innocent mischief.

She grinned. No one had ever called her beautiful before. 'Very well then.' It felt rude to refuse his invitation. Besides, it gave her more time to spend with the captivating Connor Munro.

'Splendid!' Mr Henderson held out his arm for her, and Mr Munro offered to take her parcels as the three of them walked to a nearby tearoom.

'Tell us all about yourself.' Mr Henderson helped her to be seated at a wooden table complete with white table cloth and a vase of wildflowers in the middle.

'There's not a lot to tell really. I come from York, in Yorkshire, England. My family had a farm.' She wondered how many more times she'd have to repeat that sentence.

'We know where Yorkshire is, my dear. I was born in Lincolnshire and Connor's family are originally from Scotland, though you were born in Sydney, were you not, Connor?' Mr Henderson put up his hand to attract the attention of the young waitress. 'Afternoon tea for three, please, with all the trimmings.'

'Yes, I'm a Sydney lad. My parents came from Scotland to make a new life for themselves.' Munro ran his fingers through his hair again. 'I'm sorry to hear you lost your brother.'

'Thank you. It has been a blow, and I don't think I've fully comprehended it yet. I try not to think about it.' She spoke the truth, for thinking about David hurt too much. Since leaving the bush, she'd had dreams of the shipwreck, of David being under-water calling for her. During the day she kept busy to try and forget.

'You do right, Miss Reynolds, for it'll only bring on a black depression.' Mr Henderson nodded wisely. 'And you are far too young and pretty to succumb to that.' He looked up as the door opened and two older women entered. 'Ho now, ladies. Come and meet Miss Reynolds.'

The two women looked at each other before walking to their table. Both men stood politely.

'Good day to you, Mr Henderson, Mr Munro,' said the woman wearing dark purple, her beady eyes scraping over Louisa. 'And you are Miss Reynolds from the *Blue Tulip*. What a disaster. What ever will you do?'

Mr Henderson reclaimed his chair. 'Yes, Mrs Pierce, a tragedy we don't wish to dwell on today. Miss Muir you are looking well. Won't you both sit down? Connor grab more chairs for the ladies.'

'No, no, Mr Henderson, we cannot possibly stay.' Mrs Pierce's haughty gaze swept the table before landing on Mr Henderson as though he was something repugnant. 'My sister and I have much to do.'

Mr Henderson smiled at Louisa. 'Mrs Pierce is the wife of the Reverend Pierce.'

'You *must* attend Sunday service, Miss Reynolds. Within the society of the church you may find *suitable* people to meet.' Mrs Pierce gave Mr Henderson a pointed look. 'Come, sister. We must hurry. Good day to you all.'

Once the two women had collected a boxed cake and left, Mr Henderson laughed. 'My goodness, what prudes! They never change. Miss Muir has no chance of ever being out of the yoke her sister has put on her, poor woman. They were both decent lookers in their youth.'

'Have you lived here a long time then, Mr Henderson?' she asked as the tea tray was brought to the table followed by stands of delicate pastries and small finger-cut sandwiches.

'I arrived when I was twenty-three when this town was nothing more than a whaler's outpost and a track in the scrub.' He settled back in the chair, warming to his topic. 'You see, I'm the youngest son, and my father didn't know what to do with me, common problem in large families. He gave me some money and a ticket to the colonies to try my hand at anything I chose. I went to India for a bit but couldn't settle there. Too many people. My heart was broken in Calcutta. Beautiful she was… Too good for me, obviously.' George sighed in a dreamy kind of way.

Munro shook his head slightly and grinned at Louisa.

George poured more tea into everyone's cups. 'Eventually I went to Sydney and then Hobart, where I met a fellow called John Tyler, a Yorkshire man, very clever. Anyway, John was sailing here to Albany to start farming sheep. I decided to join him.' He took a bite of beef sandwich. 'We had a partnership in the farm and weathered all the bad early times, awful they were, living in a tent, eating dreadful food, the droughts, the flies. God it was terrible, but we survived and thrived, funny enough. Then, to my utter dismay John upped and died three years after we started. Came home one day feeling ill, and within two months, dead.'

'How sad.' Louisa took a sandwich and put it on her plate, though she wasn't a bit hungry as she listened to the delightful Mr Henderson.

Mr Henderson sighed. 'Very sad, indeed. He was a good man. The best.'

'Do you still have your farm?'

Connor sipped his tea. 'Miss Reynolds, out here farms are small-holdings of a few acres growing vegetables and have milk cows. Anything bigger is called a run or a station.'

'A run or a station, like a train station?'

'There are no trains for hundreds of miles.' Munro laughed.

'How bizarre.' She smiled, enjoying herself immensely talking to these two interesting men. 'A large farm is called a station. I'm learning new things all the time.'

Connor took a pastry. 'I'm not fully sure of the meaning myself, but it stems from the homestead being the only building for hundreds of miles and it's the calling place for any traveller on their way across the country. Hospitality is key out here when homesteads can be several days between.'

'Oh, I see.' She didn't really and took a bite of her sandwich. 'Fascinating.'

'George and I have what you call "sheep runs" which are vast tracts of land,' Munro told her. 'Hundreds of acres. Some we own, other parts we lease from the government. Eventually, I want to own all of mine.'

'We are neighbours,' Mr Henderson added, 'but to get to each other's house is an hour's horse ride. Luckily, the houses were built close the boundary line between us and not in the middle of our properties, or we'd be travelling all day to call on each other.'

Louisa stared in astonishment. 'All day travelling to visit each other and you'd still be on your own land? I can't imagine such a thing. And you both have sheep?'

Munro drank more of his tea and replaced the cup on the saucer. 'Yes, about thirty thousand head for me and George what are you, twenty thousand?'

'Yes, I've been culling the flock. I'm old. Sixty-five soon. I don't have the time anymore, or the inclination to work hard in building a large flock.' He spread his hands out with a sad shake of his head.

Louisa couldn't imagine such sums. 'You have that many sheep? Your farms… er… stations must be enormous?'

'They are.' Munro took another pastry from the stand and inspected it before biting into it. 'I'm eager to buy more.'

'He'll end up owning my place at this rate.' Mr Henderson chuckled, but something dulled in his sharp gaze. 'How I wish I was young again.'

The conversation captivated Louisa. To think of people owning so much land and they weren't nobility! To ride all day and still be on land you own. It boggled her mind.

'You're still young at heart, George.' Munro nodded to him in a sort of salute.

George laughed, then he sat up straighter, a light dancing in his eyes again. 'I have a brilliant idea. I propose we invite Miss Reynolds to our stations, Connor, what say you?'

Munro hesitated slightly, his eyes downcast. 'I'm sure Miss Reynolds has better things to do.'

'Nonsense,' George barked. 'What could be more adventurous and educational for her than to visit a sheep station, or two?' He turned to Louisa. 'Would you consider coming back with me to King's Station?'

'King's Station? That's the name of your home?'

'Yes. When we first arrived, John said it was land fit for a king.' George shrugged. 'He chose correctly for I have made a good life from it.'

'I would very much like to visit your home.' She sipped her tea, smiling at the older man, thrilled at the prospect. She hoped Munro would offer the same invitation. It would be nice to have friends and to visit these huge farms.

'Champion.' George munched on a raspberry tart. 'I leave in the morning. Will that be suitable?'

'Yes. I'll pack tonight.' She glanced at Munro, but he was staring into his teacup.

George tapped the table in delight. 'Oh, it will be a treat to have female company for a while.'

'I must go.' Munro wiped his mouth with a napkin and stood. 'I've a delivery of grass seed at the warehouse I want to inspect. I'll settle the bill on my way out. See you later, George, Miss Reynolds.' He left the table, threw money on the counter and collected his hat from the stand by the door.

Disappointed by his leaving, Louisa forced a smile at George. 'How long does it take to get to your property, Mr Henderson?'

'A full day if we set off early.' He added more tea to his cup. 'Since we are to be friends and you are visiting my home, I insist you call me George.'

'Very well, and I am Louisa.'

'Splendid. I'll collect you just after six in the morning.'

'That would be lovely, thank you. I'm staying at Mrs Chokes lodging house.'

'Ah, Nessie Chokes. What a good woman she is.'

Louisa laughed. 'Do you know *everyone?*'

'Of course, Albany isn't big enough for people to be strangers, and when you've been in the district for over forty years, you have no choice but to know all who live here.' He added sugar to his cup. 'Soon enough *you'll* know everyone too.'

She liked the sound of that, of being part of a community, of having friends, and perhaps one day even a husband...

CHAPTER 6

On the first day of March, Louisa held on to the side rail of the buggy's seat. George was driving it at walking pace, and following behind them, was the station's cart filled with produce and extra farming implements bought during George's week's stay in Albany.

They'd set off from town just after dawn, and now a few hours later, they were deep in open country with the coast far behind them. The heat from the sun, which shone from a clear blue sky was hotter without the ocean breeze to cool it.

For as far as Louisa could see the land stretched unchanging. Trees, the few that grew, were stumped in growth. The soil was dry and orange, with brown tussocks of grass.

'Not much to look at, is it?' George said.

'No. It's very different again from the coast.'

'This is as close as it comes to being a desert without being a desert, if you get my meaning. However, it changes again as we get closer to the Stirling Ranges. Decent rainfall produces better grasslands for us farmers.'

'I don't see anyone close by. No farms or houses.'

'No, you won't not here-abouts. It's rather isolated between the coast and the ranges, the land isn't worth a penny as you can't grow anything in it without a lot of money spent improving it first.'

Sweat trickled down the side of Louisa's face, and she was glad of Mrs Chokes advice to buy a wide-brimmed straw hat. Small dainty hats had no place out here. 'But your fields are better than this?'

'Oh yes, much improved,' he said proudly. 'We ploughed acres and acres when we first set up and fertilised them before spreading grass seeds. Over the years we've converted more and more acres into farmland. We plough our own hay for the horses, but the sheep are hardy little souls and are happy to go out and eat the native grasses. Of course, the lambs are fattened up on the seeded fields around the farm before they go to market.'

'It's all so different to England, isn't it?' she replied, watching a small lizard dart across the track.

'Yes, very much so, but if you can get used to the heat and flies and the basic way of living, then it can provide a good life.'

At noon George stopped the little convoy beside a group of straggly eucalyptus trees near a small stream, which he informed her was called a creek. All streams and becks were called creeks here and only the very large rivers where actually called rivers. Louisa soaked up this knowledge like a sponge, fascinated to learn everything George had to teach her, just as she had with Akala's teachings.

The driver of the cart, a quiet man named Hunt, filled buckets of water from the creek and gave them to the horses before taking his food. He sat away from George and Louisa but seemed pleasant enough.

George nodded towards his man as he guided Louisa over to the shade. 'Hunt is a former convict, who has served his sentence and is now a free man. He works hard, gives me no trouble. You mustn't be frightened by him.'

Her eyes widened. 'He isn't a murderer, is he?'

George chuckled. 'No, not at all. He was caught poaching rabbits on land not belonging to him. He simply wanted to feed his wife and children.'

'My brother told me that convicts were no longer sent out to Australia.'

'That's true. However, there are many women and men still to finish their sentences.'

Shocked to be amongst a former convict, but also sad for the quiet man who had been only trying to look after his family, she remained silent. Her short time in Albany had given her a glimpse into a new world where convicts still worked their sentences and where ticket-of-leave prisoners now walked amongst the free settlers.

While George opened up two canvas stools and a small wooden table for them to eat their picnic on, Louisa strolled to the creek's edge and dampened her handkerchief to wipe over her hot face. The clear water allowed her to see its sandy bottom and the tiny fish darting about. White birds in the trees screeched noisily. She'd seen those birds before with their bright yellow tufts on the top of their heads. Akala would sometimes squawk as the did, adding to the deafening noise a flock could make.

Returning to George, she sat on the stool and poured out the raspberry cordial into two glasses. 'What is that mountain range called up ahead?'

'That's Stirling Range, I told you about. It's beautiful, isn't it? Connor's boundary is on the western edge of the range. He's climbed the highest peak. I've walked some of the smaller ones years ago.'

'And his property is west of yours?'

'North-west, yes.' George opened a linen bag and took out a loaf of bread and cuts of roast beef. 'We shall go and visit his home in a day or two, if you wish.'

She nodded, feeling a little awkward at the mention of Connor Munro, his abrupt leaving at the tearoom still caused her concern. Last night in her bed she had thought about him, remembering his dark blue eyes, the way he combed his fingers through his brown hair. She noticed the fine lines around his eyes from being out in the sunshine, the way his smile was a little crooked, and heard again the timbre of his voice. She'd never met a man who entranced her as much as he did. She hoped that she would see him a great deal while staying with George.

'My dear?'

She blinked. 'Oh, forgive me. What did you say?'

George laughed. 'I asked if you wanted pickle on your beef?'

She nodded and took herself to task. Connor Munro wouldn't be mooning about thinking of her, so she needed to do the same. If she saw him she'd be polite and engaging, nothing more, and if she didn't then well that would be fine too. He didn't need to know he'd been in her thoughts. She had to be smart and not give herself away. Besides, she had plenty enough to think about as she sorted out what to do with her future.

The sun was setting low on the horizon when they passed under the sign proclaiming they were entering King's Station. The well-trodden dirt track led them past fields of English seeded grass mown by years of constant grazing. Louisa saw no sheep, but the fields held a few cows and several horses.

As they headed for the numerous buildings in front of them, another track veered off to the right and Hunt took the cart that way.

George steered the buggy towards the house. 'Hunt is going to the outbuildings. I will show you them tomorrow.'

Excited, Louisa gazed around. The drive edged around a large brown lawn, kept short by a tethered goat in the middle. Tall eucalyptus trees grew by the west side of the house to provide shade against the setting sun, George informed her.

'The goat is Nanny.' George halted the buggy before the house. 'Produces wonderful cheese, but she has to be kept from the other goats as she's a bit bossy, like most of the females I've met in my life.' He laughed.

Louisa studied George's home, which she now recognised was a typical style for the colony, being only one-storey. Three steps went up to a wide veranda that went the full length of the front of the house. A creeper grew up the veranda's support posts giving shade and privacy. The place needed flowers, lots of them, to soften the harshness of the unforgiving landscape, and seeing the peeling woodwork, it also needed a lick of paint.

'We could do with some rain,' George said, climbing down. 'Summer has been lengthy and dry.'

The door opened, and a small old Chinese woman came out onto the steps and bowed. She wore cream linen trousers and matching shirt, her long grey hair tied in a pigtail. Her smile was warm, her eyes watchful.

George came around the buggy and helped Louisa down. 'Welcome to my home.' He escorted her up the steps to the little woman. 'Louisa, this is my housekeeper and cook, Su Lin. I simply could not do without her. Su Lin, Miss Reynolds has come to stay with us for a time.'

'Pleased to meet you.' Louisa smiled, suddenly tired.

'Welcome, miss.' Su Lin bowed again, then scuttled down to the buggy to collect the luggage.

The front door led straight into a sitting room. Lanterns had been lit on two small occasional tables, giving the room a comfortable feel as dusk descended. The furniture was solid timber, some looked handmade. The floor was also timber but varnished. The walls had been plastered and painted white like the outside of the house. Piles of books littered the floor and other surfaces, while a tower of newspapers were stacked in the corner near a door leading to another room.

An aged green velvet sofa situated at an angle to an unlit fireplace invited Louisa to sit. She felt she had to say something. 'This is a lovely room, George,' she ventured, though in truth the room was basic and sparse. There seemed to be no life in it.

'I'm sure it's not what you are used to. Being a single man, the house was not my main concern as the station grew. Buying and transporting furniture in the colony is a terribly trying and expensive business.' He looked around the room. 'The place could do with some new pieces, but…' He didn't finish his sentence as he poured them both a small sherry from a liquor cabinet near the window.

'Here's to a pleasant visit.' He raised his glass against Louisa's.

'I'm happy to be here.' She rose from the sofa, and to keep her tiredness at bay, looked at the two paintings on the wall of English country scenes.

'That one is my family home near Lincoln.' George pointed to a painting above the fireplace of a stone house set amongst flowering gardens with a church in the distance. 'My mother sent it to me shortly before she died.'

'It looks lovely. Do you miss England?'

'No, not really. I was too busy making this place a success for me to think of home, of my family. But now I'm older I think more of my long dead parents. I've not seen my brothers and sisters for so long I doubt I could pick them out in a crowd now. The letters from my siblings stopped arriving a few years ago. I guess that once my parents died no one tried hard enough to stay in contact.' George shook himself like a dog. 'Heavens that is far too emotional to be discussing on your first night!' He laughed at himself. 'Come, I'll show you to your room where you can refresh ready for dinner. Su Lin will give us a banquet. She enjoys it when I have guests.'

He guided her out of the room and down a thin central hallway with rooms on each side. 'That's the dining room, and that other little room is my study,' George informed her as they walked along. 'Here's my bedroom and there's two small guest rooms added onto the back. Let us see which one Su Lin has put you in.' He stopped by the first door past the dining room. 'Here we are. She's put you in the best room. I apologise that it is so cramped.' He stepped aside so Louisa could enter the room first.

She gazed about the pale green painted walls. A window overlooked the side of the house and against the far wall was a white iron bed with a green printed quilt on it and snowy white pillows. A fine white net hung from a circular frame above the bed to keep out the mosquitoes. A narrow handmade wooden wardrobe completed the setting.

'It's a very pleasant room, George.'

'I've added to the house as the years have gone by. I thought I could re-create a proper gentleman's residence for a family, but although I built the extra rooms, no family formed. Sad, really.'

He crossed to the tall set of drawers. 'John was a very good carpenter. He made most of the furniture here. It's something he enjoyed doing when the weather kept us inside or at night. I think he thought he was making it all for a future bride.' He lifted the flower painted porcelain jug which sat in a matching basin. 'Su Lin has brought you water to wash but if you require a bath let her know.'

He opened the wardrobe next to the drawers and Louisa's few dresses were already hung up. 'Excellent. I'll leave you in peace and go wash the dust off myself. Dinner will be about seven o'clock.' He glanced at the small carriage clock on the mantelpiece. 'Is twenty minutes enough time? I can ask Su Lin to hold off serving for a while.'

'No, no. I'll be ready.'

He nodded and with a smile left the room, closing the door behind him.

As good as her word, Louisa walked into the dining room exactly at seven o'clock. She'd washed and changed into a dove grey skirt and bodice with black lace detail at the throat and cuffs and her Whitby jet necklace on display. The style was simple but there wasn't a lot of choice that the dressmaker — a flighty woman called Miss Vincent — could make up in the week Louisa had been in Albany. Ideally, she should be in mourning black, but the dressmaker had run out of black crepe and silk, and was awaiting a new shipment of cloth coming in. Miss Vincent had been run off her feet as her assistant had recently married and left, leaving her to run the shop singlehandedly. Louisa had been grateful for the clothes she'd managed to make for her in the short time required.

George, dressed in a black suit, pulled out a chair for her at the long wooden table. A large bowl of wild flowers decorated the middle of the snow-white tablecloth and the silver cutlery shone in the golden light of the candelabra. 'You look very fetching, Louisa.'

'Thank you. I don't have many clothes yet. I'm woefully short on the most basic things other women take for granted. I don't even own a coat! However, I thought I could do without one until the weather turns colder, if it even does.'

'My dear, it does indeed. The winters here can be very bitter. Why, I have even seen snow on the highest mountain of Stirling Range.'

'Snow? Really?' This shocked her. 'Oh my, I'd best order a coat then too. I assumed the whole colony was always very hot. Since the shipwreck I've not felt the terrible cold like I did back home.'

'That's because it's summer. Remember, the seasons are the opposite to England.'

'It is difficult to get used to.'

'Did you visit Miss Vincent's shop?' George asked, pouring them some wine.

'You know her too?'

'I told you, I know everyone.' He smiled.

'Especially the ladies?' Louisa grinned.

George tapped the side of his nose and winked.

'Yes, I did visit Miss Vincent on three occasions, but she was extremely busy and her bolts of material severely lacking in variety. She'd had a run of appointments and her new stock hadn't arrived. I did well to get the three dresses I got. Thankfully Mrs Casey... do you know *her*?' She chuckled.

'Of course, she's Connor's aunt. Bit of a tartar really, likes to hold grudges. A fickle woman if you ask me.'

Louisa sipped her wine. 'Yes, well she gave me clothes from her sister who had died. Miss Vincent altered them for me.'

Su Lin entered the room carrying a tray of delicious smelling food. She placed a bowl of the aromatic soup before Louisa and then George. She bowed and then left the room.

'This will be one of her special soups.' George picked up his spoon. 'The Chinese have excellent cooking skills and use many exotic ingredients like chillies. Su Lin has her own vegetable garden and no one is allowed to enter it without her permission, even me.'

Louisa sipped her first mouthful of the soup and blinked at the sudden hit of flavours. Although mild, the soup tasted of herbs and the stock was rich with the taste of chicken. 'How delicious!'

George grinned. 'Told you it would be. Su Lin is worth her weight in gold.'

Their next course was a fried lamb and vegetable dish with a dipping sauce that was a bit spicier and Louisa only just made it through without reaching for a glass of water. George laughed at her. After that, Su Lin served roasted wild duck with rice and finished with a lime juice flavoured drink and strawberries.

'What a delightful meal.' Louisa leaned back in her chair full and fought a yawn from escaping. 'So much better than I had living in the bush with Akala.'

'Akala?'

'The aborigine girl who saved me after the shipwreck.'

'Ahh...yes.' George wiped his mouth with a linen napkin.

'She is staying with Mrs Casey. I couldn't take her to the hotel.

She's sleeping in the laundry at the doctor's cottage and helping Mrs Casey.'

'What about her own people?'

'She doesn't have any. Her mother, Kiah, just up and left to go on a walkabout.'

'Yes, they do that. I have some blacks employed here, they make very good stockmen, but they have a tendency to just leave whenever the mood suits them. They do come back eventually. There is an aboriginal camp down by the river. The tribe doesn't cause me any problems, so I leave them to hunt and fish as they wish. They leave me and my animals alone and I leave them alone. It's a harmonious relationship.'

'I feel Akala is my responsibility now, when actually she isn't. She has a mother. It seems they were not part of a tribe, at least not one close by. I'm almost certain Kiah was taken by a white man against her will. Akala is a half caste.'

George sighed as he nibbled a strawberry. 'It does happen, unfortunately. Not so much now, at least not in towns, but not so long ago it was a common thing. White women were and still are very limited in the colony, especially in far flung places such as this one.' He sipped his wine. 'The girl will adapt to any situation. Don't worry about that. Likely she'll not even be there when you return to town.'

'When I return to Albany I will find somewhere more perma-nent to live and Akala will be able to stay with me, if she wishes.'

'Have you any thoughts on that score? What you'll do?'

'Perhaps open a shop, though I don't know the first thing about business. My father was a prosperous farmer and we wanted for nothing. We had a dairy maid and a laundry maid, but my mother and I did everything else. I can run a home and cook a little.'

'What made you and your brother decide to emigrate then?'

'Our parents died within a week of each other. The landlord put our rent up. He didn't like David as much as he liked my father. David could be a tad hot-headed at times and said what was on his mind. He believed the landlord should sell the farm to us, but he wouldn't. Nor would he maintain the farm buildings or drain the lower fields that always flooded in winter. David sometimes spoke too much in our village pub about the landlord. Gossip spreads so easily. Then David caught the eye of the landlord's daughter and, well, it became difficult after that.'

'Indeed, it would.' George chuckled. 'So, you sold up and ventured across the seas.'

'To a tragic end…' She sipped more wine, her thoughts sad. How she missed David. She missed laughing with him. Her brother was always there, a stable support in her life. Now, she was on her own and she realised just how much she had taken his presence for granted.

'Try not to be too sad, my dear. Your brother would not want that.'

'I know I must be strong, and I have been since the ship went down, but there are times when I feel the loss of him dreadfully. The two of us only had each other. None of it seems real yet.'

'Perhaps that is not a bad thing. Grief can take a terrible toll on a person.'

'Can it be put off forever though?'

George shook his head. 'No, I don't think it can. You've had much to contend with since the shipwreck. You had to survive in circumstances that would break many. Be proud of achieving that and take each day as it comes.'

'That's all I can do.' She shrugged, confused and unsure of her future.

'You must go to bed, my dear.' George patted her hand. 'It has been a long day.'

'Yes, I think I will.' She smiled, and he assisted her from the table and to her room.

'Breakfast is at any time you wake. I live very informally. Please don't feel the need to be up by a certain time. I usually go out to the men early in the morning and discuss the farm's requirements, but you must sleep as long as you like.'

'Thank you. You have been very kind.' Meeting George had been a stroke of luck and she was deeply grateful for his friendship.

'That's what friends are for, my dear. Good night.' He kissed her hand and left her.

In the bedroom, Su Lin had left one lamp burning low and turned the bed down. She'd unhooked the net and wrapped it around the perimeter of the bed frame. Louisa's nightgown lay over the chair before the dressing table and the curtains were drawn. Su Lin's attention to detail made Louisa emotional. She blinked away the sting of hot tears and began to undress.

Louisa couldn't remember the last time someone had taken so much care to make sure she was comfortable. Mrs Casey had been kind, but her actions had been that of a nurse, efficient but impersonal, and Louisa had felt she was being an inconvenience staying at the doctor's cottage.

Once changed into her nightgown and in bed she pulled the net around her, liking the effect of being in a misty cloud. Turning out the lamp, she settled back and thanked the fates that brought her into contact with George. His kindness touched her deeply. Yet as her eyes closed the face she saw had deep blue eyes and a crooked smile.

CHAPTER 7

'What do you think of her?' George led a bay mare from the stable and out into the yard.

'I'll like her very much if she doesn't throw me off!' Louisa said truthfully.

'You said you can ride!'

'I can, but that was a gentle pony I'd had since I was a girl. I've seen the horses here and they move so fast.'

'They are stock horses, built and trained for that purpose. Minty is my old brood mare and ancient.' George led Minty to the mounting block next to his own horse, Firecracker. 'Right, up you get, my dear. You'll have to forgive my lack of suitable lady's saddles.'

'I've ridden astride before. I'll be fine.' Lifting her skirts, she put one foot in the stirrup and swung her leg over. Minty shifted a little, but remained calm and uninterested. 'I wish I had a riding habit though.'

'A few minutes more and I would have missed you both,' Connor Munro said suddenly, riding into the yard.

Louisa whipped around to stare at him. She'd not been expecting him and her heart thumped wildly against her ribs.

'Ho there, Connor. Good to see you.' George gave Louisa the reins. 'We were just off for a ride to the creek. But since you're here you can accompany Louisa and give my poor old bones a rest.'

Louisa's stomach twisted at the thought. Munro looked every inch of a man suited to his outdoor life wearing the usual white moleskin trousers and a checked red shirt. His hat was pulled low over his eyes, shadowing his handsome face.

'I'd be delighted.' He smiled.

She sensed a small hesitation on his part.

George patted Firecracker's rump. 'I know you've just ridden a good way to get here, so if you'd rather not then we can cancel.'

Munro relaxed in the saddle. 'No, no, it's fine.'

'Ride Firecracker and save your own beast for the journey back home.'

Munro dismounted his own horse and gave the reins to a native stable boy. He fondled Firecracker's ears as he readjusted the length of the stirrups, for he was taller than George. He murmured to Firecracker for a moment before easily mounting and turning the horse around.

Louisa couldn't take her eyes off him. Munro was a man in control, at ease in his world.

'Were you going to the pools?' Connor asked George.

'I wasn't, no. It's too far for me to ride there now, my hips don't agree with me being in the saddle for more than twenty minutes. I thought to just go to the creek down by the bottom paddock and have a gentle ride, but you must take Louisa to the pools. I'll have a drink waiting for you both for when you get back.' George opened the gate for them leading into a grassy paddock. 'Enjoy your ride.'

Munro kept Firecracker at a walk as Minty seemed in no hurry to go any faster. 'It's good that you can ride. Being in the colony and not being able to ride is a hindrance. The distances are so far and a cart can't always get everywhere, especially when the rain turns the tracks into quagmires.'

'I've ridden since I was girl. But village lanes are vastly different to the enormous spaces out here.' She felt ridiculously happy that she and Munro were by themselves on this ride. She didn't understand her feelings, only that she liked being with him. His nearness made all her senses come alive and she wanted to smile and be beautiful and clever.

'Have you been enjoying your stay with George?'

'I have. I don't know where the week has gone, really. He's so interesting. We talk non-stop, day and night.'

'George can talk, that's for sure.'

'We've been doing so much in the last few days. He's shown me the workings of the property. The shearing shed is huge. I've never seen a building dedicated to just shearing before. At home my father simply sheared in the yard.'

'Yes, but he wouldn't have had the numbers as we do here. Shearing our flocks can take weeks.'

'Amazing.' She steered Minty around a rabbit hole. 'I've met all the workers and their families. It's rather a small village here, isn't it? I've never seen the likes of such before. The station is so self-sufficient in many ways. I'm learning a great deal. Yesterday we walked to the aborigine camp near the creek.' She looked up at a tree as a crow gave a long eerie call.

'Yes, both George and I have our own camps of blacks. We treat them well, unlike some station owners who drive them off their land. But the blacks are a strange people. Have their own ways, as we do I suppose. They must think we are strange, too.'

'Yes. I used to make Akala laugh with the things I did, which she didn't understand. She thought I wore too many clothes.' Louisa smiled at the memory.

Munro waved away a fly. 'We are lucky that in this area there is no tension between us and the aborigines.'

'It is fortunate indeed. I would hate that. George thinks that black and white should get along together.'

'It's all about respect for each other, though not everyone feels the same.' He guided Firecracker around another large hole in the track.

'George said the same yesterday. He spoke with the elders and I watched the women making food. I was able to speak a few words with them. Akala taught me some of the language as best she could.'

In the distance a mob of grey kangaroos lay under a tree out of the sun. Louisa watched them, marvelling at the sight of such creatures. One male stood, he looked magnificent, tall as she was and with powerful muscles.

'I've eaten kangaroo,' she said abruptly, remembering the smell of the singed fur.

Munro laughed. 'So have I. Most people out here have.' Then he sobered. 'Was that after the shipwreck?'

'Yes. When Akala and her mother saved me. Kiah caught a small kangaroo and threw it on the coals.' She gazed into the space, recalling those weeks in the bush. 'It seems so long ago since that day, yet it was only very recent.'

She thought of her brother. He would have enjoyed being out here. This was what he'd been wanting to create for them both — their own farm. How had she endured three months without David?

'You did so well to survive out there.' Munro broke into her thoughts, his tone full of admiration. 'It can't have been easy.'

'It was hard, believe me. There were days when I wished I had gone down with the ship...'

'That's understandable.'

'Then there were days when Akala and I caught fish or crabs and we had food. The stars would shine, and she told me stories of the Dreaming.'

'The blacks are very spiritual.'

'But it isn't like the religions we know, is it?' She felt nervous being with this man. She didn't want to make a fool of herself. 'Their Dreaming is all about animals and ancestors and nature. It's a kind of religion that is mellow, not harsh like some white people's religions which cause war and hate.'

'We could learn from that.'

She blushed at her little speech, but when she glanced at him he was looking at her with such tenderness that she felt the breath catch in her throat. She looked away and stared out over the open plains. 'Everything in this country is on a large scale.'

'I'm told it is unlike England's countryside.'

'That is true.' She sent her mind back to the land of her birth. 'England's countryside is gentle rolling green hills, tumbling brooks, soft valleys and little villages. The cold of winter, especially in the north, can freeze your bones, but summer is pleasant, not at all like the heat here.' She grinned, still not used to the differences between the two countries. 'I had no idea that out here that most kitchens aren't attached to the houses but separated by covered walkways.'

'Yes, that's the case for many country houses to reduce the risk of fire. But it's not the way in the cities, where there is the chance the house will have a basement kitchen.' He shrugged as though the matter didn't really concern him.

'And the meat stores. How ingenious!' She had marvelled at the small underground building which held the aging and cured meats.

'Again, a necessity not found in England, I imagine. You will soon get used to the changes. That is, if you are staying?'

She smoothed Minty's neck with her gloved hand. 'I think I shall. I have nothing to return to England for.'

'You can do well in this country if you're prepared to work hard.'

'Even a single woman?' she asked doubtfully as their horses separated to traverse a rocky part of the track.

'Of course,' Munro said as they came back to side by side.

'Although you may not be single for very long. The ratio to men and women is unbalanced. You'll be inundated with marriage proposals before long I shouldn't think.'

'George said something similar to me. How interesting.' She blushed, hoping he'd be the first to offer and last. It was foolish to think so rashly but she couldn't help it. She'd marry him tomorrow if she could. What woman wouldn't? He was strong, good looking and owned property. He was perfect husband material.

She glanced at him and saw he was watching her. She looked away, flustered and swatted away the flies diving about her head. 'And such flies.'

He laughed, easy in the saddle with one hand on his thigh. 'Far too many of them, I agree. They are a blight on animals and humans alike.'

She relaxed into Minty's easy rhythm and looked around. The sheer enormity of the plains stretched as far as the eye could see, broken only by the ranges in the north. 'Are these pools near the mountains?'

'No, they are closer than that. The creek that runs through both mine and George's property is of decent depth and rarely dries out even in the summer because it's fed by the creeks coming out of the ranges. Along the creek, in places, there are large rock formations and in these are pools, which are great for swimming and cooling off in.'

'Sounds delightful.' She was sweating beneath her clothes and longed for a swim. She watched white birds that George had told her were called cockatoos, fly and squawk in the eucalyptus trees. She'd seen plenty of them when living with Akala and now she knew the name of them.

Firecracker suddenly skipped sideways barrelling into Minty. Louisa gasped, tightening the reins. Munro swore as Firecracker pranced about, throwing his head up and making life difficult for his rider. It took a minute for Munro to control him.

White-faced, Munro let out a deep breath. 'Are you all right? Is Minty under control?'

'Yes, she's fine.' Louisa relaxed for Minty was behaving well. She'd stopped and was eating grass, not at all concerned by Firecracker's antics.

'Sorry about that.' He edged Firecracker away a bit. 'There might have been a snake in the grass which scared him.'

'I didn't see it.' She glanced about them worriedly.

'It'll be gone now, but the horses' sense and see them before we do.' Munro took off his hat and wiped his forehead. 'I was worried Minty might bolt.'

'She's fine.' Louisa patted the mare's neck. In truth Minty looked less likely to bolt than to knit a shawl. 'But isn't winter coming? George said snakes hibernate then.'

'They do, but it's not cold enough just yet to send them undercover. Summer has been a long one this year.'

'I find it so strange that we are in March and its autumn here, where back in England it would be spring.' Louisa nudged Minty into walking again.

They rode on in silence for some way. Louisa concentrated on her surroundings and finally saw the sheep that George owned. A large number of them grazed serenely, fanned out on a huge plain. 'There's so many of them.'

'And they are not all of his flock that you see.'

'Goodness.'

Munro guided Firecracker towards some trees to the left of them and at the top of the bank he reined him in. Several yards below, the creek tinkled gently, the sun reflecting off the water as it flowed over rocks. Small waterfalls fell from pool to pool and the sound was like a musical background to the calls of the birds.

'It's wonderful.' She sighed, enchanted by the serenity and the beauty.

Munro dismounted and then helped her down, his hands lingering on her waist. She liked the close contact. He was taller than her, his chest broad. She stared up into his dark blue eyes and wished he'd kiss her.

Minty snorted and Firecracker moved away content to pull at the grass.

Connor turned to the creek. 'Do you fancy walking down there? The bank is a little steep, but we can manage it, and it's worth it.'

Holding her skirts with one hand and placing the other hand in Connor's, she followed him down the sandy bank to the edge of the creek. Thin-leafed trees overhung the water, creating shadows.

'What trees are these?'

'I don't know the scientific names, but the common name is black wattle. They have bright yellow flowers which bloom about September. And those,' he pointed to the trees on the other side of the creek, 'they are called Tea-trees. The Aboriginals use the oil from the leaves to help with cleaning wounds.'

'How fascinating.' She stepped towards the water, the sun warm on her back.

'Early settlers apparently used to boil the leaves for a kind of tea, too.' He took her hand as naturally as if they'd known each other for years instead of days and led her along the bank towards one of the pools. She liked that he'd done that. He could have taken her elbow, which was considered polite, but he'd taken her hand, creating an intimacy she welcomed. She felt very aware of him, of them being alone out in the middle of nowhere.

'Sometimes, if you're quiet, you'll see a platypus,' he whispered as he stepped onto a flat sandstone rock at the top of the next little waterfall.

'Oh, I've read about them. They have a duck's beak but look like a small otter.'

He smiled, helping her to stand a little closer to him. 'Yes, something like that.'

For a few moments they were quiet, watching the small

waterfalls trickle from pool to pool. Birds called and flittered in the trees. A small lizard darted on spindly legs across the rocks, its head held high as though it was in a great hurry. Louisa smiled, thinking Akala would have chased it if she was here. In the clear water, small fish swam lazily. It was serene, peaceful and she didn't want the moment to end.

'I like this place.' Louisa sighed in contentment. 'Thank you for bringing me here.'

'You're welcome.' He looked down at her. 'It's a special place. I'm glad I was the first person to show it to you.'

'I am too.' She desperately wanted to touch his face and quickly tucked her hands behind her back to squash the urge. 'Is your home very far from here?'

Munro glanced away. 'Yes, in the other direction. However, I don't have pools like these, the creeks on my property are all boringly flat. But if you wander up into the ranges, the scenery is rather spectacular. You can see for miles.'

She gazed at him. 'I'd like to visit the ranges.'

'I can take you. Shall I arrange a day then? George might not venture that far, but we could travel up one of the smaller mountains, if you wished?'

'I'd like that very much.' She felt giddy at the thought of spending another day with him.

'Good. We'll do it then, soon, before you return to Albany.' He walked along the edge of the pool. 'Are you hot, do you want to swim?'

'Swim?'

'Yes. You could swim in this pool and I'll go further down to the next one.' He pointed to the next large pool, covered by a large overhanging tree. A small waterfall and a drop of a few feet separated that pool from the one they were standing next to.

'I wasn't prepared to go swimming. I don't have a towel or change of clothes.'

He laughed. 'You don't need them. Strip down to your shift,

and once you've finished swimming, just lie on the warm rock and the sun will dry you.'

She was hot, but to undress with him so close? A wicked part of her wanted to do it, for she'd done it with Akala plenty of times. However, now she was back in civilisation there was a proper way to behave.

'I didn't think you were the kind to turn away from a little adventure, not after everything you've already done,' he teased, mischief in his eyes.

She thrust her chin up, glaring at him. 'I'm not frightened in the least.'

He gave her a sardonic smile and left her to walk down to the other pool.

Behind a tree, she undressed down to her shift and bloomers. Then, watching for Munro, she crept from the shade and into the sun. She slipped into the pool, shivering as the cool water coated her heated skin.

Bare-chested, Munro stood further down, wearing only his moleskins.

She stared at his body and felt an exciting sensation in the pit of her stomach at the sight. He looked magnificent, lean and taut with only a smattering of chest hair. She couldn't take her eyes off him.

He smiled at her across the distance. His hands went to his trousers. 'Turn your back, please, Miss Reynolds, to protect your modesty,' he called out with laughter in his voice.

Her smile froze as she realised he was going to go naked. 'Oh, my!' She swivelled in the water and looked the other way. Blushing, she listened for the sound of him entering the water. Her imagination ran riot as she pictured him with no clothes. Her heart raced, and her breath deepened.

'You can turn around now.'

She turned back around and saw only his head sticking above the next pool. Taking a deep breath, she tried to calm herself and ignore his presence and just enjoy the moment. Her pool was waist deep and she swam a little in the middle before floating on her back and closing her eyes to the bright sun.

After a while, she climbed up onto the rock and laid down on its hot surface. She listened to the birds, the insects humming, the tinkling of the water. The heat of the rock beneath her seeped through her bones like warm treacle and made her sleepy.

She woke with a start. Covering her eyes from the sun, she squinted across the pool where Munro stood doing up the buttons of his shirt. He had his back to her and she studied the strong width of his shoulders as the muscles flexed.

She hurried over to her clothes and dressed as quickly as she could, despite her shift still being a little damp. Flustered, she was all fingers and thumbs.

'Do you need some help?' His voice carried over the noise of the waterfalls.

'No, I'm perfectly fine, thank you,' she lied. By the time she was decently dressed, she was sweating and hot again.

'You look ready for another swim.' He smirked as she emerged puffing and panting.

'Next time I'll be prepared and have a towel and a change of clothes.' Her hair had come loose from the combs that held it and hung straggly down her back. She tucked it up the best she could but felt dishevelled and unladylike. Her mother would be horrified by the sight of her and being so in a man's company!

'Ready for the ride back?' he asked.

'Yes. I'm longing for a cup of tea.'

'Drink from the waterfall. It's fresh water not polluted.'

She did as he said, and cupping her hands, drank thirstily at the cool water.

'Good?'

'Yes, lovely.' She wiped her mouth with the back of her hand and pulled on her gloves.

He took her hand and helped her climb the bank up to the

horses. By Minty's side, Munro stood close to her. Louisa was keenly aware of him, her heart seemed to suspend its beating.

'I have enjoyed this afternoon,' his quiet voice reached her on a murmur.

'Me too.' She glanced up at him, searching his face for a clue as to how he was feeling.

'Perhaps you could call me Connor?' His tender gaze held her spellbound.

'Yes, all right. I'm Louisa.'

Connor bent and laced his hands for her to use as a mounting block. In one swift movement she was up on Minty's back. His fingers held onto her foot and helped her put it in the stirrup. He adjusted her skirts and her skin tingled where he touched her above her boot.

'Thank you.'

He paused, took a breath, and turned to mount Firecracker without looking at her.

On the ride back, Louisa felt more comfortable on Minty. She didn't feel the need to concentrate so much on keeping in the saddle. 'So, your family come from Scotland?' she asked to break the silence.

'That's correct. My grandfather couldn't make a living on his farmland in the Highlands. He told my father to emigrate, which he did along with his sister, Mrs Casey, and they ended up having a sheep property a day's ride from Sydney. That was where he married my mother. They had me and my sister, and then my mother died. My father couldn't cope with a farm and two young children, so we were sent to Melbourne where my mother's sister had gone to live. My Aunt Mary brought us up.'

'You have a sister in Melbourne?'

'Yes, Martha. She looks after Aunt Mary and runs a small shop. My father is Mrs Casey's brother.'

'Is your father still alive?'

'No, he died when I was ten. I don't think he ever got over my mother dying. He couldn't make his farm successful and eventually sold it. I think that was the final straw for him.'

'So how did Mrs Casey come to be in Albany?'

'Her late husband, Albert Casey, was a captain of a whaling ship. He was a good man, like a father to me really. He was the reason I came to Albany. He wanted to set up an office here for his whaling business. Albert wanted me to run the business, but I decided office work wasn't for me and headed out here to try my hand at sheep farming, like my father had done.'

'Is that why Mrs Casey doesn't speak to you, because you left the business?'

'Yes, she feels I betrayed Albert. Not long after I bought Munro Downs Albert grew ill and died. She's never forgiven me and said I brought stress to Albert.'

'How tragic.' Louisa swished away the flies hovering in front of her eyes.

'I offered for her to come live at Munro Downs, but she declined and started working for Doctor Jamieson. I think she prefers being in town rather than out in the country. There's not enough gossip for her out here.'

They'd returned to the homestead quicker than Louisa wanted. She relished listening to Connor and learning about him. She was sad when they arrived at the stables.

George was waiting for them on the house's veranda with a tray of Su Lin's delicacies. He poured a whisky for Connor and a sherry for Louisa as the orange sun slipped further below the horizon. 'How was the ride, my dear?'

'Delightful. The country is so spacious, so vast.'

'And the pools?'

'They are beautiful. We each had our own pool to swim in!' She laughed, touching her wild hair.

'Wonderful! It's an excellent bathing spot.'

Connor leaned against the veranda post, drink in hand. 'We didn't see a platypus.'

'That is a shame. Shy creatures.' George sipped his whisky. 'How did you find Minty?'

'A good ride. She was well behaved and made it easy for me.'

'I thought she'd suit you.' George looked pleased with himself.

'Would you mind if I rode her again tomorrow?'

'Not at all, my dear. She needs the exercise, has got too fat. Consider her yours while you are at King's Station.'

'Thank you. I enjoyed being in the saddle again. I've missed it. Although the country is very different to England, and I never had to worry about the horse treading on a snake!'

'That happened?' George looked at Connor in dismay.

'Firecracker noticed it before we did. The snake slid away, and all was well.' Connor downed his whisky. 'I've promised Miss Reynolds a ride into the ranges. You will join us, George?'

George frowned. 'Perhaps.'

'Right, I'd best be off. It'll be dark before I'm home. I'll send a rider over with a date for the ride.' Connor placed his hat back on his head and smiled at Louisa. 'Thank you for your company today.'

'Thank you for taking me.' She blushed, not knowing why, but savouring the fact that he looked at her so intensely and soon they would have the chance to have another ride together.

Connor patted George on the shoulder and headed down the steps.

George leaned forward in his chair. 'Take care on the journey back. And give my regards to Nancy. We all must have dinner together soon.'

Connor's stride checked as though he stumbled, but he kept walking and simply raised his hand in farewell.

Louisa sipped her sherry, basking in the events of the day. 'Who is Nancy?'

George stared down into his drink before giving her a sorrowful look. 'Nancy is Connor's wife.'

CHAPTER 8

*L*ouisa sat in the buggy next to George as he drove them over a rough dirt track towards Munro Downs. She wasn't eager for the visit. In fact, she wished she could jump off the buggy and run back to the hotel room in Albany. Since George told her two days ago that Connor had a wife, she'd been in a flux of moods and emotions. She'd been so stupid to allow her feelings to get the better of her.

As much as she enjoyed being with George and staying at his home, it was now ruined. Worse still, George had noticed and tried harder to make her happier, until today when he suddenly decided they needed to go to Munro Downs.

'You know why I'm taking you, don't you?' George gave her a sideways look.

She sighed, picking at her gloves. 'No, not really.' It had taken an hour of George wearing her down to make her climb into the buggy. She had no wish to see Connor and his wife. The thought made her stomach queasy. 'I think it is time I went back to Albany.'

'You need to see Nancy, make her real in your mind. I know you've developed an affection for Connor. However, he can never be yours. So, before you become too involved...' He cleared his throat and adjusted the long reins in his hands. 'I'm not doing this to be cruel, my dear, far from it. Both Connor and Nancy are special people to me. I don't want any of you to be hurt. This is as much for Connor as it is for you. He needs to see you and Nancy in the same room, too.'

'We haven't done anything wrong,' she defended, feeling hot, rattled.

'No, not yet. But you could have. I can tell by the way the news hit you that you expected Connor to be free. No one can blame you for admiring him. He's a good man and has the kind of looks that attract women. He's never behaved like this with anyone before. But he forgets that I know him very well, better than he even realises. And I could see in his eyes the interest he has in you. The way he has been acting. Something in *him* saw something in *you* that day when you walked down the street destitute and lost. Some inner response made him leave the men he was talking to and go to your rescue. Whatever that feeling was... well, it was strong, and he acted on it. What else will he act on?'

'Nothing. Nothing at all. He's just being decent and kind.'

'Trust me on this.' George nodded wisely.

She didn't know what to make of anything anymore. 'Then why encourage him to take me to the pools?'

George scratched his chin. 'I can't explain why. It was like I needed to know if what I thought was true.'

'You tested us,' she accused.

'I did.'

'You had no right.'

'Agreed. However, as soon as you come up on the veranda with happiness shining from your eyes, I knew you felt something for him. I also knew he'd not told you about Nancy.'

'No, he didn't.' It hurt that he hadn't. She wished he had told her right from the beginning, the day in the tearoom. It would have saved her thinking about him, dreaming of him, of hoping for something that would never happen. 'What am I going to do?'

'Hopefully, these feelings will taper off soon enough, especially once you've seen Nancy.'

'I'll have to leave. Go on to Sydney.' She felt the loss of friendships already. George had become someone dear to her. Once again, she'd be alone.

'That would be a shame, for I've grown fond of you, but I can see why you'd want to.'

'I don't want to. I really like it here.'

He patted her knee. 'Let us not be hasty, for after today you may feel you can stay and live in Albany. It's not as if Connor is in town every day. He barely goes into Albany more than once a month and would have no need to visit you.'

They drove over a rise and spread out before them was the homestead and numerous farm buildings of Munro Downs. The track turned to the left at the bottom of the small hill and they travelled under a wooden arch with the station's name on the top. The fields on either side of the track held herds of cows.

George pointed to them. 'Connor is building a good size dairy herd. Nancy is creating a name for herself in cheese and butter making.'

Louisa turned away and stared into the distance. She didn't want to know how clever Nancy was.

Stone built, unlike George's timber house, Connor's large home had a wide veranda wrapping around the front and sides of the house. Mature fig trees grew on either side of the drive. In the middle of a lush green patch of lawn was a bronze statue of a horse and foal. Lush gardens filled with abundant flowering bushes bordered the veranda. The homestead was impressive and didn't fail to show it to visitors.

Louisa saw at once the stark difference between George's humble home and the grandness of Munro Downs. George's home was neat, serviceable, a bachelor's home. Whereas Connor Munro was a wealthy man, and that wealth was evident in the elegance of not only outside but inside his grand home as they entered it.

The housekeeper, a woman dressed in grey and with a stern face, showed them into the drawing room. It's blue papered walls and brown leather furniture was lightened by its polished cedar timber floor and white lace curtains at the windows. Paintings of horses decorated the walls.

'Mrs Mac. How lovely it is to see you again.' George beamed at the housekeeper. 'Allow me to introduce you to Miss Louisa Reynolds.' He turned to Louisa. 'Mrs Mac is a daughter of Scotland. Her late husband was the overseer here and her son is one of the best stockmen in the district. Isn't that so, Mrs Mac?'

George's charm was wasted on the housekeeper, who merely scowled at him and after a brief nod to Louisa, turned and left them.

George laughed. 'God knows how her husband, Cameron, survived been married to her for so long. She's a face like a trout and a manner to match!'

Louisa, despite her nervousness, chuckled. 'She does seem a bit fierce.'

'Her husband though was a good man. The tales he told around a camp fire at night. Brilliant. A natural born storyteller. I'll tell you some of them later.'

The sound of wheels on the wooden floorboards made Louisa turn from studying a painting of a sailing boat on the ocean, which seemed so out of place amongst the horse paintings. The timid smile on her face faltered as she stared at a thin woman sitting in a wheelchair.

'George! How nice to see you? This is a surprise.' The woman's dark eyes revealed a wariness as she smiled and received George's kiss on the cheek.

'Nancy, delightful as always.' George kept hold of Nancy's

hand. 'This is Miss Louisa Reynolds. A new friend of mine who is staying with me.'

'It's a pleasure to meet you, Miss Reynolds.' Nancy held out her hand and Louisa shook it gently. She could feel all of the bones in Nancy's pale thin hand. Everything about Nancy was petite and delicate. Her dress was a soft rose colour edged with at least six inches of white flounces. It was a dress for a young girl, not a married woman. Her abundant black hair was bound high on the top of her head, exposing a long graceful neck. She had a clear pale complexion and dark brown eyes which showed shrewd intelligence. If Louisa was asked to describe Nancy Munro she would say a regal cold beauty. In comparison, Louisa felt very much an unrefined country maid.

'I'm pleased to meet you, Mrs Munro,' Louisa murmured, finding her voice at last.

'You must call me Nancy. We don't stand on ceremony around here, do we, George?'

'Absolutely not. I've told Louisa that on more than one occasion,' George answered, giving Louisa a I-told-you-so look.

Nancy wheeled her chair about. 'Shall we take tea out on the veranda? It's a lovely day. Though Connor feels we'll receive some rain tonight.'

'Clouds are building up on the ranges, so no doubt we'll get a splash or two. It's always needed,' George replied as they went through double French doors and out onto the wide veranda.

They sat at a table already set with tea things and a stand of cake slices and sandwiches. Mrs Mac had been busy in a short time.

Nancy wheeled her chair to the table and began pouring out the tea. 'So, Louisa, I may call you that?' She paused, the delicate china teapot suspended above a cup.

'Yes, of course.' Louisa pulled off her white gloves and placed them on her lap. Nancy was nothing as she expected. She hadn't known what to expect really. In her head no vision had formed of

Connor's wife, yet her being in a wheelchair certainly had thrown her.

'So, you're fresh from England I take it?' Nancy poured the tea into three cups.

George passed the cake stand to Louisa. 'Louisa is a survivor from the *Blue Tulip*. Did Connor not mention her to you?'

Nancy's eyes widened. 'Good grief. I had no idea. No, he didn't. I had read about the shipwreck in the newspaper a while ago. You were one of the two people they rescued?'

'No, I'm the third survivor.' Louisa took a sandwich, though she had no appetite. Would Connor join them soon? She wished that he wouldn't as she didn't think she could stand it. To see him and Nancy together would make everything real. He would never be hers now, even though she thought of nothing but him. She had to sort herself out. She needed to put him from her mind.

'How incredible.' Nancy stared at her kindly. 'What an experience for you.'

George added sugar to his cup. 'She lived with the blacks, you know, for months. Terribly brave.'

Louisa sipped her tea. 'I had no other choice. I couldn't have survived on my own, I'd have died without Akala, I'm sure.'

'Akala?' Nancy asked, adding sugar to her cup.

'A young native girl who befriended me.'

'That's truly amazing.' Nancy stirred her tea. 'Though not surprising. The local aborigines around here are very friendly. You hear stories of stealing and skirmishes elsewhere, but we have been lucky in this part of the country, haven't we, George?'

He nodded with a mouthful of food.

'Though we make sure to treat them with respect. We have many working for us. Connor is a big believer of helping them as they in turn will help us. He trusts their knowledge about the country and respects it, whereas a lot of British settlers dismiss their ways.'

'Best trackers in the world are the blacks,' George declared.

'Absolutely,' Nancy agreed. 'Connor has relied on them to find a lost flock, and even the odd stockman, more than once.'

Louisa picked up the triangle of sandwich from her plate, eyes downcast. She envied Nancy being able to speak of Connor so easily, so informally. They were married, a couple who shared each day and night together. Jealousy curled inside her like a deadly snake, striking randomly and disabling her thoughts.

As if her thoughts had conjured him up. Connor came out through the French doors further down the veranda. His step faltered on seeing them.

'This is a surprise.' His smile didn't reach his eyes as he neared the table.

George wiped his mouth on a linen napkin. 'Thought I'd bring Louisa out for a drive and call in to introduce her to Nancy. If Louisa moves on to Sydney I didn't want her going without seeing Munro Downs and all its beauty.'

'You are moving on, Miss Reynolds?' Connor rotated his hat in his hands.

'Quite possibly, yes.' She stared at him, waiting for his reaction, but his face gave nothing away. He seemed as though he was chipped from stone.

'Sydney's gain will be Albany's loss,' Nancy said over brightly, watching Connor. 'Do you want some tea, Connor?'

'No, sorry, I cannot stay. I'm about to ride to the western boundary. There's been reports of some wild dogs killing some of the flock there.' He took a step backwards, half turning.

'Can't you send someone else?' Nancy's tone became strained. 'We have guests.'

'No, let the man go, Nancy.' George waved him away. 'We called unannounced and mustn't hold him up. Feral dogs are the last thing we need in the district.'

'Yes, but we hire a great number of men, surely there is someone who can go instead?' Nancy's eyes grew cold. 'Come, Connor, stay and socialise for a few minutes. The dogs will wait.'

'But can my sheep wait to be killed?'

'Excellent point, good man,' George said jovially. 'Go and take them to task. We have no need for packs of flea-riddled scavengers killing our stock.'

'Well, if you'll excuse me.' Connor nodded his head in farewell. His last glance was at Louisa and her insides melted with longing.

'Don't forget your promise to take me to the ranges,' Louisa suddenly blurted out, not wanting him to go.

He placed his hat on his head, shadowing his face. 'Of course. I'll arrange a day.' With a final nod he descended the steps and walked around the side of the house.

An awkward silence fell over the table.

'A day at the ranges? Connor never mentioned it to me.'

'It's not important, I understand how busy Connor is,' Louisa muttered and seeing Nancy's face was tight with tension she refrained from mentioning the trip to the pools.

'After tea, I can show you around, if you wish?' Nancy said, though her flat tone belied her wish to do it. 'We've had a foal born, George. Beautiful she is.'

'Excellent.' George selected a piece of cake and gave Louisa a small smile.

* * *

CONNOR GRIPPED the reins and swung his leg over the saddle. Prince, his bay, waited patiently for the command to walk, but Connor sat for a moment. His heart and head were thumping fit to burst, and both were linked to each other by the same cause. Louisa.

Why in God's name had she come into his life? He hadn't needed this complication. His life had been ordered, structured for the last five years. Since marrying Nancy, he'd accepted his fate and thrust himself into making Munro Downs the best sheep station in the district, even the whole country if he could, or he'd die trying. That's all he'd focused on, all he needed in his life. Work fulfilled him. He lived and breathed Munro Downs. He knew he could have nothing more in his life than his station, and up until meeting Louisa he had been content with that, accepted it.

Yet, since meeting Louisa on that very first day, he had been thrown into confusion and doubt. Why had he crossed the street to her when she first stumbled along looking like a captive of the natives? When he'd first seen her, barefoot and dressed in rags, something had twisted in his heart and instinct made him go to her. Her tanned face, dry lips, tangled hair had given her an aura of helplessness, yet when she spoke to him, he'd sensed a strength within her. She had achieved what most people would think impossible. She'd survived a shipwreck and then months living in the bush with a young native girl to keep her alive. That showed so much courage. He was in awe of her.

Then later, when he saw her in the street, dressed as a lady, her beauty radiant and glowing, it had felt like he'd been hit in the chest. A weird feeling, really. Not like anything he'd ever experienced before, not even with Nancy. Not ever with Nancy.

Nancy.

His thoughts shattered, and his gut clenched. He loved Nancy. Who could not? They'd been best friends since he first arrived in Albany aged twenty. She'd laughed at his quips, shown him how to mix and mingle with the men of the town who would make good connections. He liked her enormously. The daughter of a wealthy man, and a delightful person to be with. He couldn't recall ever falling in love with her. Over time they had just grown to be always in each other's company. He enjoyed being with her. She was clever and interesting, with a sharp wit. He expected her to get married to one of the many suitors who hung on her every word, but as the years went by she never did. Then she had the accident...

Prince shifted beneath him, shaking him out of his reverie. With the slightest pressure with his legs, he urged Prince into a trot, then a canter. He lowered his head to keep his hat on as they covered the dry dusty ground easily. Riding Prince gave him a joy that he couldn't find anywhere else. He knew he spent too much time in the saddle, leaving Nancy in the house for days on end with only Mrs Mac to talk to, but he couldn't help it.

The house, as beautiful as it was, made him feel trapped. Out here in the bush, he had freedom. Out here he wasn't married to a woman he wasn't in love with. Out here he was a man working hard to create an empire. Out here he could mix with the men, share a joke, and sleep under the stars. Out here he didn't have to see the sadness in Nancy's eyes.

He slowed Prince down to a walk and sighed. Today, seeing Louisa unexpectedly, sitting in his own home with Nancy, had rocked him to the core. Guilt raked at his insides. Ever since the day at the pools, when he'd desperately wanted to kiss Louisa, he'd felt like the biggest cad. He was married to Nancy. He *couldn't* have feelings or desires for another woman. He had made the choice to marry Nancy five years ago. He'd never looked at another since then. He'd never had the slightest interest in going elsewhere like other men did to ease their bodies' urges. He accepted Nancy's disability and the separate bedrooms. Their marriage had never been consummated but that was fine by him. Nancy was his friend, had been for years, he could no more sleep with her than he could with his own sister.

However, Louisa had awakened something inside of him that wouldn't go back to sleep, and it tortured him.

He slumped in the saddle dreading the day when Louisa would leave for Sydney, but yet hoping it would come soon so he could return to normal.

CHAPTER 9

*L*ouisa sat on the veranda at King's Station and watched the rain fall. Her mind empty, she sniffed the cool air, relishing the smell of fresh eucalyptus. The rain had washed away the dust, refreshed the landscape. Water dripped off the roof eves, the sound a constant pattern.

She sighed.

She should be making decisions about her future, but nothing would form. Yesterday, when they had left Munro Downs, she'd been determined to leave for Sydney straight away and start a new life there. But on reaching George's home, and eating a lovely meal cooked by Su Lin, her eagerness had dwindled with each sherry George poured for her. Sydney loomed as a big friendless place, and with no set idea what to do there, she felt overwhelmed by the prospect.

By the morning she was still no wiser and her future stretched out into a dismal lonely fog. In a short space of time she'd gone from being high on life, dreaming of being with Connor, then back to the depths of despair as she had been after the shipwreck.

'There you are, my dear.' George came out of the front door

and sat beside her. He shook his right hand and winced. 'My arthritis is playing up today. The cool weather always does it to me.'

'Cold weather?' She smiled at his exaggeration. 'Hardly cold. It's not even winter, just a rainstorm.'

'Don't mention winter. I loathe winter. I cannot hold a pen for longer than a few minutes.'

'Is that what you've been doing, writing?'

'Yes. It's another thing I loathe. Writing cheques, writing letters, adding figures in ledgers. Bah! The whole lot of it drives me crazy. It's worse when my arthritis affects my hands. So, my letters will have to wait for another day.' He massaged his knuckles, the pain reflected in his eyes.

She frowned, upset that he suffered. 'May I help you? I can write your letters or any other correspondence, if you wish?'

'Really?' He seemed surprised by her offer. 'Why would you wish to do such a tedious task?'

She chuckled. 'It's not that bad, and of course I'd like to help you. I'm here doing nothing but enjoying your hospitality. I'd like to do something for you in return.'

'You are great company to me, that is all I ask.' He stared out over the wet fields. 'You being here has been such a delight. I dread the thought of you going.'

'Well, while I'm here why don't I be of use? I've spent the last couple of weeks being lazy. I should earn my keep.' The idea of doing anything was better than moping around the house thinking of Connor.

'If you're sure?'

'I insist.'

'Excellent.'

She stood and entered the house. 'Show me all you need help with.'

George's study was a room she'd not spent much time in. It was his sanctuary, a very male room. The walls held bookshelves of thick farming tomes and pictures of country scenes. A red oriental rug covered the floor and in the corner was a small fireplace burning brightly. Heavy leather chairs sat either side of a mahogany desk, which was covered in mounds of ledgers and papers.

Louisa took a deep breath as she stared at the piles of correspondence piled haphazardly on the desk and floor. 'Heavens, George. How do you find anything in this mess?'

'Mess?' His eyebrows rose. 'This is highly organised. I know where everything is.'

'Really?' She disbelieved him. The room was warm from the fire she felt wasn't needed, but that George added another log showed how the slightest change in temperature affected him.

She sat down and picked up a sheath of letters. 'Do these need answering? You could tell me what you want me to write, or where to start?'

He made himself comfortable in a chair by the fire and picked up a farming journal from the floor and flicked through the pages. 'What is the first one on the pile?'

Louisa shuffled through the letters. 'Should we not start from the earliest date?'

'That should be last week.' George nodded.

'No, the earliest date is…' she reached the bottom of the pile '… two months ago, from Mr John Fletcher.' She looked up at him as he stared at her. 'Or have you answered this letter?'

'Er…no…' He rubbed his forehead. 'John Fletcher, he's a friend who lives in India. I thought I'd answered him.'

'Shall I read his letter to you and then it's fresh in your mind to compose a reply?'

'I think we need some coffee while we do this.' He rang the bell for Su Lin. 'It's going to be a long afternoon.'

The afternoon of office work turned into three days of concentrated sorting out.

Louisa uncovered a non-existent filing system and ledgers not updated for months and bills left unpaid. George became more concerned as Louisa involved herself deeper in the station's paperwork left unattended and found the situation was out of hand. She had written a dozen letters for him to friends and acquaintances, but it was the bills of fare that were unpaid that frightened her.

'George, this tax bill is six months overdue,' she told him on the evening of the third day.

'Another one?'

'Yes. The one we paid yesterday was for the third quarter for last year. This is for the fourth quarter for last year.'

George's eyes glazed over. 'No more. I cannot think of this anymore.'

'But you are behind in so many things.' She picked up a sheath of papers. 'All these are bills from stores in Albany and Perth. They are all overdue.'

'I don't care about any of it.'

'You have to care. You'll be summoned by the debtor's court if you ignore them for much longer.'

'Nonsense! Enough!' He threw his hands up in the air and left the study.

She gave him a few minutes and then went to find him. After searching the house, she left it and crossed over to the outside kitchen, but Su Lin, busy making bread, hadn't seen him.

Louisa headed for the outer buildings. He wasn't in the stable yard, barns or single men's sleeping quarters. She visited the family cottages, nodding to the odd stockman's wife she saw, before stopping by the pig sty, the dairy and chicken coop.

Finally, she walked towards the shearing shed; a large open sided building on the outskirts of the main hub.

Inside the huge timber building, she walked across the large platform. Standing against a rail overlooking the empty holding pens, George stared out across the grassy plains, shoulders slumped.

'George?' she asked tentatively.

He gave her a small tired smile as she joined him. 'I'm fine, my dear. Please forgive my outburst.'

'I didn't want to upset you. I'm sorry.'

'Oh, you haven't upset me, believe me. It's all my own fault. I've let everything slip. I've lost interest. There's no drive left in me to make this place thrive like it once did. What is it all for? I'm an old man all alone.'

She felt sorry for him, and understood how he felt, for she was alone as well. She slipped her arm though his. 'It'll be easier now the ledgers are up to date.'

'And my bank balance is in the red.'

She thought for a moment. 'Did you deliberately not pay your bills so your money stayed in the bank?'

'Perhaps. Seeing a healthy bank balance meant I could pretend everything was as it used to be.' He sighed. 'I've nothing left to give, Louisa, and that's the truth. This place thrummed with life years ago. I lived and breathed this station. It was my life's blood, especially after John died. I needed to honour his hard work and his memory. However, with neither of us marrying and having children... well, as I say, what was it all for?' He sighed heavily. 'Connor reminds me of how I was back then, full of energy and passion to create something larger than me, something that would be passed on. But I have no one to pass it on to, and actually nor does Connor. Ironic, isn't it? We work so hard for all these years and for what?'

She laid her head against his shoulder. 'You're talking as though you're giving up.'

'I have no one. In my will I've given this place to Connor. For he has been like a son to me, and there is no one else I care about. He will have this place and as the boundaries are joined to his, he'll be one of the largest landowners in the southern region.'

'He's a lucky man.'

'He works like a man possessed and deserves it. Unlike me.

For the last ten years I think I've just been going through the motions of living, waiting to die.'

'You could live for another twenty years or more!' she admonished.

'I don't think I want to, not alone. I'm tired of my own company. I dread the thought of you leaving, of being on my own again. During the day, it's not so bad as I can talk to the men and Su Lin, but at night…'

'Then I won't go, not yet. I can stay.' The words flew out of her mouth.

He reared back. 'But what of Connor?'

'What of him? He is married, untouchable. My feelings can fade,' she said it more to convince herself than George. 'It's not as if I'll see him every day, is it?'

'I wouldn't want you to stay for me. You've your whole life ahead of you.'

'Exactly, my whole life. I think I can spare some time here to keep you company. I really feel at home here.' That was true. She loved being at King's Station.

He took her hand and squeezed it. 'You fit in as though you've always been a part of King's Station, but I don't want you to stay out of pity, but because you *want* to.'

'You are my friend. We'll help each other. Besides, if I leave, your accounts will become a huge mess again!' She grinned, lightening the mood. She hated seeing him so down, especially when he was always the jolly one keeping everyone's spirits up.

'It would make me so happy if you stayed.' He patted her hand, the relief evident in is voice.

'Then it's settled. I'll stay until you grow tired of me.'

'That'll be never.' He grinned. 'This will give the gossips in town something to talk about, won't it?' A spark of the old George returned.

'Yes, it will.' She shuddered, hating to think of being gossiped about again.

Arm in arm they walked out of the shearing shed. Over the last few days, she'd been aware of George not being as robust as he was when she first met him, which saddened her. The accounts and bill paying had eroded his happy manner. If by staying she could make him content, then she could fight her own battle regarding her feelings for Connor. Hopefully, she wouldn't see too much of him.

The following day they made the trip into Albany to collect her few belongings she'd left at the hotel and to pay for the room they'd held for her. George laughed when she placed the deckchair in the back of the buggy, early the next morning.

'What is that for?'

'It came off the shipwreck. I can't leave it behind. It's special to me.' She couldn't explain the attachment she had to the deckchair. She wanted it with her and that's all there was to it.

He shrugged. 'Who am I to deny a woman her little fantasies?'

'I must see Akala. I'm worried she'll have run off from the doctor's cottage. I've not been a good friend, leaving her like that.'

George took her arm as they walked the long dusty street to the doctor's cottage as the sun was rising above the rooftops. 'You said she was happy there.'

'Mrs Casey said she could stay with her, but I don't think it would be something Doctor Jamieson would tolerate. I didn't think I'd be at King's Station for so long. Akala might think I'm not ever returning.'

'Well, she is welcome to come home with us. I'm sure Su Lin would like more help in the kitchen.'

'Thank you. I would like to know she's close.'

Louisa knocked on the cottage's door and after a moment Mrs Casey answered.

Her eyes widened on seeing Louisa. 'Miss Reynolds. It's very early, but nice to see you again, and you, Mr Henderson.' She frowned at George and Louisa in confusion. 'Is there something wrong? Do you wish to see the doctor?'

'Apologies for the early hour, Mrs Casey. No, there's nothing wrong, I've come to see Akala.'

'You have?' Mrs Casey lifted her chin. 'I'll not have you upsetting her. It's taken me weeks to settle her down after you left. She's happy now.'

Feeling guilty, Louisa raised her hands at the older woman. 'That's all I want, for her to be happy. Is she still here?'

'Of course. Where else would she go?'

'Her mother hasn't returned?'

'Heavens, no. She is of no use to Akala. She's damaged that one.' Mrs Casey tapped her head. 'You know what I mean?'

Louisa frowned at the other woman's tone but made no comment on Kiah. 'Akala can return with us to King's Station if she wishes to.'

Mrs Casey paled. 'No. She is happy here. Why disrupt her?'

George coughed into his hand. 'Perhaps we should ask the child herself what she wants to do?'

'Wait here.' With a huff, Mrs Casey turned and left the room. She was gone a few minutes before she returned with Akala holding her hand.

Louisa stared at the native girl who'd been her saviour for months in the bush. Akala seemed taller, fuller in shape, no longer skin and bones. She now wore a light blue dress and her wild curly hair had a white ribbon in it, which clung lopsidedly to her head. She wore no shoes and that made Louisa smile.

'Loo… sa.' Akala grinned shyly.

'I've missed you.' Louisa felt under pressure from Mrs Casey's beady-eyed glare. 'That's a pretty dress you're wearing.'

Mrs Casey's head snapped up. 'She wears decent clothes now. She's taking lessons from me to talk better English and I'm hoping to start teaching her to read and write.'

'Is that what you want, Akala?' Louisa asked gently. 'Do you like living here with Mrs Casey?'

'Missus good. Feeds me well.' Akala glanced up at the house-keeper. 'I become whitefella.'

Stiffening, Mrs Casey smiled with thin lips. 'Akala, do not say whitefella. Remember what I told you.'

Akala shrugged.

George stepped forward. 'Akala, my name is Mr Henderson and Louisa is coming to live with me at King's Station. Would you like to live with us too?'

Akala looked up at Mrs Casey. 'Missus says she'll teach me. I white…girl.'

Louisa folded her arms, knowing full well that the house-keeper had promised Akala a lot. 'Do you care for Akala, Mrs Casey?'

'What are you implying?'

'I'm implying nothing, simply asking a straightforward question. If I am to leave Akala here long term, then I want to know she is being cared for properly.'

'What? Better than you can? You left her without a backward glance. You've no rights over the girl.'

'I was down the street in an hotel, she knew where I was.'

'For only a week before you took the opportunity to be gone!'

George held up his hand. 'Louisa was visiting my home for a welcomed rest after all she had been through.'

Mrs Casey's eyes widened, and she smirked. 'And now she's returning with you. Do you fancy being an old man's mistress, do you? Got an offer too good to refuse, did you?'

'How dare you!' Louisa spluttered, shocked and alarmed anyone would think that way.

'Akala stays with me,' Mrs Casey snapped. 'I'm taking care of her. She's happy here.'

'And what of Doctor Jamieson? Does he approve?'

'In fact, he does. I told him I needed help and Akala is young enough for me to train.'

'Does she still sleep in the laundry?'

'For the moment, but that will change. I'll turn one of the outbuildings into a room for her. She'll be fine, and better than she was in the bush.'

George placed his hand on Louisa's back. 'Come my dear, we can do no more here.'

'Akala.' Louisa bent down in front of the girl. 'Do you want to stay with Mrs Casey?'

Akala nodded, giving Mrs Casey another glance. 'I be a whitefella,' she whispered to Louisa.

Louisa squeezed the girl's shoulder softly, knowing the argument was lost. 'As long as you're happy. But if you need me I'm at King's Station with Mr Henderson. Remember that, won't you?'

'King's Station. I will, Loo... sa.'

Without another word, Louisa left the cottage and walked down the street, which was becoming move alive as people started their day. In the hotel stable yard, two young boys where mucking out the horse stalls.

'Have I done the right thing?' she asked George as they reached the buggy.

'My dear, only time will tell.' George helped her up onto the seat. 'The girl believes that old hag will make her white.'

'But that's not going to happen. Akala will be treated as a native no matter if she speaks good English and wears a dress.'

'True.' George shook his head sadly and walked around the buggy to climb up into the seat.

'I don't understand Mrs Casey. She was so nice to me when I was there. Now, she's like a different woman.'

'That's because for the first time in her life she has a child to take care of. She's being a mother at long last and she won't give that up in a hurry. Becoming a mother changes some women, they become possessive. I've seen it happen before.'

'But Akala isn't a white baby for her to nurture into a version of herself. She's a native girl who can survive in the bush by herself. She doesn't need Mrs Casey.'

George released the brake. 'Perhaps that's what makes Mrs Casey so determined to keep her. She can be the one person to *save* Akala.'

'Save from what? She doesn't need saving, she just needs a home, someone to care for her.'

'Gee up there.' George slapped the reins. 'Louisa, my dear, to some people that's all and the same.'

'I feel as though I've let her down.'

'My dear, stop torturing yourself. At the end of the day, Akala is a native. She'll go bush when it suits her, they all do at some point, and Mrs Casey will not be able to do a thing about it.' He drove the buggy away from the hotel stable yard. 'Now shall we stop and have some breakfast before we make the trip home?'

She nodded, thirsty but not hungry, her mind in torment. Had she done the right thing leaving Akala?

A few streets away, closer to the bay, George stopped the buggy and helped her down. They were at a different place to the one they stopped at with Connor. Louisa glanced up at the sign above the door. 'Mrs MacDonald's Lodgings.'

George opened the door for her with a smile. 'Fiona MacDonald is a lovely woman, a dear friend and she makes very good honey cakes. She's another Scot, there's loads of them in Albany. She was unwell last time I was in town and that's why we didn't come here with Connor.'

Louisa nodded and followed him through a communal room with sofas and tables and out onto a back veranda that over-looked the bay. A cool breeze came off the water but not unpleasant for the sun held warmth already. Small wooden tables and chairs lined the wall interspersed with barrels of coloured geraniums. At the end of the veranda a door opened, and a pretty woman about fifty years of age came out with a smile.

'George!' She hugged him and kissed his cheek. 'This is a lovely surprise.'

'Fiona, my darling girl.' George kissed her hands. 'You are fully recovered?'

'Oh yes. I have to be to run this place, don't I?' She laughed and waved them to a table. 'And this must be Miss Reynolds?' She shook Louisa's hand. 'The whole town is in a flutter about you.'

'I wish they weren't.'

'Well, fancy surviving a shipwreck, then months in the bush and then scarpering off to King's Station!' She grinned, showing no malice. 'The busy-bodies of the town are in high dudgeon about it all.'

Louisa blushed, hating that she was the talk of the town.

George laughed. 'Good!'

'What can I get you both?'

'The full breakfast works, dear Fiona, and I want you to eat with us too. We need to catch up,' George announced, pulling out Louisa's chair for her.

An hour later, replete from a good breakfast, Louisa and George paid the bill and readied to leave.

As Fiona cleared their table, a small party of women came out onto the veranda chatting away only to stop and stare at Louisa and George. One woman cupped her hand over her mouth and whispered to her friend standing next to her.

Louisa wanted to crawl inside herself and disappear.

'Good morning, ladies. A late breakfast is it?' Fiona stepped away to sort out the ladies, placing them at the furthest table.

'Take no heed of them, my dear.' George patted Louisa's hand. 'The gossip will die down eventually.'

Louisa kept quiet, wishing they were back at King's Station, away from the whispers and glances. Out in the country they were left to themselves and society could be ignored.

Fiona passed them on the way back to the kitchen. 'The church ladies' society,' she whispered. 'They are here for morning tea, but it's really breakfast they indulge in. They love my livers and scrambled eggs.'

Louisa looked up as another woman came out onto the veranda with apologies for being late and she recognised Mrs Pierce. She groaned as the reverend's wife made for their table.

George sighed. 'Winifred Pierce. That woman is as welcome as an ant at a picnic.'

'Miss Reynolds. Mr Henderson.' She gave them a curt nod, dressed in severe dark grey. 'I am pleased to see you, Miss Reynolds.'

'You are, Mrs Pierce?' George tilted his head. 'Why so?'

'To warn you, of course.'

'Warn us?' George frowned.

'Not *you*, but Miss Reynolds.' Mrs Pierce eyed them down her sharp nose. 'I feel it is my duty to warn you about the gossip your association with Mr Henderson is creating within the town. I'm sure you are aware of it yourself, and you must feel beholden to put a stop to it? I have just come from Miss Reynold's hotel where I have been informed that her room has been paid up.'

Louisa was lost and stared at the woman. 'I don't understand.'

Mrs Pierce sighed dramatically. 'Of course, you *understand*, how could you not! I warned you when we first met that you should join the church and meet people who would be of an acceptable acquaintance, but you didn't listen. Instead, your actions become even more disgraceful by going into the country with a single man and no chaperone!'

Louisa looked to George and for the first time she saw anger in his eyes and a tightness around his lips.

He stood before the odious woman. 'Enough! You have always been a nosy old goat!'

'I take offence at that!'

'Good, as I'm giving offence, just as you have given it to me all these years. I turned your advances down decades ago, and since then you've gone out of your way to speak ill against me, and anyone concerned with me.' George's eyes blazed with unconcealed distain.

'How dare you imply such a thing!' Her face paled.

The women of the church society stared from their table and Fiona came out of the kitchen, carrying a tea tray.

'I dare, madam, because I tire of it, of you and all the fire and brimstone you sprout. You're hell-bent on making as many people's lives as miserable as yours is.'

Mrs Pierce blinked rapidly at his words. 'Your actions condone you, sir. People have eyes and ears and see for themselves what is happening here.'

'And if they don't, you make sure that they soon do!'

Hatred filled her voice. 'You are no good George Henderson, and this young woman here needs to see that! You disgrace her by taking her to your home without thought to her reputation.'

'Do I? Really, Winifred? Do you really think that?' George heaved a deep sigh and retook his seat. 'How disappointing you are, Winifred.'

'Don't call me that, you have no right to use my Christian name,' she spat at him. She turned to Louisa. 'I strongly suggest, Miss Reynolds that you stay clear of this man, for he cares about no one but himself. I, again, offer you the hand of friendship and guidance. You are very welcome to come over and join our table and we, the society, will give you shelter as the Lord would want us to.'

'Thank you, Mrs Pierce.' Louisa summoned a stiff smile of thanks. 'However, George is my friend, and he—'

'He is a false friend, Miss Reynolds. You don't know him as well as I do.'

George laughed. 'You don't know me at all, Winifred.'

'I know you as a woman chaser, a joker, a man who plays false, a liar and who is free with his words to soften the misdeeds he does!'

Silence descended, all shocked by Mrs Pierce's outburst.

Fiona put down the tea tray on their table. 'I think that you should return to your friends, Mrs Pierce.'

'I have a duty as a member of this parish to give aid and advice, my husband would wish me to do so.'

'Perhaps he would *if* the advice was asked for first?' Fiona gave a brief nod, her voice firm.

Mrs Pierce held her ground. 'Miss Reynolds needs guidance.'

Louisa could take no more. A slow-burning anger at the woman's audacity to think she knew better than everyone was too much to bear. 'Thank you, Mrs Pierce, for your concern for my welfare, but I am twenty-one years of age and am quite capable of taking care of myself.'

'I beg to differ. What would your parents say to you living with a man old enough to be your grandfather?'

'The man you refer to is a gentleman, and… and soon to be my husband. I am in no danger from my fiancé.' Louisa dared not look at George as a collective gasp echoed around the veranda.

Fiona smiled, laughter in her eyes. 'May I be the first to offer congratulations?'

George, covering his shock well, sat straighter in his chair. 'We had come here for a quiet breakfast to celebrate our betrothal before we return home.' He gave Winifred a withering glare. 'Do you offer your congratulations as well, Winifred?'

She took a step back, knocking into the rail behind her. She stared with loathing at George and then at Louisa. 'Congratulations? To you two? *You* are nothing but an old man and *she* is obviously nothing more than a fortune hunter. You deserve each other.'

'Come now, where is your charity, your benevolence to your fellow man?' George grinned.

Mrs Pierce stuck her nose into the air. 'Miss Reynolds, don't say I didn't warn you. I gave you the chance to be integrated into decent society. You rejected my offer of help. On your head, be it.' Without another word, she left the veranda. Her flock of society women quickly rose from their chairs and hurried out after her, with one complaining that they hadn't eaten yet.

'Well!' Fiona grinned. 'Shall I bring out some cake, or a bottle of something stronger than tea?'

George reached for Louisa's hand. 'How do you feel, my dear. That was a nasty episode.'

'I'm fine, truly.'

'So, *are* you engaged?' Fiona asked.

Louisa looked at George. 'I had to say something to stop her vile words. I'm sorry if I embarrassed you.'

'You didn't, not at all. But, my dear, this news will be all around the district by nightfall.' He gave her a loving smile. 'You've set the cat amongst the pigeons.'

'Is it any worse than what they were already saying?' Fiona asked, as she left their table to return to the kitchen.

'No.' He sighed. 'I had no idea Winifred would be that cruel.'

Louisa knew the encounter had taken it out of him. 'She hates you, George. Whatever did you do?'

'Many years ago, I quite liked the look of her. We went to dances and for walks along the bay, but I soon realised she was not as nice as I first thought. Her sister, Miss Muir, who you've met before, she was much sweeter, more shy. Winifred didn't like that I paid any attention to her sister, and she became ruder, more manipulating. In the end I stayed away. Winifred put it about that I had broken a promise to her that I would marry her. It was all untrue, of course.'

'She's very bitter.'

'Yes. She's hated me ever since and my name is mud on her tongue. Over the years I've started to treat it all as a joke, really. How can someone carry such hate for so many years just over a few walks and a couple of dances? It bamboozles me. So, as time went on, and each time I came into Albany and would see her in the street or at social functions, I would be overly nice to her. It infuriates her when I do it.'

'Where you a woman chaser?' Louisa smiled.

He shrugged, a grin spreading on his face. 'I like women. They are beautiful and wondrous creatures. Over the years I have had many female friends, and this is a small town. What can I say? I am a man. But those days are long over.'

Fiona came out to them once more carrying a bottle of wine. 'It should be champagne, I know. But this is good quality. Take it home and have a toast, my gift to you both.'

'That is most kind.' Louisa smiled.

'Speaking of home, we should be going, my dear,' George said to Louisa. 'We'll be arriving after dark as it is.' He took Fiona's hand. 'Thank you, lovely lady, for your friendship.'

'You know you always have it, George. Goodbye.' Fiona nodded with a smile to Louisa and then disappeared into the kitchen once more.

George took Louisa arm and led her outside to the buggy. 'You know, we can pretend this engagement is real for a while, until you grow tired of me.'

Louisa settled herself into the seat. 'What if I don't grow tired of you?'

His eyes widened as he climbed up beside her. 'You want to be engaged to me?'

She didn't know what she wanted, but something deep inside her was saying yes. She wanted a home, somewhere she could relax and be happy. Connor was lost to her as a potential husband, the man she wanted to have children with, the man who she could spend the rest of her life with. Therefore, without Connor, she needed to reassess what would make her happy, and living with George at King's Station could do that. She could be mistress of the station, George's companion, and wouldn't be alone any more – neither of them would.

George leaned forward, his expression earnest. 'I will take care of you, if you want. King's Station would be your proper home if you became my wife.' His voice lowered. 'And I wouldn't expect my husband's rights, you understand.'

She nodded, grateful he mentioned it. 'Thank you. Are you

certain you could live without those rights a husband is meant to have from his wife?'

'I could. I'm far too old for that kind of nonsense now. I'm past my prime, but can you? To not have children, can you live without that?'

'I've never been one to hunger after children. Naturally I thought they would arrive after I married, but marrying wasn't something high on my list. My energies were focused on creating a farm with my brother. A husband and children were too far away in my future to be of any importance to me. Until I met Connor...'

'And Connor can never be yours.'

'No.'

'You'll be sacrificing your youth to be lumbered with me.'

'I don't see it that way. Though people will say I'm only after your money.'

George laughed suddenly. 'You've seen my accounts. I don't have that much!'

'No, you don't.' She gave a small smile. 'Do you want to be *lumbered* with me as your wife?'

He leaned back in the seat and stroked his chin in thought. 'Actually, I think I do. We are both alone in this world. Why shouldn't we share our time together? A woman by herself is hard enough, but more so when you are in a new country.'

She thought of David, her parents, their little farm back in England. What would they have said to her for considering such a proposal to a much older man? She stared out over the water, the blue bay shimmering in the sunshine. Her family would want her safe and secure. By marrying George, she would have that.

She turned to him and gave him a brilliant smile. 'I think we'll be very happy together.'

CHAPTER 10

Connor watched Louisa arch her back a little in the saddle. They'd been riding for hours and she was undoubtedly getting stiff and sore.

'Not much further,' he said, riding beside her along the red dusty track.

'Then a nice cup of tea,' George added from the buggy he drove. 'I'll set up camp while you two stretch your legs.'

Connor focused on the ranges looming up before them. The blueness of the tallest peaks was framed against the cloudless blue sky. It was perfect weather for exploring, not too hot. Birds called from the eucalyptus trees, and as they entered the ranges properly, they encountered rock wallabies bounding through the bush and lizards darting from rock to rock.

'Will there be time today to climb one of the peaks?' Louisa asked him.

He gave her a warm smile. 'No, probably not, but we can walk up one of the smaller ones before the sun sets, and then in the morning leave early to trek one of the higher peaks.'

'I'm so excited to do that.' The joy radiated from her.

His gut clenched at the beauty of this woman. He wanted her

like he'd wanted no other. Yet, the news of the engagement brought him fresh heartache. He knew he could never have her, he wasn't free, but the crushing blow that she will marry his best friend wouldn't leave him.

It was stupid of him to suggest this visit to the ranges. Yet, he thought if he could get her away from George and talk sensibly to her, she would rethink her decision. He couldn't let her throw her life away on being shackled to George, a much older man. Of course, he pretended he was happy for them but inside he ached with sadness. Louisa was the kind of woman who needed to be loved and who would have children and a long life with a man who could take care of her. George couldn't provide all that, not at his age. He believed George to be selfish in marrying Louisa. If the man wanted a companion then he should pick one of the old widows in Albany, who would jump at the chance to be Mrs Henderson.

'We have left the flat lands behind,' Louisa murmured, gazing around at the hills. 'It's such a contrast, isn't it?'

Connor nodded, not trusting himself to speak. However, the tranquil splendour of the ranges called to his romantic side and he gazed about noticing the odd flower still blooming from summer. The quietness of the ranges always affected him. The only sound was birdsong, the squeak of leather and rhythmic rumble of the buggy's wheels and he liked that after the busy atmosphere of Munro Downs.

Eventually they stopped to make camp at the base of a large hill and close to a narrow creek.

George climbed down from the buggy and stretched. 'This seems a decent spot. I'll get a fire going to boil some tea.'

'I'll pitch your tent, Louisa.' Connor turned away and tethered his horse to a nearby tree.

'Am I the only one having a tent?'

George laughed. 'Yes, my dear, for Connor and I are used to

sleeping under the stars, though I've not done it for years, but I'm looking forward to it tonight.'

'I could have done the same. I didn't need a tent.' Louisa took out a crate of provisions from the buggy. 'I did sleep in the bush with Akala for months.'

'True,' George nodded, 'but with us men about it's more respectable for you to be in a tent, wouldn't you say?'

Once the basic camp was sorted, they left George to water the horses. Connor led Louisa away into the bush and up the gradual slope of the nearest hill. Single file they didn't talk as they climbed higher. At times when the terrain became steep and rocky, Connor would take Louisa's hand and help her. The touch of her, even through her leather riding gloves, made him want to pull her tight into his arms and never let her go. This feeling he had must be a kind of madness, he couldn't rationalise his thoughts when it came to her.

'Are we at the top?' she asked him from behind, puffing.

'Nearly.' He rounded a jutting boulder and turning to take her hand once more, guided her up until they reached the summit.

They were both breathing hard. Connor watched her chest rise and fall with each breath and quickly glanced away to take in the view. 'Isn't it beautiful?' he whispered.

'Yes. Glorious.' She stood by his side, shading her eyes from the sun to gaze out over the rolling landscape. 'I can't see our camp.'

'No, it's behind us. Those boulders we edged around means we're on the opposite side to the camp.'

Louisa stared ahead, and Connor watched the emotions play on her face. He wanted to know her thoughts, her feelings. Did she think the same of him as he did of her?

He pointed to the blue-grey ranges flowing away from them like a stormy wave. 'Those peaks are so much higher than here. But we can climb that one tomorrow.'

'Which one?'

He moved closer to her and pointed over her shoulder to the nearest peak. 'This one.' His breath seemed to leave his body as she turned and smiled up into his face. Desire rippled through him.

'I don't know if I'm capable. I'm out of breath just from this short climb.'

Her face was inches from his. 'You don't have to do anything you don't want...'

'Connor,' Louisa's voice barely reached him as they stared into each other's eyes. He didn't know who moved first, but suddenly they were holding each other and kissing. His body responded to her touch, her light floral smell and the way she curved into him.

'Louisa...' he mumbled her name against her lips, then kissed her face, her neck, squeezing her against him. He was hard for her, wanting her now, on the dirt, on top of this hill. He unfastened the buttons of her blouse, his fingers clumsy and needy. He revelled in her kisses, as passionate as his own. When her tongue touched his, he thought he would explode.

'Connor, we must stop...' she spoke into his ear as he tried to free her from her corset.

'Why must we?'

'Because you're married.'

The words hit him like a bucket of cold water. He stepped back, putting distance between them. 'You are correct, I am,' he snapped, breathing fast. He felt foolish to have given in to his urges so quickly. The ache in his loins throbbed and he walked away, sucking in deep breaths of mountain air.

'I shouldn't have let you... I shouldn't have wanted you...'

He closed his eyes at the pain in her voice.

'Connor, we can never be, as much as I wish it otherwise.'

'Is that why you are marrying George?' He clenched his jaw to bring himself under control.

'Yes. I would wish it were you, but that is impossible. So I must think of the future.'

He swung around to her, angry and frustrated. 'Why him though? Why stay here and torture us both? Wouldn't it be better to go onto Sydney or Melbourne and start again?'

Her eyes widened in surprise. 'Why must I be the one to leave? To walk away from the chance to be happy and safe with someone who cares for me? You are asking me to give up an opportunity of a loving home just to ease your burden!' She marched past him back down the way they'd come.

'Wait.'

'Leave me alone, you selfish oaf!' she flung over her shoulder as she descended quickly down the hill.'

'Louisa, stop! You'll fall and twist an ankle, for God's sake.'

As though his words conjured up the action, he watched in horror as Louisa slipped on loose stones and fell sideways.

Her scream pierced the air and seemed to echo around the ranges forever.

'Louisa!' Without thought he jumped after her, reaching for her as they both tumbled down, banging against rocks and shrubs until he managed to grab her skirt hem and slow her down.

They slithered a little more amongst the bushes as he pulled her towards him. 'I've got you. Look at me. See? I have you.'

For several moments they lay still, dazed at what had happened.

'Are you hurt?' Connor asked, not wanting to let her go.

'I don't know,' she murmured.

Connor glanced about them. They were nearly at the bottom of the incline. He pushed himself to his feet and then pulled Louisa up beside him.

She whimpered a little as she put pressure on her right foot. 'I've hurt my foot.'

'Take it easy, you'll be fine. Hold onto me.' Connor put one arm around her waist. 'Can you walk at all?'

Louisa tried to take a step and collapsed in pain. 'No! Please tell me I've not broken it?'

Guilt racked him. 'Don't worry. Lean on me. We'll take it gently.'

'I'm so sorry.' Her face was white as a bedsheet. 'I shouldn't have rushed off like that. It was stupid.'

'The fault is mine. If I had behaved as a gentleman you'd have no need to run off like that.'

'And I should have been a lady and not kissed you back.' She looked sheepish. 'We are both to blame.'

'Don't marry George, I beg you. I couldn't bear to see you tied to him as I am tied to Nancy. I married her for the wrong reasons and you are doing the same.'

'I'd rather have a nice life with George and see you when I can, than to walk away from you both and be alone in a strange city. Do you understand that?'

He nodded and knew he had no right to insist anything of her. 'It will be hard, having you as a friend only,' he whispered, desperate to kiss her again.

'We have to try, for everyone's sake.'

Feeling as though he'd lost everything that mattered to him, he helped her to stand. 'I am here if you need me, remember that.'

Arm in arm they began the agonising walk back to George at the camp.

LOUISA STARED around the sitting room, smiling in general to the gathered guests, mainly male friends of George's who'd come from Albany or further out in the country. They had all witnessed their wedding ceremony, performed by a young vicar newly arrived from Perth. He'd married them in the garden under a large eucalyptus tree. George hadn't wanted to be married in a church in Albany and definitely not by Reverend Pierce. Perversely he'd sent an invitation to Miss Muir, but not to her sister Winifred. Naturally, Miss Muir didn't attend. Not many had attended from town. The long trip out to King's Station wasn't worth the effort to see George marry a nobody, a ship-wreck survivor who had the audacity to marry one of their own.

She and George had spent the day before decorating the veranda with bunting, while Su Lin cooked up a feast. Louisa had kept busy, cleaning and sorting, knowing they'd have guests staying over. Being winter she didn't have many flowers to pick to brighten the rooms. The small garden lining the front of the veranda held a few sparse rose bushes, which had been neglected for years, but no flowers grew in June to give her the option of a bouquet.

At times, in a quiet moment, she would think about Connor, or her family. She'd go over in her head the reasons why she was marrying George. Nerves made her stomach cramp and she found her appetite all but disappeared. Was she doing the right thing? What alternative did she have? As George's wife she'd be respected, secure, mistress of the station, a person of rank in Albany's society and in the district. As a single woman she'd have none of that. She'd have to find her own way of earning a living, of making the money she had stretch.

No. Becoming Mrs Henderson was the right thing to do. She would take care of George as he grew older and he would take care of her. But could she live here for the rest of her life, side by side to Connor, especially after that kiss at the ranges and knowing he felt the same about her too?

The ceremony had gone without hitch. A weak winter sun shone, the birds chirped in the trees, the guests appeared happy and dressed for the occasion. She'd said her vows quietly, confi-dently. George's smile made her happy. She brought him comfort and that was a fine thing to do for someone.

'You look lost in thought,' Nancy said, wheeling up beside Louisa.

She had tried to avoid Nancy as much as possible, for the guilt she felt at kissing Connor must surely be written all over her face? 'I'm just thinking. I can hardly believe it is my wedding day.'

'Not one you would expect to be like?' Nancy sipped from her wine glass.

'I never really gave much thought to my wedding day before. None of the boys in my village back in England took my fancy. Then when my mother and father got sick and died, it was just David and I. Looking after the farm and him kept me busy. Then we made the decision to come out here…'

'And you were suddenly alone.'

Louisa stared at her, waiting for her to say what most people whispered. 'Yes, I was alone.'

'George is one of the best men I know,' Nancy said, her gaze searching for the groom who stood amongst friends near the window. They'd come inside for the clouds had swallowed up the sunshine of the day and threatened rain.

'He is a good man.' Louisa watched George as he stood drinking with his friends. Although he was sixty-five, he stood tall and proud. His shock of white hair was neatly combed and the black suit he wore fitted him perfectly. At a glance a person would think him ten years younger than he was, and today he seemed to have a new lease of life. It pleased Louisa enormously that she made him happy.

'You two are the talk of the district. No one can believe you have married him.'

'Do they say I've done it for money?'

Nancy drank more of her wine. 'I'm afraid so.'

Louisa nodded. 'We expected it. It's not true, of course, but they won't think that.'

'I can understand why you agreed to marry George. You're

without friends or family. He is kind and on paper a good catch, if you ignore his age.'

'His age doesn't bother me in the slightest.'

'What about children?'

'We've married for mutual companionship, you know that. We told you at dinner weeks ago.' Louisa glanced down at Nancy.

She'd seen her once since she'd become engaged. Nancy had invited them over for dinner, but Connor had not been there. He'd stayed out in the bush, hunting wild dogs who were killing the sheep. Louisa had been glad he wasn't there that night. She didn't want to sit across a table from him while Nancy asked her about wedding plans. And today she'd only said a brief good day to him. Connor kept himself separate from her, cool and aloof, and she was glad he did. She could cope with her trembling heart as long as he wasn't too close.

A tall man with a black beard came up to them. Louisa knew him to be Nancy's cousin, Alfred, a dour man with a deep voice. 'Ladies, would you care for some refreshments?' he asked.

'Thank you, no.' Louisa gave him a tight smile. 'I must check on Su Lin and make sure she is managing. Excuse me.'

She made her way through the guests and out of the back door. The kitchen was built detached to the house and reached by a covered walkway. Ivy, a native girl a few years older than Akala helped Su Lin. She smiled at Louisa as she passed her with a bucket full of slops to feed to the pigs.

'Is everything fine in here, Su Lin?' Louisa asked, just as the rain started falling.

'Good, Miss Louisa.' Su Lin faltered on arranging salad into a large earthenware bowl. 'Missus I mean, Missus Henderson.' She bowed an apology at the name mix up.

'I think it'll take time for us both to get used to my new role.' Louisa stared around the brick building with its stone floor and large pine table. 'Do you need more help?'

'No, missus. All good.' Su Lin used a large knife to cut slices of ham from a cured leg. Chinese lanterns hung from the ceiling and a sign with Chinese writing on it was nailed to the back wall.

'What does that writing say, Su Lin?'

Su Lin read aloud in Chinese and then paused. 'He who fears suffering is already suffering from fear,' she said it in English perfectly as though she had been practising. She gave Louisa a long look before turning her attention back to slicing the ham.

Feeling a little useless, Louisa returned the way she had come, only to stop half way along the covered walkway when Connor came out of the house.

For a long time, they stared at each other. He looked handsome in his dark grey suit, which was so different from his usual white moleskin trousers.

'You look beautiful,' he spoke softly, and she only just heard him over the noise of the rain hitting the tin roof.

'Thank you.' She reddened self-consciously, glancing down at her pretty white lace dress. Miss Vincent, the dressmaker in Albany, had made it for her at short notice.

'I understand why you've done it... married George. I accept it, but as I said in the ranges. If you ever need me, don't hesitate to contact me.'

She nodded. Was she imagining the sorrow in his eyes was a reflection of her own? Her heart ached. She couldn't drag her gaze from his blue eyes which seemed to speak to her the words his mouth didn't utter.

'Louisa! Ah, there you are.' George stood behind Connor in the doorway. 'Some of our guests are leaving. The rain is forcing people home.'

'Yes, I'm coming.' She sidled past Connor, her eyes closing at his nearness, before she pasted a smile on her face and went to George.

'Are you all right?' George took her hand as she reached him, looking over his shoulder at Connor.

'Absolutely.' She smiled wider, making herself believe it too.

'How many people are going, and who is staying over for the night?'

George's reply distracted her from all thoughts of Connor. She threw herself into being the perfect hostess and only relaxed when Connor and Nancy finally left as well.

* * *

COLD JULY WINDS battered the house as Louisa ran her finger down the line of figures, frowning. 'I've added it up three times and come to three different answers.'

'And I've read three different articles about Ned Kelly in this newspaper. For the love of God will they not leave the story alone? He's a criminal and deserves to hang. Shame they didn't kill him in the shoot-out, then there wouldn't be such hysteria about him.' George folded the newspaper and looked over at her.

Louisa barely listened to him. The fortunes of the rogue bushranger, Ned Kelly, didn't feature in her thoughts. She cared little for what people said about the man, who'd taken the law into his own hands.

'Leave the books for today, dearest. You've been working on those ledgers all week.'

She scratched her forehead, then jumped when the gale tossed a large leafy twig up against the window. 'This is serious, George. The price of wool has dropped. If we shear next month, we'll lose money. If we wait another month and shear in September we risk the lambs the ewes are carrying, don't we?'

'It'll be fine. The team of shearers I usually employ are careful with the ewes and the lambs they carry. We'll wait. The price will go back up.'

She rose from the desk and stared out of the window at the cold racing winds. It was hard to understand that in Australia winter was in July, whereas back in England it would be summertime. 'What is Connor and the other farmers doing?'

George fished a note out of his waistcoat pocket. 'Connor has written that he's shearing the first week of August. It's a gamble to do it in August, for we can still get extreme cold weather, but he has a bigger flock and he's yarding his sheep before turning them back out.'

'Yarding?' she asked, hating that she didn't know everything about sheep farming in this country, even though George had explained so much to her over the last month since they were married.

'Holding yards next to the shearing shed. He can keep his flock in the yards to protect them from the cold after they've been shorn. He has the money to hand feed them for a week or so before turning them back out to lamb.'

'I see.' She thought of their own shearing shed and the few pens they had next to it. Their station was smaller than Connor's in every way. 'So, we aren't doing that?'

'No. We'll bring the flock in during September when the weather is warming up.'

'And what if the ewes have begun lambing?'

'I'm not shearing next week, Louisa. It's too cold and the wool prices are too low. Another two months will be worth the wait.'

'But if Connor is—'

'Connor is different. His concern is larger than ours, he has more money than me. Trust me on this.'

'You know best, George.' She sighed and left the room. George could be so stubborn at times. He stuck to his ways and would hardly listen to her if she had a new idea in regards to the running of the station.

She walked into her bedroom, the one place in the whole house that she felt was completely hers alone. Su Lin was the only person who came in here to either clean or hang up Louisa's clothes.

Flopping onto the bed, she listened to the wind howling around the buildings. A sheet of tin roof had loosened somewhere and flapped with an annoying creak. The sound grated on her.

She grabbed her diary from the set of drawers next to the bed. She flipped through the months of August and September, the pages were bare of invitations. George said it was because of shearing time. People didn't entertain during shearing, but she felt differently. They were being outcast from society. Winifred Pierce and her followers were making it clear that Louisa and George weren't on anyone's guest list. Not that she cared. However, it would be nice every now and then to go and visit other people. Since the wedding a month ago she'd not left the station and was finding it a little constricting at times. She was bored.

A long sigh escaped her. In the corner of the room stood the deckchair and she went to sit on it. The wood creaked as it took her weight, but the canvas still seemed in good condition. She had placed it where she could see it every day. Like her, it had survived the shipwreck and was, to her, the symbol of surviving. When she felt low in spirits and was missing David or her parents she'd sit in the deckchair and feel closer to them. She told no one of this little oddity of hers, least they would laugh at her. It was her secret. But even today, the deckchair brought her no comfort.

She closed her eyes, her heart heavy. She missed David, especially on days like this when she was stuck inside and didn't have enough to occupy her. Su Lin ran the house brilliantly, leaving Louisa with nothing to do but sewing on an evening. George didn't have a very interesting library, the books being mainly about farming. She had no letters to write, for she didn't know anyone who'd want a letter from her. With no invitations to break up the monotony of the weeks, she had too much time to spare to think about her loss of family. She missed David's cheeky laugh, his ability to turn every day into something worth living. She'd never met anyone like him before who had the talent to make her laugh.

Su Lin's frantic calling bolted Louisa upright. She scrambled off the deckchair to meet Su Lin at the door.

'Missus! Missus!' Su Lin's eyes were wide, her grey pigtail swished as she slid to a stop. 'You come quick!'

'What's happened?' Louisa followed her down the hallway and out the back door.

'Come quick!' The little housekeeper dashed away despite her advancing years.

They raced along the covered walkway and across the yard towards the outbuildings. Wind tore at Louisa's hair and she lost pins from her hair bun, but she ignored that and kept running. Some of the men were running into the largest barn on the property where much of the farming equipment was stored.

Inside the barn, Louisa skidded to a stop. A large eucalyptus tree had crashed through the roof on one side of the building, smashing onto a cart and some barrels.

Hunt, George's most trusted man, and leader of the men on the station, pulled away the broken pieces of barrels, spreading grain out over the ground. Instructing the other stockmen to get through the tree's branches, he chopped away with an axe at the larger limbs. The wind howled through the jagged yawning gap in the building, blowing things over and dust into their eyes.

Hunt turned as Louisa reached his side. 'Mr Henderson is in there!'

'What?' Horrified, Louisa stared into the multitude of branches and at the enormous trunk. 'George? Are you sure?' It seemed only minutes ago she had left him in the study.

'He came out to talk to me about the shearing.' Hunt hacked away at another branch. 'I left him to go and secure the barn door and then the tree came down.'

'George!' she yelled, frantic. 'Find him! Get him out!'

A native stockman called, Sammy, carefully climbed over the

trunk, nimble and quick. He squeezed through the shattered wreckage of the tree and the tin roof sheets.

Louisa waited, breath held, her eyes searching through the leaves looking for George.

Sammy disappeared beneath the tangle of branches. Moments later his shout was heard over the whacking of Hunt's axe chopping the smaller limbs.

'You've found him?' Louisa strained to see.

Hunt jumped into the leaves, following the path Sammy used.

Louisa looked at Su Lin. 'Go get bandages ready, quickly now.' She turned to another stockman, called Carter. 'We need something to carry him on back to the house.'

'I'm on to it, missus.' He dashed away leaving her with another station hand called Turner.

'Saddle a horse, Turner. I want a doctor here.'

'A doctor?' Turner gave her a stare as though she was mad. 'Where will I get a doctor from? There ain't one for miles.'

Louisa rounded on him, temper flaring. 'I don't care! Find one. Munro Downs has a doctor, don't they? If he can't come, then ride into Albany if you have to! Just go!'

'Yes, missus.' He ran from the barn.

Hunt's head and shoulders emerged. 'Missus! The boss is trapped. A large branch has him pinned down. Can you pass me the axe?'

She picked up the axe and climbed over a broken barrel to pass it to him. 'Help me get to him.'

'No, missus, it's too dangerous.'

'Don't be soft, man.' She lifted her skirts and hitched herself over the branch nearest to her, then she ducked under another large limb. Hunt reached out his hand, guiding her through the maze of broken timbers and the tree canopy. Her skirts caught and ripped on a broken branch and she pulled at it angrily until she was free.

'You have to get down low on your knees and crawl under the

trunk.' Hunt lifted leafy branches aside to show her the hole she had to go through.

On her hands and knees, she inched under the trunk, keeping low.

George lay on his back, eyes closed. Blood seeped from a cut on his forehead. From the waist down, he was pinned.

'Cover his face, missus.' Hunt started chopping at the branches while Sammy took the strain of the weight off George's legs.

Louisa knelt beside George's head, using a handkerchief to press against the bleeding cut. 'George? Can you hear me? It's Louisa.'

His eyes remained closed.

Frightened he might die, Louisa kissed his cheek. 'George, can you open your eyes?'

With no response, she held his hand and watched as Hunt worked hurriedly to free him. Several minutes went by before the first of the branches were yanked away.

George moaned.

'George!' She bent closer to him. 'It's all right. Try not to move.'

'Louisa?'

'Yes, it's me. We're in the barn. The wind blew a tree onto it and it's trapped you, but Hunt is going to get you free soon.'

He nodded once and closed his eyes.

'Quickly,' she urged Hunt.

After another fifteen minutes, Hunt and Sammy had removed the last of the branches and timber posts, clearing George's legs and a path to the barn door.

Carter stood waiting with a hand cart and they carefully lifted George onto it. Louisa held his hand, but he didn't make a murmur, though his face was grey with pain. Slowly they pushed the cart across the yard to the covered walkway where Su Lin waited.

Once they had him on his bed, Louisa sat beside him. She gave him a tender smile when he opened his eyes. 'I've sent Turner for the doctor. Where do you hurt?'

'All over, but I'll be fine in a little while.'

'Special tea.' Su Lin stood on the other side of the bed with a tea cup filled with a browny-green liquid that didn't smell like tea.

Louisa helped him up to sip at it, then he lay back exhausted.

'Su Lin's special tea is all I need,' George murmured.

'Your legs could be broken, which will take more than tea to fix,' she admonished him gently.

He smiled. 'I've endured worse than this and survived, haven't I, Su Lin?'

'Yes, boss.' Su Lin nodded vigorously. 'Tough boss. I make soup.' She bowed and left the room.

'Is the pain very terrible?' Louisa asked, worried how severe his injuries might be.

'Tolerable. My legs mainly.' George squeezed her hand.

She made him sip more of the tea.

'No one else was hurt?'

'Only you.'

'That's a relief.' He winced in pain. 'More tea, please.'

'What is in it?' She helped him to sip again.

'Su Lin won't tell me, but I'm guessing poppy juice, as she only brings it out when someone is in great pain.'

'As long as it helps you I don't care what is in it.'

George closed his eyes and she let him sleep for some time. Sitting by his bed, she watched his face relax. He was a dear man, her best friend, and she hated to think of him in agony.

She must have fallen asleep as she woke with a start at the sound of rapid heavy footsteps on the floorboards.

Connor hurried into the room followed by another man in a black suit.

Louisa stared at them both.

'Louisa, forgive us, we came as soon as we heard.' Connor's stare went between her and George. 'Is he…?'

George stirred and opened his eyes.

'You're still alive then, old man?' Connor joked, though the worried expression stayed on his face. 'Edward and I were riding into Albany together when we met Turner on the road.'

'Out in this gale?' George quizzed. 'Madmen.'

Louisa ignored her thumping heart and stood on legs that were suddenly weak. She wasn't expecting to see Connor and it unsettled her and after the shock of George's accident she was feeling decidedly delicate. She held out her hand to the man standing beside Connor. 'I'm Mrs Henderson.'

'Doctor Edward Milton. Pleased to meet you.' He shook her hand and then opened his medical bag. 'Now then, Mr Henderson, let me have a look at you.'

'You're a doctor?' she asked, relieved. He surprised her by his young years. Most doctors she knew were the age of George, but Milton was barely thirty years of age in her estimation.

'Perhaps we should leave them in peace, Louisa?' Connor said, making for the door.

She hesitated slightly, giving George a lingering look before leaving the room and joining Connor in the sitting room.

'Would you… would you care for some refreshment?' Her words seemed stuck on her tongue. She was acutely conscious of him being in the room, standing only a yard from her.

'No… yes…' He shook his head, his eyes intent as he looked at her. 'I'll stay until we know George is going to be fine, then I must go.'

'Of course.' She rang the bell for Su Lin, and when she stood at the door Louisa ordered tea.

Louisa felt uneasy being in the room alone with him. Could he sense her conflict? She wanted his company but was frightened of it as well. She wanted to say something interesting, but her mind was blank.

'The gale isn't so strong at Munro Downs, otherwise we wouldn't have journeyed out. We didn't encounter the winds until we reached the Albany Road. It's been cold though.' Connor watched the wind punish the trees outside.

'It's fortunate that you had a doctor with you.' Louisa straightened a cushion on the sofa, needing to do something.

'Yes. Edward is my friend, and Nancy's cousin, from Melbourne.'

'A friend from Melbourne? How nice.' She walked to the fireplace and added more wood to the fire.

'He's not long finished his studies and thought to come out to me for a time before he settles into a practice. He wanted to see some of the country. He's not visited Albany since our wedding, when he could only get away for a few days, and hasn't seen Munro Downs at all.'

'And instead of having an easy time of it, he's administering to George.' She watched the flames lick at the wood.

'He will be happy to help. I've put him to work on my station these last few weeks. I've offered for him to stay permanently.'

She turned to look at him. 'Do you think he will?'

'No.' He gave a small smile. 'I think we are a little too remote for his tastes.'

'Shame.'

'Oh?' He raised an enquiring eyebrow.

She blushed. 'He seems a nice enough fellow.'

As though a shutter came down over his face, his expression went neutral. 'May I remind you that you are a married woman now, Mrs Henderson.'

'I didn't mean that at all, only that doctors are limited in number here.' Did he think she admired the doctor? How could she forget she had married George? She had only done so because the man she wanted was already married!

'True. I would feel better having a doctor permanently at

Munro Downs. Is there anything you need my help with?' His tone was business-like.

'I don't think so.'

Connor glanced out of the window. 'George will be off his feet for a while. You've got shearing to contend with.'

'Not for two months.'

'Why shear in September? That's late.'

'The wool prices are too low, George said.'

'His ewes will be lambing.' Connor frowned. 'I'll speak with him. My shearers arrive next week, then can come here when they've finished my flock.'

'He's made his mind up. We had this discussion only hours ago.' She took the tea tray from Su Lin and placed it on a small round table by the sofa. Connor stood close to her as she poured the tea.

'If George is out of action for a while, you'll need my help.'

'I'm sure we'll handle it. Hunt and the other stockman are very capable, I'm sure.' She passed him a teacup with a hand not so steady.

'Those men are paid labourers and don't have the same dedication as an owner. Someone will need to keep an eye on them.'

'And that will be me.'

'You?'

'I grew up on a farm. I've done my share of lambing.' She smarted at his lack of confidence in her. 'My brother and I often stayed up all night in the barns with the ewes as they birthed their lambs.'

'You will be needed to take care of George.' Connor stared at her. 'I'm offering to help you.'

'Thank you for your offer, but I'm sure I can manage. You have your own station to oversee.' Why didn't he understand that she couldn't have him here?

Before he could comment, Doctor Milton entered the room.

'How is he?' Louisa asked, knowing that Connor was annoyed with her response.

'Mr Henderson has got severe swelling and bruising on both legs. I couldn't detect any broken bones, but he's in so much pain it's hard to tell. There could be a minor fracture near the left ankle. The swelling in that area is rapid. I've bandaged the cut on his head, but I don't believe it needs stitches. We need to watch for concussion.'

'What can I do?' She poured the doctor a cup of tea. He was a good looking man with dark auburn hair and kind eyes. His presence relaxed her, unlike Connor's.

'Nothing for the moment, but to monitor him.' He took the tea. 'If it pleases you, I'm prepared to stay here tonight and watch him. I cannot rule out internal bleeding and I'd be happier if I could stay with him.'

'Of course. Thank you for your kindness. I'll have Su Lin make up a bed for you.' Louisa went to leave the room.

'Oh, Mrs Henderson? Cold compresses would be useful for the swelling.'

'I'll ask Su Lin.'

When she returned from the kitchen, she looked in on George who was asleep, and continued into the drawing room. Doctor Milton was alone.

'Connor said he'd return tomorrow to talk to George.'

She nodded, saddened he had gone without saying goodbye. He was a complex man and she didn't know how to handle him.

CHAPTER 11

*L*ouisa stood on the bottom yard rail and watched the stockmen bringing in the sheep. Dust rose in the air. She gazed out over the flock of bleating ewes. The noise was deafening; mounted stockmen's whistles to the working dogs, the yells, the bleating sheep, and the general clamour of horses' hooves striking the hard ground vibrated through the air.

'That's the last of them from the southern paddocks, missus. They look good. The percentage of pregnant ones is high as well,' Hunt said coming to stand on the fence with her. He hooked his arms over the top rail.

'It's been a great effort, Hunt, thank you.'

'We've just got one more section of the northern paddocks to clear and put through the river and they'll all be in.'

'When is that happening?'

'Carter and Sammy are on with it today. They'll be at the river shortly. I'll go and give them a hand.'

'Ask someone to saddle Minty for me, will you? I want to see the sheep go through the river, too.' She stared over the backs of hundreds of sheep. 'Am I doing the right thing, bringing them in now and not next month?'

'I would say so, the weather isn't too cold and should hold. Mr Munro says the same.'

She glanced quickly at him. 'Mr Munro?'

'I saw him out riding the boundary yesterday.'

'You told him what we are doing?'

'Aye, and he agreed.'

Louisa nodded, relieved to have his approval. She just hoped George would agree.

Since his accident last month George had not recovered as fast as Doctor Milton liked. The good doctor, who insisted Louisa call him Edward, still lodged with them, for George hadn't left his bedroom and each day seemed to bring more health problems. It was as though the fight had gone out of him. For the first time George's body had let him down and he couldn't cope with his fragility.

Louisa had no choice but to take command of the station while George remained bedridden. The prospect was daunting. She'd never had to control men before or run a farm as large or so different as King's Station. Her family holding back in England had been so much smaller and so much easier to manage. Her father and brother worked the seasons like second nature.

Here, however, was different. Farming in Australia was on another scale. Everything was bigger, the land space larger, the weather more extreme, the numbers of labourers greater, and the sheep, a brand called Merino, more expensive and treated like walking gold, could change a man's fortune overnight.

Since George's confinement, she had thrown herself into learning everything she could about the station. George had no interest in anything and told her to do as she wished. So, feeling she had no choice, when the end of August came, she had gone ahead and sent the stockmen to herd the sheep into the yards for shearing – a whole month earlier than George had planned. She just hoped the weather wouldn't turn cold again.

'Mrs Henderson.'

She turned to smile at Edward. 'Have you come to see the sheep?' she asked, knowing after a month of living with him that he had no interest in animals or farming at all.

He laughed, easy in her company. 'No. I've come down to tell you that Su Lin is upset about something, possibly something I said.'

'Again?' Louisa sighed. Edward and Su Lin had been at logger-heads over how to care for George. Su Lin had Chinese medi-cines which she swore by and dismissed Edward's Western ways. No matter what they both said or did though, George remained uninterested in anything around him and made no attempt to leave his room. He picked at Su Lin's wonderful food, half listened to Edward's advice, and forced a smile at Louisa when she sat with him.

Nothing would entice him back into normal life again, he left everything to Louisa to sort out, even the odd visit from Connor failed to rouse him. The man she had grown to know as energetic and living life to the full was slowly becoming someone else. His age had never been a factor to her, but now every one of his sixty-five years showed on his lined face. He'd lost weight, despite doing nothing but sitting in bed. His lack of enthusiasm worried her.

So, she was determined to give her all to the station to show him that he had much to live for.

Edward turned his back on the sheep, the dust and the yells of the stockmen. 'George was asking for you.'

Soberly, she climbed down from the rail. 'I'll go to him.'

Walking back with Edward, Louisa noticed things that before she'd have not taken any notice of. Now she knew the names of the four milking cows, Clover, Sunshine, Rosie and Buttercup. She knew they were in calf, serviced by Connor's bull months ago. She was aware of the chickens, the number of hens which laid their eggs every day, the rooster who attacked Su Lin quite often and who Su Lin threatened with the axe to cut off his head. She knew of the geese which had a habit of chasing the stockmen and squawking so loud it hurt her ears, of the vegetable garden that Su Lin guarded with her life, growing her herbs and vegetables which provided fresh goodness for the table.

Louisa knew the work that happened in the dairy, the tasty butter and cheese that Edith, one of the stockman's wives, produced. She'd met Hattie, the laundry woman, again another of the stockman's wives, and her aborigine helper, Sunnie. She'd toured the workers' little cottages when she first arrived at King's Station, but she'd not paid much attention to the workings of the farm. Back then she'd been a visitor, now she was George's wife, and since his accident, the sole person in charge.

She felt the responsibility keenly. The shearing had to go well, and the wool prices must go higher. Without the wool clip money, she'd not be able to pay the wages which supported all these people. Without the wool clip she'd not be able to pay the bills to keep the station running.

'You seem lost in thought. You aren't unhappy about my spats with Su Lin?' Edward asked.

'No, Su Lin can take care of herself, as I'm sure you can,' she reassured him. 'I'm more worried about George. How long will it be until he's back to being himself?'

'He is very gloomy, that's true. Talks about death a lot. It's to be expected. He's found that he's not indestructible.'

'He often mentioned his age when I first met him, but it was always like a joke. He still did everything he needed to and ran this place.'

'When people are in constant pain, it alters their personality. Once he has healed, he'll be the man you knew again.'

'But I need him to be back running things now. We have to show him that he is important still, remind him that he is wanted, needed.'

'Naturally, but he's feeling sorry for himself at the moment and can't see a way past it yet.'

'Is that all? Are you sure he hasn't some hidden injury?'

Edward swatted away a fly from his face. 'I'm certain of it. He sprained an ankle and there was plenty of bruising, but it's gone now. It's been a month, he should be back on his feet now. I had him hobbling around the bedroom this morning and he handled it well, though he said it still hurt. I'm at a bit of a loss really. If he has a broken bone then it must be slight, as I can't feel it and the swelling has gone.'

'What can I do to help?'

'Nothing. Time will heal his ankle. Basically, I think the accident has just knocked the stuffing out of him. He doesn't want to get better.'

'But why? I don't understand it.' They'd reached the back of the house.

'I don't have that answer, I'm afraid. Just be with him. Give him things to look forward to.' Edward gave her a tender smile, his eyes kind. 'He is very lucky to have you.'

'Thank you.' She squeezed his arm gently in gratitude. She liked Edward very much and couldn't imagine how she'd have coped without him in attendance. He was attentive to his patient, but when George was asleep, Edward would seek her out and they'd spend each evening talking, playing cards or reading quietly together. She liked his company, his conversation. However, she had noticed that Edward's gaze would linger on her a little too long at times, and sometimes his hand would brush hers. She hoped it was all in her imagination, but she could sense it was perhaps something more on his part.

She left him and went into George's bedroom. George sat propped up in bed, a book opened on his lap. 'How are you feeling?'

'Can you stop asking me that? I don't change from day to day.'

'But you will soon.' She sat on the chair beside the bed. 'Your ankle will heal and—'

'And what? I'll be running about again? I'm old, Louisa. My days are numbered. I'm ready to die.'

'Why must you talk so negatively?' She jerked up again, angry with him. 'Do you enjoy making me upset? Do you think that is what I want to hear?'

At once his face softened and he held out his hand to her. 'I'm sorry, my dear. Upsetting you is the last thing I would ever want to do.'

'Then why say it?' She took his hand and sat back down.

'I don't know, honestly I don't.' He shrugged helplessly. 'I don't understand myself anymore.'

She sighed tiredly. 'I married you because we are friends. We needed each other. We can take care of each other. I like being with you, but not when you are like this.'

'I apologise. Forgive me, please?'

'Promise me I'll not hear such talk from you again.'

'I promise,' he replied, eyes downcast, suitably chastised.

She stood and threw back the blankets. 'Now get up.'

His grey eyebrows rose nearly into his hairline as he scrambled for the blankets again. 'What?'

'Get up. Come on. You're going to have a shave and a bath and join Edward and I for dinner tonight.' She went to his wardrobe and pulled out clean pressed trousers and a white shirt.

He looked horrified by the thought. 'I don't think I'm ready for that.'

'You are!' She found his polished black shoes. 'I'm not asking you to walk into Albany. I'm requesting you to step back into the life you live, which is beyond this bedroom.'

'Louisa…'

'No, I'll not listen to you.' She turned for the door. 'I'll have Su Lin bring the bath in. Edward will assist you.'

Before he could utter another word, she strode out of the room, bumping into Edward in the hallway.'

'Bravo.' He clapped lightly.

'You heard?'

'Your raised voice carries, I'm afraid.' He grinned. 'I'll go in and help him.'

'Thank you. I want him up and about again. Then you'll be able to return to your life as well.'

Edward's expression dropped a little. 'I'm in no hurry. I've enjoyed my time here with you. I don't wish to leave you.' He lingered a moment, his grey eyes watching her reaction and then he stepped into George's bedroom.

Louisa walked slowly out of the back door, her mind replaying Edward's words. She hadn't imagined his growing affection for her then. He had revealed too much. She didn't want his admiration. Edward's feelings towards her were a complication too many.

Leaving the covered walkway, she headed for the stable. She wanted to ride out to the river to the men – a small part of her wanting to just keep riding and not stop.

Suddenly, Connor rode into the yard and Louisa struggled to contain her excitement and also dread at seeing him. Connor was both pleasure and pain.

'Louisa. Good afternoon.' Connor dismounted and gave Prince's reins to an aboriginal lad who came out of the stable yard.

'We weren't expecting you, Connor. Aren't you busy shearing?'

'We will be finished today and that's why I've come to see if you'd like to visit Munro Downs to watch the process before the shearers come to you, so you know what to expect.'

'Oh.' She hadn't expected the sudden invitation.

'Also, we have a party to celebrate the end of shearing.'

The idea thrilled her. To spend more time with him is all she wanted, though for her own sanity she needed to stay well away from him.

When she didn't answer he continued, 'Edward might like a break from his patient too. Can Su Lin take care of George for one night?'

'Yes, she could, but I don't think I should go.' It was hard for her to say those words.

'Why?'

She stared into his questioning blue eyes and wished he would kiss her, but she had no right to want such things. 'I'm needed here. There's too much to do. But do take Edward. I'm sure we can cope without him now. George got up this morning.'

'That is excellent news about George. Are you sure you don't want to go?'

'Yes, quite sure, thank you.' Her heart disagreed with her head, but she held firm.

'I'll go speak to Edward and see George.' He turned for the house but paused when she didn't join him. 'You aren't coming in?'

'I've things to attend to. We're washing the sheep in the river.' She turned away, heading for the stables. She sensed his stare on her back.

* * *

CONNOR WATCHED LOUISA WALK AWAY, wishing she'd stay longer to talk to him. She was never off his mind. Perhaps it was a good thing that she didn't return home with him. She was a complication he didn't need.

Sighing, he went towards the house but stopped by the back door and waved to Su Lin who sat in the kitchen garden plucking a chicken. He stepped inside feeling like a traitor to his best friend. George didn't deserve to be treated like this. Although Connor

146

hadn't done anything, he had impure thoughts regarding Louisa and that wasn't fair to George or Nancy. Louisa was like a madness inside him. Staying away from her drove him mad thinking about her constantly. However, to be in her company was another type of torture. To see her smile, hear her voice, the smell of her…

Feeling a fool, he took his hat off and went along the hallway. In George's bedroom he found his friend sitting in a chair by the window, a window that overlooked the yard and buildings. George would have seen him and Louisa talking.

'How are you today then?' Connor forced the jollity into his tone.

George, looking older each time he visited, merely gave a glimmer of a smile. 'I've been hobbling about and now my body is throbbing with a dull ache.'

'That's not good news. I'm sorry to hear it.' Connor stood beside him. 'Where's Edward?'

'Filling a bath for me. I'm to re-join the living apparently.' George stared out through the window. 'You should be busy shearing, why are you here?'

Connor remained standing by the door. 'I came to invite you all to Munro Downs to witness the end of the shearing and attend the party. I thought both Louisa and Edward would like to see what happens.'

'They will see it soon enough here.'

'True, but my end of shearing parties are legendary,' he boasted with a grin. 'You always enjoy them every year. Remember a few years back when we drank two bottles of that very expensive Scottish whisky? We stayed out all night and watched the sun come up. We outlasted everyone, didn't we?' Connor shook his head recalling the night. 'What a time we had. Mrs Mac did a jig on top of the dray and nearly fell off, remember? But we paid for it the next day. I've never felt so sick in my life.'

George stared down at his hands. 'Not this year. Louisa is too busy, and I need Edward.'

Connor's lips twitched. George sounded like a spoilt child. 'You don't need Edward at all. Let him go and enjoy the night.'

'Take him if you must, but Louisa will stay here with me.'

'Very well. I simply thought it would help Louisa to learn how it all went about before the shearers arrive here next week.'

'She's watched sheep being sheared before back in England.'

'But not on the scale we do it here.'

'She'll be fine. Between her and Hunt they will sort it out.'

'So, you won't come for a night? A change of scenery might do you some good.'

'What use am I to anyone when I can do nothing but hobble about?'

'For a start you can sit and talk to Nancy. She's in a wheelchair and manages to be of enormous use.' Connor couldn't help but remind him that he was being a baby about his injuries compared to all that Nancy went through and dealt with every day.

'I'd rather just stay at home.'

'Very well.' Connor sighed. 'I'll come back and help Louisa in a few days when the shearing starts.'

'I'm sure you have enough to do on your own station.'

'Are you saying you don't want me to help her?'

'I'm saying I don't want you hurting her.' George's stare held a message that Connor couldn't fail to recognise.

His gut clenched. 'I don't want to hurt her.'

'But you will.'

The simple statement made Connor wince.

George's stare didn't waver. 'As a friend, I'm asking you to stay away. There is enough gossip about her because she married me, an old man. Don't let the nosy beggars in town hear of anything else.'

'There is nothing else, you know that.'

'Then keep it that way, I beg you.'

Silence stretched between them for a moment.

Connor turned for the door, wishing he'd not wasted the time in riding here today. 'I hope you're feeling better soon.'

'We'll see.' George glanced away, dismissing him.

Frustrated and annoyed, Connor left the room and nearly bumped into Edward as he came out of another room. 'Ah, there you are. Are you nearly ready to return to Melbourne?'

Edward shook his head. 'Why is everyone so insistent I leave? I'm needed here. For the moment anyway. Louisa can't manage George on her own.'

'She's not on her own. There's a dozen people right outside the door.'

'You know what I mean.'

Connor didn't, not really. 'I thought you wished to return to Melbourne by the beginning of September?'

'I can postpone my plans.'

'Why would you?'

Edward stepped towards the bedroom. 'I told you. Louisa needs me.' With a nod he walked into George's bedroom and shut the door.

Suspicious, Connor left the house and strode to the stables for Prince. Edward wanted to stay here even though the emergency was over. What could possibly make him want to stay?

The answer was simple and knocked the wind from his chest. Louisa. Edward wanted to stay because of Louisa.

Mounting Prince, Connor let the horse have his head and he urged him towards the river.

Louisa stood watching the sheep being encouraged to wade into the river as he rode up. He dismounted and smiled when she turned towards him.

'Isn't this such a wonderful sight?' Excitement shone from her eyes. 'Look at that, Connor. So many sheep going through the water. I've never seen such a thing before. Hunt says the river is at the right height to wash through the fleece but not endanger the ewes.'

'Hunt knows what he's doing. He's been a stockman long enough.'

'I don't know what I'd have done without him. He's been an enormous help to me.'

He felt a tinge of jealousy. He needed to get a grip on himself. Now he was being jealous over a bloody stockman!

She gave him a glance. 'Are you on your way home?'

'Yes.'

'Without Edward?'

'Yes. He feels he is still needed here.'

'I'm certain we could manage without him now. George needs to not rely on him so much. Edward should be with you or return to his life in Melbourne.'

'I don't think he remains here because of George.' He watched for her reaction and noticed her blush. It seemed he was right.

The bleating of a nearby sheep drowned out everything else for a moment. It had become separated from the others and made its displeasure known. Connor clapped his hands sending it along the bank to where Carter stood waving the wet unhappy ewes towards the farm buildings.

On the other side of the bank, a blanket of dust rose stirred up by hundreds of hoofs. Stockmen cracked whips and called to dogs working the sheep.

'I don't think I could ever tire of watching this,' Louisa murmured.

He let the matter of Edward drop. 'I agree. It has its own charming qualities. City folk don't understand it.'

'I pity the city women who spend every day by the kitchen fire and never witness the outdoors, or nature properly. How boring for them.'

'I think you'd find many are happy to do just that. This,' he waved his arm at the spectacle before them, 'this isn't for every woman, or man for that matter. You have to be strong out here to survive it.'

'And now I wouldn't want to be anywhere else. Life is strange, isn't it?'

He nodded, staring at her lovely face as she watched the sheep in the water. Without a doubt he would do anything for this woman.

'Thank you for coming over. I know how busy you are.' She clapped her hands as another ewe headed their way.

'George says you're managing just fine, that you won't need my help for the shearing. But I'll come if you want me to.' Desire flared in him as her eyes widened before she glanced away.

'I'm certain we will have it under control. I'm hoping by next week George will be able to walk and supervise.'

'Louisa ...'

She stared up at him and he nearly lost all reason. He saw the longing in her green eyes, the rapidness of her breathing. He wasn't imagining it. She felt the same as he did and the elation it brought him sucked the air from his lungs. It took an enormous effort to not drag her into his arms and kiss her until his mind was lost completely.

'You must go, Connor,' her voice was barely a whisper.

He nodded, not trusting himself to speak. Words weren't needed though. He knew what she felt, what they both felt, and it was enough, for now.

CHAPTER 12

*L*ouisa wiped the sweat from her forehead and bent to collect another armful of fleece from the floor of the shearing shed. The cavernous space was filled with men and some of the stockmen's wives as they worked hard to get all the ewes sheared. The gang of shearers were needed at another station tomorrow. The race against time gave her anxiety. She didn't stop helping, even though she wasn't as strong as the others, or as quick. But every pair of hands was needed to finish the job.

They'd been shearing for nearly two weeks – weeks in which the station had come alive. The team of shearers and their cook were a rowdy noisy bunch of big rough men. They slept in the huts near the shearing shed and didn't venture near the house. However, their infectious laughter and spirited presence changed the vibe of the station, making everyone cheerier, eager to get the back-breaking work done during the day and then at night have a singalong by the campfires.

Louisa found the team fascinating and spent each day in the shearing shed helping as much as she could. She closed her ears to the curses and swearing, the ribald comments and the bad language. Yet, despite the impropriety of the workers, she enjoyed the atmosphere of the shearers being on the property and the laughter they brought.

George refused to leave the house and meet the shearers. Louisa had apologised on his behalf and they had wished him a speedy recovery. She thought they might have protested at her, a woman, being in charge but they had simply got on with the job which paid them handsomely.

Despite not being interested in venturing down to the sheds, George had left his room and joined her and Edward for dinner each night. His company was welcomed by Louisa, as it kept Edward's attentiveness to a minimum when George was present. Not that Edward did anything untoward, more a case of lingering looks that were becoming uncomfortable for her. He was a gentleman in every way, and Louisa did like him, for his intelligent conversations were interesting and his manner quiet. If only he wouldn't look at her as though she was a delicious treat he wanted to eat.

Although she knew of Edward's feelings towards her, Louisa enjoyed his company. He'd written a poem about her, but she begged him to not read it aloud, her embarrassment would be too much. As George's wife she was protected from Edward's advances and that gave her a sense of compassion towards Edward. Wasn't she in just his situation but with Connor? So, she forgave his awkward adoration and remained his friend. But secretly she hoped he would return to Melbourne very soon.

Waving away another pestering fly from her face, she continued gathering the fleeces and carrying them to the sorting table. The cold weather of July and August had disappeared as though it never was, and a spell of unusually warm weather, or so she was told, had heralded September and spring.

Carter and Turner rolled another full bundle of fleeces past her, ready for loading when the dray arrived. Sacking covered her dress to protect it, but she was still filthy and sweaty. Thankfully, the shearing shed had a high roof and only walls at each end of the building. The open sides allowed whatever breeze there was to come through.

She smiled at Edward who insisted on lending a hand too, though he was worse than her and mainly got in the shearers' way. He took their cursing lightly, always having a laugh and a joke, enjoying the physical work he'd never done before.

She paused to stretch her aching back and looked out over the clean creaminess of the newly shorn sheep gathered in a large pen on the other side of the shed. Their bleating filled the air. Sammy daubed the back of the ewes with green paint to identify them as belonging to King's Station, she knew red painted sheep belonged to Munro Downs. Then the ewes were released back out into the home paddocks in readiness for lambing.

A shout from one of the men to another broke her daydreaming and she continued gathering fleeces. The heavy air foreshowed a storm.

'Lightning,' someone observed.

Curses of the weather became louder. No thunder cracked, or rain fell, just lightning forked through the unthreatening clouds. Louisa had never seen such a storm before.

'Is lightning all we'll get?' she asked Hunt. To speed up the process he was wrestling an ewe up the ramp for the shearer, who stood sharpening his cutters.

'I hope we don't even get that. Too dangerous.' As if his words conjured up the lightning gods, a fork of lightning dazzled in the distance, hurting their eyes and scaring the ewes.

'I don't like it,' one of the shearers mumbled. 'Good job we're nearly finished.'

Edward came to stand beside Louisa as they watched the sky light up behind the clouds. 'It's like the gods are putting on a show for us.'

'The gods?' She laughed. 'There is more than one?'

'Well it depends on which religion you consider important.'

'My father wasn't a religious man, which got him into more strife than I can remember. He always said that religion caused too many wars, too many deaths.' She glanced up at him, noting the sweat darkening his auburn hair to nearly black. 'Nature is causing that light show in the sky, not gods.'

He bowed like a gallant knight. 'I stand corrected, madam.' He grinned. 'You are a true Darwinian.'

'And proud of it.'

'Missus!' Su Lin called for Louisa from the end of the shed.

Wiping her hands on her sack apron, Louisa went to her. 'Yes?'

'Boss ask for you.' Su Lin turned away. The little woman was of few words, and Louisa was yet to have a proper conversation with her about anything outside of food or cleaning.

Lightning cracked again as Louisa strode up the dusty track towards the house. She hurried, not liking the closeness of the strikes. On entering the house, she went straight to George's bedroom, but it was empty. She looked in the other rooms and finally found him sitting out on the front veranda sipping tea. It delighted her that he was slowly returning to the old George. In the last week while she had been busy at the shearing shed, he'd ventured further on his sore ankle. A solid walking stick had been fashioned for him by Sammy, who had smoothed and polished it with beeswax.

She sat down opposite him, hot and tired. 'You sent for me?'

'I wanted to know how you are getting on. I only see you at night and you and Edward are too exhausted to sit and talk to me for long.' He pouted like a child.

'We can't help that. It's tiring work, as you well know.'

'Of course, you're tired. I feel bad you have to do it.'

'It won't be for much longer. We have done well.' She hid a grin. 'Are you feeling neglected?'

'I am, yes.' He chuckled softly as he poured her a cup of tea.

'This damn ankle is so weak I don't trust putting my weight on it. I'm sorry for acting like an old crotchety man.'

'I forgive you.'

'I'll be back to normal soon, I promise. I feel bad giving you more things to worry about.'

'It would be good to have you up and about with me again. I need your guidance.'

'And you'll have it.' He sipped his tea as the sky flashed with sheet lightning.

Louisa watched it for a moment. 'I've never seen anything like this before.'

'It's common in this country. Storms that aren't real storms, no rain or thunder just lightning. Powerful.'

'Incredible.' She relaxed against the chair, worn-out. 'I needed this,' she said, sipping the tea.

'You need to eat more, too.' George sliced a lemon sponge cake. 'Many left to do?'

'No, about a half day more tomorrow should see it finished so Hunt tells me.'

'Excellent. The shearers will be gone by nightfall tomorrow.'

'Hunt has a keg of beer to tap for them this afternoon. Apparently, Munro Downs has the best party at the end of their shearing. However, we can put on a bit of a spread for them before they leave.' The party at Connor's was a sore point, for she had wanted to go. Instead, she'd stayed at home and played cards with Edward, but wishing she was dancing with Connor.

Eating his cake, George looked out over the drive. 'Shearing is a great job to have finished. Damn hard work for all concerned. They'll enjoy a night of ale before they head off to another property. We all can't be as good as Munro Downs.' He sounded irritable at the mere mention of Munro Downs lately.

Louisa changed the subject. 'Hunt says Peters, the bullocky, and his team will be here this afternoon to take the wool into

Albany tomorrow. I'll be interested to see a team of bullocks in action.'

'Wonderful beasts.' George relaxed in the chair. 'Peters has been carting my wool clip since John and I first used him at the very beginning of building this place. He has eight bullocks and they all respond to their names. Unbelievable. Like dogs they are.'

'How fascinating.' Louisa tried to imagine what a bullock team would look like and was looking forward to seeing them arrive this evening.

George waved away a few flies that seemed intent on landing on their cake. 'One of us should go into Albany with the wool clip. Though Wilf Copeland is a good assessor and wouldn't cheat me, but still, I'd like someone to make sure all goes well.'

'I can go. I'd like to visit Akala.' She was eager to visit Albany and do some shopping. She'd not been since before her wedding months ago.

George's reply was drowned out by the snap of a lightning strike somewhere close by. They didn't see it but heard the crack of it. He frowned. 'That was close.'

She ate a piece of cake. 'I don't like these lightning storms. I'd much rather have rain and thunder.'

'Me too.' George cut himself another slice. 'I was looking through the accounts earlier. The farrier will be here next week. You've not met him yet, obviously. He's called Ollie Manns. He comes every couple of months or so. He's also a blacksmith. We need a list from the men of the tools that need repairing.'

'Does this Mr Manns stay overnight?'

'Usually he's with us for a few days. Depends on how much he has to do. He sleeps in the men's quarters. Su Lin feeds him. Hunt knows what—'

Sudden shouts made them both turn. Sammy came tearing around the side of the house and up the stairs, the whites of his eyes wide in his dark face. He gabbled too quickly, slipping into his native language and Louisa strained to understand what he was saying.

'Slow down, Sammy.' George leaned forward in his chair. 'What's happened?'

'Fire!' Sammy burst out.

George paled. 'Good God!' He jerked to his feet, his bad ankle crumbling beneath him. He cried out in agony as he fell to the floor.

'George!' Louisa shot up, spilling her tea and went to him. 'Sammy help me!'

Together they lifted him up. With his arms around their necks they got him back into his bedroom and on the bed. His face strained with pain.

'Go get Doctor Milton! Hurry!' Louisa told Sammy.

'But missus, fire!'

'Go! Now!' She grabbed cushions and propped George's leg up. She slipped off his house shoe.

George groaned and pushed her away. 'I'm all right, Louisa. Go see what is happening. Quickly!'

'Are you sure?'

'Go!' He closed his eyes, his face a sickly pale colour.

She rushed from the room, her heart in her mouth. She lifted her skirts high and raced across the yard, groaning in anguish as she saw the dark plume of smoke above the buildings. Fires were such dangers and could spread so quickly in such a dry climate. She prayed it was only a small one.

She rounded the end of the stables and missed a step as mayhem reigned in front of the shearing shed. The men were throwing buckets of water onto the burning shed, but their efforts were inadequate as the blaze took hold of the dry aged timbers.

The heat from the flames was a physical force, and scorched anything within a few yards, beating back the men. Red and orange flames went high in the air, the cracking and splitting of timbers like a roar. She'd never seen a fire as large or so intense.

Gasping, Louisa stopped beside Edith who was filling another bucket from the horse trough. 'What happened?'

'Lightning struck the shed. We all were jolted.' She was crying as she worked. The poor woman was filthy. 'It stunned us.' She wiped away the tears leaving dirty streaks on her cheeks. 'The doctor …' She indicated to where Hunt and some of the shearers knelt on the ground near a fence.

Edward! Louisa rushed to them and pushed through to kneel beside him. 'How bad is he hurt?'

Hunt pulled her back gently. 'He's gone, missus. We carried him out here, but there was nothing we could do.'

'Gone? How? What?' She stared at Edward, unable to believe it. He looked like he was sleeping. 'Are you sure? He might be stunned?'

'No, he's gone, missus. I checked his pulse. He's not breathing.'

'But how? How did he die?'

'He was sweeping. The lightning hit the shed and we all felt it, but I think the doc was right in its path, for he dropped like a stone.'

She laid her head against his chest but couldn't hear a beat or feel the rise and fall. Her breath caught in her throat. 'Did he suffer?'

'No. I think it was an instant thing. Tommy over there saw it happen.'

Louisa looked to a big shearer who sat on the ground, dazed and with a lost look in his eyes. 'Who else is hurt?'

'Some of the others have burns to their hands. We tried to get the sheep out of the yards, but it all went up so quickly. Too much dry timber and the wool.'

As if to remind them of its presence, the fire roared, and more roof beams cracked and fell. The plume of smoke rose high into the sky, darker than the clouds which were receding and taking the lightning with them.

The heat forced away those who were trying to throw buckets of water onto the flames. The fire was out of control, a living beast intent on destroying everything.

Louisa didn't know what to do. She knelt beside Edward, her mind blank and stared at the raging fire, hating the heat on her face, the red scorching menace that was destroying an integral part of the station, and which had killed a lovely man.

'Shall we take him up to the house, missus?' Hunt asked quietly. 'We've got one of the cots from the men's quarters to carry him on.'

She nodded numbly. Turning her back on the fire, she walked with them and held Edward's hand, not letting go until they reached the back of the house. She went in ahead, a silent nod at Su Lin was enough to get the other woman busy.

At George's bedroom open door, she paused. He was resting on the bed, his bad ankle still elevated on a cushion. The swelling evident.

'My dear?' His voice carried a world of worry and pain in it.

'Lightning strike.' Her throat clogged with unshed tears. 'Edward is dead.'

'No.' George closed his eyes. 'God in Heaven. Why? How?'

'The shearing shed is lost, too.' It was hard to tell him such dreadful news.

'No! What a disaster. I don't want to believe it. A good decent man…'

'The fire was too much, too big. We couldn't save it. Edward, he… lightning.' She wasn't making sense, her words tumbling out.

She dithered by the door, hearing the others murmuring as they put Edward in his room. She should go and see to things, but her feet wouldn't move.

'Poor Edward,' George's voice came from far away. 'Such a kind fellow. A gentleman.'

'They've put him in his room...' Her voice broke.

'Come here.' George held out his arms to her and she fell into them and cried for the lovely man who had become her friend. Emotion swamped her. The quickness of life and death astounded her. One minute a person could be laughing and talking and the next they are gone, as David had and now Edward.

Sometime later, she sat up and wiped her cheeks. 'I'm sorry. I don't know why I cried so much.'

'I have a feeling it was more than just for Edward, possibly for your brother, too. You told me you've not allowed yourself to mourn David. Maybe this accident was a trigger.'

She gave a little shudder. 'You might be right. I miss David so much.' Tears filled her eyes again. She didn't know what was wrong with her. She wasn't usually a crier and now she couldn't stop.

George patted her back. 'We must send someone to Munro Downs to inform Connor of what's happened to his friend, and he was Nancy's cousin. It'll be such a blow to them.'

She left the bed and took a deep breath to steady her feelings. Lord, she would have to see Connor on top of everything else.

A knock on the open door interrupted them. Hunt stood there, hat in hands. 'Sorry, boss, missus.'

'Come in, Hunt.' George pushed himself up straighter. 'Is the fire out?'

'No, sir. It'll burn for days I should think. There's a lot of wood and wool to feed it.'

'Wool?' George's eyes widened. 'The clip? You got the bales to safety, didn't you?'

'Not all of it, sir, no.'

George groaned in despair.

Hunt, covered in dirt, sweat and smoke grime, looked

defeated. 'We tried, but our main concern was Doctor Milton and getting everyone out of the shed. The lightning hit the shed and it went up so fast, like a firework. We saw the doctor had been hit and others had fallen to the ground, shaken up they were, and some with burns. I thought to get everyone out as fast as possible. We carried the doctor out, but he was gone.'

'None of it is your fault, Hunt.' George shook his head sadly.

'Me and some of the lads went back in, but the fire had already taken hold. Some of the sheep were on fire... We've lost about eight, most I think just had a heart seizure from the fright. Turner managed to open the yard gates and got the others away for they were going mad with panic. Then we thought of the bales. They were on the platform ready to load on the dray when it arrives. We pushed a few off and they landed on the ground, but we had to get out of there for the fire was nearly upon us. The other bales are lost, I'm afraid.'

George remained very still. 'Thank you, Hunt. I'm sure you did your best.'

Sensing George's distress, Louisa stood tall. She'd had her five minutes of sorrow now she had to be strong. Losing the wool clip would have devastating effects on them all. 'Hunt, would you send someone to ride into Albany and inform the constable of police what has happened today and that there has been a death on the property. Have my horse saddled too, please?'

'Why?' George reached for her hand.

'I must ride to Munro Downs and inform Connor of what's happened to Edward. He can't receive the news from a stranger, can he?'

'But it'll be dark by the time you get there.'

'I'll take Sammy with me, I'll be fine with him.' She squeezed his hand, then had a thought. 'Perhaps... perhaps we should take Edward's body with us? Connor would wish for him to be buried at Munro Downs.'

George nodded with a sigh. 'That's exactly what he'd want.'

Louisa turned back to Hunt. 'Have the cart prepared instead. Sammy can drive it.'

'I will go with you.' George swung his legs over the side of the bed, grimacing. 'I don't want you doing this by yourself.'

'Don't be silly, George, you can't even walk.'

'No, but I can hobble, and I can sit in the cart beside Sammy. I'll not argue. My mind is made up. I was the reason Edward stayed with us for so long. In a way his death is my fault.'

'Nonsense. I won't have you blaming yourself. Edward stayed because… because he wanted to.' She blushed, knowing that he stayed because he enjoyed her company.

'Nevertheless, I'll go with you. Hurry now, the afternoon is advancing.'

CHAPTER 13

*C*onnor stood in the small graveyard, the sun warm on his black-suited back. Mourners, mainly his work force, had walked the mile from the homestead to the open area he'd set aside for a graveyard on the station. They stood around the outskirts of the white picket fence, leaving him and Nancy inside the fence next to the gaping hole. On the other side, Edward's coffin rested on two wooden plinths. Reverend Pierce waited at the end of the grave, a slight breeze blowing his black robe. His annoying wife, Winifred, stood a few steps behind him, her pious glare scrutinising the gathering.

'It is unlike George to be late,' Nancy murmured beside him. She sat on a chair brought from the house.

'No, it isn't.' Worry filled him. He glanced over his shoulder, over the fields to the track coming from the house and buildings.

'Perhaps Louisa has held him up. Very rude of her if she has,' Nancy added.

'Why would you think it was Louisa's fault?' Connor scowled at her.

'Everything is her fault. Last time I spoke to Edward, he did nothing but praise her, as though she is the first female to ever work on a station. *She* was the reason he stayed at King's Station, and *she* is the reason he died in that fire.' She crumbled up her handkerchief, but her eyes were dry, cold.

'You're talking nonsense and you know it.' Despite believing it himself, he'd never say it out loud. Nancy was bitter about Louisa and nothing would make her think differently.

'He was a doctor working in a shearing shed! *Why?* Why would he be doing that? For *her*, that's why!'

'Be quiet,' he hissed, noticing the reverend and Mrs Pierce were staring at Nancy. 'Say no more about it. What's done is done.'

'I bet she offered him all sorts of *enticements* to stay with them.'

Angered, he bent down close to her face. 'What are you saying?'

'Do I need to spell it out? I saw Edward just once in the month he was at King's Station when he came back here to get more clothes and a few books. He did nothing but speak of her like a love-struck fool! Louisa killed *my* cousin, *your* friend!'

'Shut your mouth, Nancy,' he whispered, dangerously close to losing his temper with her. 'I'm sick of your snide comments. You've not had a decent word to say about Louisa and I'm tired of it!'

'Shall we make a start?' Reverend Pierce asked a little loudly.

Connor glanced once more at the track and sagged in relief when he saw George's buggy break from the barns and slowly make its way towards them. 'Here they come.'

'Good. Now take that worried look off your face.' Nancy's smile was brittle.

Connor gave a nod to Reverend Pierce. 'The last guests are coming now, then we can start.'

'Very good, Mr Munro.'

Within ten minutes, and full of apologies, Louisa slipped down from the buggy and ran around to help George down too. Connor leapt to help him also, his hands touching Louisa's as they assisted George to the graveside and to sit in the chair beside Nancy's.

'Shall we begin?' Reverend Pierce's voice carried well as he started the service.

Connor took a deep breath, slid a sideways glance to Louisa and seeing her fussing over George turned his attention to the friend he'd lost. He thought of Edward over the years, the shared nights of carousing, the days fishing. Then the witty letters they wrote to each other after Edward moved to Melbourne to train as a doctor. He would miss him.

Afterwards, back at the house, Connor stood on the veranda, holding a plate of food he didn't want, as he watched Nancy play the perfect hostess to their guests, especially to Louisa, as though they were best of friends, but he knew different. He knew that a rage burned inside Nancy and it worried him.

'I'm so sorry to hear you've suffered another setback with your ankle, George.' Nancy poured out the tea.

'I was forgetful of it and stood up too quickly on it.' George shook his head. 'Foolish. It feels the same as it did when I first hurt it. I have undone all the healing.'

'And no Edward to attend you this time.' Nancy sighed sadly. 'We will miss him, especially Connor, won't you? Although he was my cousin, ever since I introduced him and Connor they have been the best of friends.'

Connor winced at her soft words. 'I am finding it hard to believe it is real. To never see my friend again, to never receive another letter from him. I can't believe it. Edward's letters used to give me a chuckle when he wrote of his professors and their ways of trying to instil knowledge into him, knowledge he believed he'd never remember as he struggled through the years of training to be a doctor.'

Connor stared down at the sandwiches on his plate. 'But he had done it. He'd done all those late nights of reading thick books, the lectures that he slept through, the long days in hospitals, the never-ending studying. One book, he told me, was so thick and weighty that he used it as a doorstop most days.' He looked up at Louisa who smiled wretchedly.

'He was a good kind man, who will be remembered,' she said quietly.

He nodded, giving her a smile of thanks.

Nancy coughed. 'I recall him arriving late at our wedding, didn't he, Connor? Apparently, he'd been attending a surgery on a man's brain!'

'Yes, he told me that.' George nodded. 'He'd spend many nights sitting up with me when the pain was terribly bad after my accident. Excellent man.'

Louisa picked up her teacup, her gaze on George. 'Are you in pain?' she whispered to George, but Connor heard her.

'A little bit,' he whispered back.

Connor's heart constricted at the tender way they conversed. He wanted that for himself.

Nancy smiled dreamily, oblivious to the whispers as she topped up Winifred's teacup. 'We were married in Perth, where my mother's family come from.' She stared at Louisa, her tone changing. 'That's where my father is at present, in Perth, visiting my late mother's family, otherwise he would have been here for the funeral. He will be devastated about Edward.'

'He normally lives in Albany, yes?' Louisa asked.

'Yes. That big white house by the bay. You must have seen it?'

'I can't say I have,' Louisa replied.

'No, likely you wouldn't have ventured that far around the shoreline. There are no shops there, it's very exclusive, naturally, so you'd have no need to visit that side of the bay.' Nancy's stinging words hung in the air.

Louisa sipped her tea and looked away and Connor felt like strangling Nancy's scrawny neck for her rudeness.

Reverend Pierce leaned back in his chair. 'Edward's family? They couldn't get here in time for the burial?'

Connor put the plate on the table, tired of holding it. 'No. I had a telegram sent to them, but his parents are elderly, and the trip would have been too much for them in such a short space of time.'

'Edward's mother is my late mother's sister,' Nancy butted in. 'They have a lovely place on the Yarra River. My uncle was a judge before retirement.'

Winifred Pierce nibbled on a tart. 'I do wish to travel to Melbourne again.'

'I am to travel to Melbourne tomorrow, as it happens, to take Edward's possessions to his parents,' Connor said.

'You are?' Nancy's eyes widened at him.

He felt a twinge of guilt for suddenly announcing this to her, but he knew she'd not want him to go and by telling her in front of their guests then she'd not make a fuss. The truth was he wanted to see Edward's parents, talk to them about their son, tell them of his funeral, where he is buried, and he could do that better in person than in a letter. He also wanted to see his sister and aunt. Besides, he needed a break from the station, from Nancy, from everything. He'd not been to Melbourne for some years and was eager to visit the city and see the changes since his last stay.

'You'll give my regards to Martha and your aunt, won't you?' George reached for his walking stick.

'I will.' Connor stepped forward to help George up from his chair.

'Louisa, I think we should be going.' George gave a tired smile to Nancy. 'I'm sorry to not stay longer, dear girl, but I need a rest in my bed.'

'We understand, don't we, Connor?'

'Of course.' Connor pulled back Louisa's chair, her light perfume, the scent of rose and something else floral he couldn't identify, filled his nose. Whenever she was near him, he had to fight not to reach for her. A break in Melbourne was very much needed for his sanity.

Louisa smoothed out her black skirts. 'Thank you.' She gave him a quick glance then went to aid George down the steps to the buggy.

Frustration filled him. He wanted so much more from her, even though he wasn't entitled to it.

'Enjoy your time in Melbourne,' George said, puffing hard after climbing up into the seat. He gathered the reins in his hands. 'How long will you be gone?'

'I don't know yet,' Connor answered. Behind him, up on the veranda Nancy sat in her wheelchair watching them and he knew that as soon as their guests were gone she'd have something to say about his decision. He wished he was leaving now.

'Safe journey home.' His gaze rested on Louisa and her small smile burned into his brain, branding into his memory.

Her eyes stared into his for a moment and then George urged the horse on, breaking their contact. He watched them for a long time until Nancy called for him.

Sighing, he went up and sat at the table opposite her. Things had changed between them, his fault entirely. He loved her as a friend, like he'd always done. He'd married her as a friend, and she him. He'd felt sorry for her when she had her accident and she believed her life was over. As her best friend he wanted to show her that wasn't the case. She could still be a bride, some-one's wife. He asked her to marry him out of guilt and pity, but also because he didn't want to see her upset or feel worthless. She was one of his dearest friends and if by marrying her then they could carry on as before. Only, now, that wasn't enough. Five years too late, he'd realised you shouldn't marry someone out of pity or guilt.

Half an hour later, Reverend and Mrs Pierce left, and Connor was alone with Nancy.

'How long will you be gone for?' Nancy crumbled a biscuit on her plate, not looking at him.

'A month or so.'

Her hand stilled. 'A month?'

'The shearing is done now.'

'You never miss the lambing.'

'I've never had my friend die before and I have to visit his parents. It's the decent thing to do.' He eyed the teapot, wishing for a beer instead.

'He was *my* cousin. I will happily go with you to see Aunt and Uncle.'

'The trip is too much for you. Look at the difficulties you have just visiting your father in Albany. Such journeys exhaust you and Melbourne is many times that distance. Besides, it's been too long since I've seen Martha. My sister is asking me to stay awhile with her ...'

'And you don't want me to go with you.' It was a statement not a question.

He had no reply and felt like a bastard.

* * *

Louisa sat at the desk in the study and sighed. The bills arrived with dreadful regularity and she felt ill every time the post came with the deliveries from Albany.

Money was seeping out of George's bank account like water out of a leaking bucket. She didn't know how to stem the flow. The money from the wool clip, those few bales which they'd salvaged from the fire and sold, didn't get close to meeting the demands of wages and bills.

'There you are. Did you go for a ride while I read my book?' George limped into the study with the aid of his walking stick.

'I was going to, but it was getting too late, then Hunt returned from Albany and he had some post...'

George sat on the chair opposite the desk. 'More bills?'

'Yes. Too many. We can't cover them all.'

'Some will wait.'

She tightened her lips in annoyance. 'That doesn't solve the problem. I can't ignore them all. For a while I think we should cut out unnecessary spending.'

'What do you deem unnecessary?'

'Well…' She shuffled the bills in front of her. 'We could eliminate the buying of so many crates of whisky and wine.'

'Oh, no, now steady on!'

'Drop your book subscription from that publisher in London.'

'I adore my books!'

'You have a wardrobe full of clothes, you don't need to visit the tailor for years.'

'You know my weight fluctuates.'

'You have a standing order of cigars sent to you.'

'What's wrong with a good cigar after dinner, I beg?'

She sighed, knowing whatever she suggested would meet with negativity. 'George, we have to be sensible about this.'

'I'll not go back to living like a pauper as we did when John and I first built this place. We had years of living rough or doing without any niceties. I'm too old to go through it again.'

'Living rough? Don't be so theatrical. You've got a comfortable house and good food. You won't be roughing it in tents and eating from a camp fire as you did back then. All I'm suggesting is to cut back on things we don't truly need, for a short time.'

'I'll reduce the flock.'

'Fine, and then we can put off some men, too.'

'What? No!' He banged his cane on the floor. 'We can't let people go.'

'We can't afford to pay them, George!' She was losing her patience with him. Why couldn't he see the need to do this? She flipped though the pile of papers on her desk, looking for more ways to trim the spending.

'Then we sell.'

Her head snapped up at his words. 'Sell?'

'We sell everything, the whole lot and go live in a cottage in town, or elsewhere. I don't care.' He threw his hands up and pouted like a child.

'You can't *really* want that?'

'I do.'

She could tell he wasn't serious by the high tone of his voice. 'I don't think we need to be that dramatic. If the bank can give us a loan until we can sell the lambs, then—'

He sighed deeply. 'No, it won't be enough. I only scrape by each year when I sell the wool clip *and* the lambs. This year we only have the lambs, but we need to keep some to improve the stock as the older ewes become worthless. On top of that we don't want a debt to the bank.'

'I have money. We can use that.'

George banged his stick on the floor again. 'I will not!'

'It's not just you who can make decisions, George. If I want to pay bills with the money I have in my bank account, then I will.'

'No! I'll not have it.'

Su Lin stood in the doorway and bowed. 'Visitors. Outside.'

'This late?' Louisa looked at the clock. 'It's nearly five o'clock.'

Slowly, George got to his feet with the aid of his cane and waiting for Louisa to take his arm they followed Su Lin out to the back of the house.

Five men stood holding their horses' reins. On seeing George and Louisa they took off their hats and one man stepped forward.

'Good day to you both.' He held out a hand and George shook it. 'I was wondering if me and my men could stay the night? We've ridden for days and are done in.'

Louisa's gaze roamed over the dusty bearded men. Their ages ranged from a teenage boy to the oldest man with grey in his beard who spoke. Each man's horse was sweating.

'I'm George Henderson and this is my wife, Louisa. You're welcome to stay in the barn tonight. Su Lin, our cook will rustle up some food for you.'

'Thank you kindly.'

'Your name?' George prompted as the man went to turn away.

'Geoffrey Porter.'

'If you follow me, I'll show you to the barn.' George limped towards the buildings on the other side of the wide yard.

Louisa stood watching them walk away, leading their horses. She knew there was a code out here in the bush that you gave strangers a place to stay and those men looked tired, their horses beaten.

She went to the kitchen and spoke to Su Lin about extra meals, then returned inside. The sun was setting, throwing long shadows across the rooms. She lit some lanterns and added more wood to the fire in the drawing room. Although it was the end of September, and spring, the nights were still cool.

Her sewing basket sat beside the sofa, waiting for her attention. She'd torn the lace on the hem of her petticoat and that needed sewing, but she felt no inclination to do it. Staring into the flames, she tossed around George's idea to sell the station. She didn't want to. The station had become her home, she felt needed here. When she could, she enjoyed riding Minty across the fields, along the creek, embracing the harsh dry land because it was hers now. Marrying George had given her a sense of place, and she was loath to give it up.

'They seemed settled enough,' George said, coming into the room.

'I've spoken to Su Lin. She'll feed them after she's served us.'

George poured out two glasses of sherry and passed one to her. 'They've ridden from Adelaide, can you imagine? Over a thousand miles. It's taken them a long time.'

'Why are they in this area? Why come so far?'

'They didn't say. Very quiet they were. Tired, I expect. Food and sleep is what they need.'

'They aren't the only ones.' Louisa yawned.

'You should go to bed after dinner. Get some rest. You do too much.'

'I feel like I do nothing at all.' She pondered the flames.

'Nonsense, look at all you did with the station accounts, and you run this house.'

'Only after arguing with Su Lin to give up control. Even now, there's not much for me to do.'

George laughed. 'It has been her domain for many years. But she gave in gracefully, in the end.'

Louisa eyed him doubtfully. She and Su Lin had finally agreed to comprise in the running of the house. Su Lin with the help of a couple of aboriginal girls did all the cooking, Louisa was happy to leave that to them, and most of the heavy cleaning of the house. Louisa selected when the bedding needed to be changed, organised the fresh laundry when it came back from the laundry house, she picked flowers for the rooms and did all the accounts – something which Su Lin was delighted to give over to Louisa. Most days everything ran smoothly, and Louisa respected Su Lin's advice on many things, and as long as she stayed out of the kitchen, Su Lin was happy too.

George relaxed in the chair. 'You've been riding a lot. Hunt says you've a keen eye for the ewes, picking out the sick and reporting dead ones and whatnot.'

'I enjoy riding and if I can help the men, then I will.' She didn't tell George that she hoped that by riding out she might see or hear something about Connor. She'd not seen him since Edward's funeral a month ago. Was he home from Melbourne? Did he think of her as she thought of him?

'It's more than that though, isn't it?' George asked softly.

'Pardon?'

'Connor rides out every day, often camping out and not

returning to the house for days. He says he likes his freedom, but truthfully it is because he doesn't want to be reminded of the mistake he made.'

'What mistake?'

'Marrying Nancy.'

She swallowed. Connor regretted marrying Nancy? 'What does my riding have to do with that?'

'Do you ride each day to be free of me? Do you regret our hasty marriage and being tied to a broken old man such as me?'

'Oh, no, no, George. You mustn't think like that, not at all.' She rushed to kneel beside his chair. 'I wouldn't want to be without you in my life. You are very dear to me.'

He patted her hand. 'And you are to me but getting married was a mistake. I shouldn't have agreed to it. I was selfish, like Nancy, and said yes to please myself and not thought of you, as she didn't think of Connor.'

'We are different to them.'

'No, we aren't. Not really. Connor married Nancy because he dared her to a race when they were out riding. He teased her that she couldn't jump a deep ditch. Nancy never refused a dare. Her horse stumbled, however, and she fell into the ditch, her horse landed on top of her, nearly killed her. Connor took the blame. No one else blamed him, of course. It was an accident and Nancy should have known better than to push her horse to do some-thing it was incapable of, but the result was she ended up in a wheelchair and Connor never left her side. Best friends they were. Inseparable since the day he arrived in Albany and met her at a party hosted by her parents that same night. He gave up his freedom, so she'd never feel unwanted or unloved.'

'That was a very generous thing for him to do.'

'I think he wishes he hadn't now. Just like you must wish the same.'

'No. I don't wish that at all. I'll not listen to that kind of talk. Their marriage was built on a tragedy.' She gripped George's hands. 'But I haven't done that with you. We both wanted to care for each other.'

Sadness entered George's eyes. 'I saw how Edward behaved whenever you were in the room. He was enamoured by you, and he would have been such a catch for you, a doctor. You could have lived in Melbourne and enjoyed all the comforts.'

'I didn't want Edward in the slightest, you must know that. Besides, I have all the comforts here, with you.'

'But no children, not a young man who can love you properly in the marriage bed. Why should you miss out on that?'

'I cannot miss something I've never had.' She shrugged, not wanting to focus on that, or imagine what it would be like to be loved in the physical sense. She didn't know how it felt, so she could pretend it didn't matter. And if Connor's blue eyes came to mind the she pushed them away.

CHAPTER 14

*L*ouisa woke to something pressing against her neck. She moved, annoyed and opened her eyes. In the grey light of pre-dawn, it took a moment for her to realise someone was standing beside the bed.

Alarmed, she reared back, only to be grabbed roughly. Hauled from the bed, she tried to scream, but a hand was clamped over her mouth before a sound escaped. Dragged protesting and scared, the man kept her in front of him as they staggered into the front room.

George was in his chair near the fireplace, Geoffrey, the leader of the band of men who'd rode in yesterday, stood next to him, a pistol pointed at George.

'Don't harm her!' George barked as Louisa was thrust onto the floor at his feet. 'You all right my dear?' George murmured, taking her hand.

'What's happening?'

'Quiet!' Geoffrey demanded, coming around to stand in front of them. 'I don't want this to be unpleasant.'

'Unpleasant?' George puffed. 'Are you mad? What is the meaning of all this?'

'We need money.'

Louisa laughed mockingly, trying to be brave. 'You've come to the wrong place! We have none.'

'I find that hard to believe.' Geoffrey smiled. He walked around the room in the half light of dawn. 'We want to be gone from here, and you'll not report you've seen us at all. If you do, we'll come back, and we won't be so friendly next time.'

'Take what you want and go,' George snarled.

Geoffrey bowed. 'I'm glad you're being so approachable.'

'Robbing decent folk who've worked all their lives is despicable,' George fumed.

With a nod to the men standing by the door, Geoffrey gave them permission to move about the house. In sacks they put anything they could grab. From the dining room, Louisa heard them rattle the silver tea service that had once belonged to George's mother and she was enraged.

Geoffrey paced the room, the pistol never not pointing at George. 'I'm sad there isn't more for us to take. I've searched the study while you both slept and was disappointed you have no money about. If you have a hidden safe, I suggest you tell me where it is.'

'We don't.' George glared at him. 'We lost our wool clip and shearing shed to fire. We'll not make the men's wages this year. We're struggling.'

Geoffrey's laugh rang out in the still room. 'You think I'd believe that? I'm not a fool. You farmers think us chumps to believe you're all poor. You've fields full of beasts. Sell them to pay your workers.'

'We will!' Louisa snapped. 'But what of next year and the year after that?'

He peered down close at her. 'I'm sure you'll survive. The likes of you don't know how it is to go without!'

'You know nothing at all.' She wanted to hit him, the feeling so strong she hid her hands under her legs and gripped her nightgown.

'Take what you've got and leave us,' George demanded.

Swaggering around the room, Geoffrey picked up the odd book, his manner nonchalant. 'We'll go when I'm ready. I did think to leave this morning but I've a hankering for another of your cook's dinners. For a chink she's a good cook.'

'I'll get her to pack you up one,' Louisa said, rising from the floor.

Geoffrey waved his pistol at her. 'Sit.'

'You want food! I'll wake Su Lin.'

'I'm in no hurry, missus. Sit down!'

Perching on the edge of George's chair, Louisa gave a small grimace to George. He squeezed her hand as they faced Geoffrey.

As each man came back into the room with full sacks, Geoffrey inspected the goods. He turned to Louisa. 'No jewellery?'

'No. It's been sold,' she lied. In fact, her mother's pieces were still in the pouch which she had kept in the bank. George had said he'd buy her a pretty jewellery box when they next went to Albany, but it had never been high on their list of purchases.

Geoffrey looked quizzically at George. 'What kind of husband doesn't buy his wife precious gems as beautiful as the woman he loves?' He moved closer to Louisa and touched her hair, which hung down her back. 'If I was married to such a beauty I would shower her in diamonds.'

'Stolen ones?' Louisa taunted, brushing her hair out of his hands and conscious she wore only her nightgown.

'Louisa.' George squeezed her hand with a gentle shake of his head.

'Listen to your husband, Louisa. It wouldn't do to anger me.'

'Please just take what you have and go,' George said.

Glancing at his men, Geoffrey took another stroll about the room. 'So, men, what say you all about staying a bit longer?'

A mixture of yeas and nays filled the room.

One man leaned against the doorjamb. 'There's some good horses out there. I say we get gone, Geoff.'

'Aye,' said another. 'The longer we stay in one place the easier it'll be to be caught.'

'Perhaps…' Geoffrey nodded. 'But no one knows we are here, except those few men outside.'

A dirty, black-bearded man stepped forward. 'I say we kill them all and take the sheep and sell them in Perth. Then get a boat for America.'

'We can't sell them. They are marked,' the oldest man of the group spoke. 'Let us just take fresh horses and go. If we're caught we'll be hanged no matter what, so let's take food and fresh horses and get away from here.'

'I'm not going back to Adelaide.' Black beard glared at the older man. 'I'm done with traipsing through the bloody desert.'

'Enough!' Geoffrey commanded. 'Out, all of you. We're taking their horses, so get them ready. Tie our horses to the saddles and then we've got spares.'

George swore under his breath, but Louisa heard him, and she felt the same injustice. Her anger built higher. How dare they take their good horses!

'Dan,' Geoffrey called to the older man as he went through the door. 'Take as much food as we can load on the horses.' He turned back to George and Louisa. 'Thank you for your hospitality. You'll not be seeing us again, unless we hear you've gone into town and told the constable about us. Then we'll be back, and we won't be so nice next time.'

'We'll not tell a soul,' Louisa murmured.

Suddenly a gunshot rang out making them jump.

Geoffrey dashed out of the room and as Louisa went to follow, George held her back.

'Go into my room. There's a loose floorboard under the curtain. There's a loaded pistol inside. Take it and go for help to Munro Downs.'

'Not go to Albany and the police?'

'Munro Downs is closer. Get them to ride for town. Stay there, don't come back.'

'What about you?'

'I'll be fine. I'll stall them as long as I can.' George rose and leaned on his walking stick. 'Go quickly now. Just put your boots on and go.'

She dithered, frightened, then kissed his cheek and ran from the room. She went straight into George's room and knelt by the window. She pressed the floorboards, her heart in her throat. Another gunshot sounded, and she smothered a cry.

Pressing the end of one board, she realised it was loose and using the heel of her hand she pressed on one side of it to pry with her fingernails to lift it up. The pistol was wrapped in an oil cloth.

Yells came from outside and she hurriedly grabbed the pistol and ran to her room. Her riding boots were at the bottom of her wardrobe and she pulled them on not bothering to button them up. From the end of the bed she took her dark blue shawl and wrapped it around her. She had no time to dress.

At the door, she paused to listen and hearing nothing in the hallway, she ran to the front room to see George, but he wasn't there. She eased open the front door and ran down the steps.

No one was at the front of the property, but the trees were sparse giving her little protection. She ran to the last tree before the wide expanse of fields that usually held the horses not in work. Hiding behind the trunk, she quickly buttoned up her boots.

Taking a deep breath, the pistol heavy in her hand, she ran as fast as she could down the long dirt drive. At the sign proclaiming King's Station, she leaned against the fence, puffing as though her lungs would explode. She looked back, but the drive was clear of men following her.

If she turned left now, she could head for Albany and the

police, but it would take her too long. She headed right for Munro Downs. She ran again, not as fast this time, but a steady pace until a stitch in her side slowed her down to a walk. Alone on the track, the numerous bird calls heralded a new day. The sun was rising, the pink sky clear of clouds.

She kept looking back, fearing she'd be chased. Soon, Geoffrey would know she was missing. Were they good trackers like the aborigines? Would they shoot her on sight? Her skin prickled.

After an hour of walking she heard hoof beats pounding the hard ground. Scared, she sprinted into the low bushes beside the road and squatted down. A rider rode into view and she recognised him as one of the five gang members, the one with the black beard. He reined in his horse and walked it some yards along the road, his eyes scanning the either side.

'I know you're in there!' he yelled.

He had seen her. She stayed as still as possible, even though ants ran over her boots. She dared not breathe as he turned his horse about and rode back a little way.

'You might as well come out. We'll find you eventually.' He turned the horse again, coming back towards her. He kicked the horse into the bushes, but it shied nervously and backed out. The man swore and slapped his mount. Back on the road, he dug his heels into its sides and trotted past where Louisa hid.

'I'll be back, woman, and if I don't find you, you'll die of thirst soon enough!' He laughed like a madman, then urged his horse to canter away back towards King's Station.

She waited, watching the rider grow smaller the further away he went, a cloud of dust rising behind him. Knowing the gang would have to come back this way if they wanted to ride to Perth, she could no longer use the road to get to Connor's home.

Turning into the bush, she half ran through the gangly trees and shrubs, trying to keep the dirt track on her right the whole time. Her footprints showed on the sandy soil, but there was nothing she could do about that. An aboriginal tracker would find her in minutes, but hopefully the men were not as clever.

A spiky bush tore her nightgown and the shawl about her shoulders made her hot. Without stockings, her boots rubbed her feet and she winced every time she trod on a stick that cracked loudly.

A wild pig dashed from underneath a bush, squealing, frightening her so much she thought her heart would stop completely. Its black furry hide disappeared into the undergrowth and Louisa ran faster, scared it might come at her. She had heard they were dangerous animals. The stitch in her side cut like a knife. Then, taking a deep breath, she remembered Akala's training.

She stopped, listened and absorbed the bush around her. Instead of running blindly, she placed her feet carefully, avoiding the sticks and dried leaves. Her movements became sharp, purposeful.

She edged further away from the road but kept it within eyesight between the trees. She took off her dark blue shawl and wrapped it around her waist, covering the white of her nightgown and making her harder to spot.

Steadying her breathing, her ears tuned to any sudden noise, she crept on. After a while, she came to a small creek, and followed it upwards. Munro Downs had a great many creeks snaking through the property. She prayed this one would be one that wound close to the house. Everyone told her to stay close to water as waterways would always lead to people eventually.

She knelt at the creek's edge and drank handfuls of cool, clear water and splashed her face to wash the tiredness away. Refreshed, she continued on, hoping she was going the right way and not getting lost.

The sun was high in the sky when she finally stumbled out of the bush. Before her lay the wide expanse of grassy paddocks and, in the distance, the hub of Munro Downs.

Nearly crying with relief, Louisa carried on, heading for the house. Blisters on her feet gave her agony and she craved a drink of water.

As though the fates were against her, she saw no one until she was within a hundred yards of the house. An old man, who she guessed was the gardener since he pushed a wheelbarrow came around the corner of the house and stopped as though he'd seen a ghost. He dropped the handles of the wheelbarrow and fled as fast as his bandy legs could go.

Louisa made it to the veranda steps before the door burst open and Connor was catching her as she stumbled on the top step.

'Good God! Louisa!' He held her to him and she sagged against him. 'What's happened?'

'A gang… thieves… going to kill us.' Her throat was dry, she could hardly speak.

Connor scooped her up in his arms and carried her inside, calling for Mrs Mac. He glanced down at her. 'You're safe now.'

'Water, please.' She closed her eyes and leaned her head against his shoulder. 'George.'

Nancy wheeled towards them with Mrs Mac close behind her. 'Connor! What's happened? She's barely decent!'

'A gang of bushrangers are holding up King's Station.' He told Nancy and Mrs Mac as he placed Louisa carefully on a sofa in the drawing room.

'Bushrangers? Here?'

'Yes, Nancy! I'm sure Louisa isn't making it up!' He unfolded a blanket from the end of the sofa and placed it carefully around her shoulders. 'I'll take some men with me and ride over there now. Mrs Mac have someone ride to Albany for the constable, quickly.' He crossed the room to the drinks cabinet in the corner and poured her a glass of water from a decanter.

'But it could be dangerous for you to go there.' Nancy stared at him as Mrs Mac hurried from the room. 'Just send for the constable and his men. It is their duty to get involved, not yours.'

'George is in trouble, Nancy. Do you expect me to do nothing?' Connor knelt beside Louisa and watched her drink. 'Of course, I must go help.'

Louisa struggled to sit up, her body aching with protest at her movements, but the water was cool and refreshing. 'I'll come with you.'

'No, you won't!' Connor snapped, worry in his eyes. 'You'll stay here where you're safe.'

'George needs me.' She finished the glass and put it on the small table beside the sofa. She had to go back and see how George was faring.

Connor's jaw clenched. 'I'll help George. He wouldn't want you in any more danger.'

'If she wants to go home, then she should, Connor.' Nancy butted in. 'She's not hurt.'

Impulsively, Louisa reached out for Connor's hand. '*Please*, take me back with you.' She didn't want to stay here with Nancy and spend the whole time tormenting herself with what might be happening at home.

Connor squeezed her hand softly. 'Are you strong enough?'

She gave a glimmer of a smile. 'You doubt me?'

He cracked a weak smile. 'No, not at all. You're constantly reminding people how strong you are. I'll organise the men and be back shortly.'

She watched him walk from the room, her chest tightening with emotion at his concern and gentleness.

'My husband is a good man,' Nancy said coldly. 'Always rushing about helping others. He enjoys a good drama, does Connor, and saving damsels in distress.'

Louisa looked at her, saw the cool regard, the hardened stare and felt again the tingle of awareness that Nancy wasn't always as friendly as she liked to make out. 'We are lucky to have such a considerate neighbour and friend.'

'Oh yes, Connor is most reliable to his friends. Tell me, why did you run here and not ride into Albany for the police?'

'Munro Downs is closer. Besides, I couldn't get to a horse. I had to escape on foot. It was the natural decision to come here.'

'To Connor.'

Defensive, Louisa sat straighter, tightening the blanket about her shoulders. 'I came to Munro Downs as I knew *someone* would help me, help us. I didn't even know Connor was home from Melbourne.'

'He arrived home yesterday.'

Louisa waited for Nancy to say more, but Connor marched back into the room.

'We're ready to go.' He offered his arm to Louisa and helped her up from the sofa.

Pain from her boots made her wince. She hobbled outside to the cart where Connor helped her up onto the seat before climbing up and taking the reins. Eight men on horseback, their faces grim, turned their horses about at Connor's nod and the serious party headed down the dirt drive at a good pace.

Holding onto the seat, Louisa stole a glance at Connor's set face.

Connor looked at her, the brim of his hat low over his eyes. 'Are you sure you feel up to this? You've had an exhausting and terrifying morning.'

'I am fine. I just want to know everyone is safe.' She stared straight ahead at the long dirt track leading back to her home. What would they find there?

'My men and I will get the situation under control. I've brought Jimmy with us.' He indicated the aboriginal rider behind them. 'Jimmy's a really excellent tracker. If they've gone bush, he'll tell us where.'

'I hope they have gone and never come back.' She shivered.

'Tell me everything that happened.'

186

Her eyes not leaving the road, Louisa told him about the unwanted guests at King's Station.

'And they've ridden from Adelaide?' Connor asked once she'd finished.

'That's what they said.'

'Such a long way. Likely they're on the run having broken the law in that area too.'

'They seemed so normal at first. Obviously, their plan all along was to steal from us.'

'I'd be surprised if they'd kill though. They'd get no peace from the law if they did that. The police would hire every black tracker they could find to hunt them down.'

They fell silent as the outer paddocks of King's Station came into view. Connor slowed the horse to a walk and turned to speak to his men who rode up alongside the cart. In ones and twos, the men peeled away and went cross country, leaving one rider on either side of the cart.

The hair stood up on the back of her neck as they turned into the long drive to the house. Louisa peered into the distance trying to find any sign that something was wrong.

Halfway up the drive, Connor stopped the cart and turned to her. 'I'm leaving you here. It's too dangerous to take you any further.'

'But—'

'No arguments. Get down.' The determined tone of his voice made arguing redundant.

In a huff she gingerly stepped down and glared back at him.

'Lie down on the grass. I don't want anyone to see you.' With a snap of the reins he set the horses on and she was left alone.

She did as he said, mainly because standing hurt her feet. She lay on her stomach and watched them ride closer to the house. She expected to hear gunshots and shouts, but the eerie quietness alarmed her even more.

What if Geoffrey and his gang had shot everyone before they

left? What if they hadn't gone at all and waited in ambush? Connor could be killed?

She sat up and slipped off her boots, trying not to cry out at the agony of the bleeding blisters on her heels, which were a mess of fresh and dried blood and split raw skin. She tossed her boots to the side. Walking in bare feet, she crept along the drive, wishing it was tree-lined to give her protection. She felt exposed and a target but kept going until she reached the cart in front of the house. No one was about.

Nervously, she edged away from the cart when suddenly the front door opened, and Connor hurried down the stairs.

'I told you to stay away!'

'What's happened? Where's George?'

Connor took her elbow and walked with her into the house. 'He's well. The gang had tied everyone up in one of the stable stalls before they left. They've shot one of the men, Turner, but he'll live.'

'Thank God.' She hurried into the front room and found George sitting in his chair nursing a brandy. 'George.' She ran and knelt beside him. 'You're hurt? You're bleeding.'

George touched the small cut on his forehead and the swollen lip. 'It's nothing, my dear.' He patted her shoulder. 'You made it through. Well done. I knew you could do it.'

'Nothing was going to stop me.' Now it was all over she felt a ridiculous need to howl like a baby, but she stopped herself.

'They've taken all the horses.' George stared into his brandy.

'It doesn't matter as long as everyone is safe and well.'

'We've only got the two horses left that are being used by the men out with the sheep,' he spoke as if he'd not heard her. 'Can't afford to buy more. Disaster.'

'We'll work something out,' she whispered.

The bleakness in his eyes spoke of his despair. 'We'll have to sell up.'

'Let us talk about it later.' She was very aware of Connor

standing close by. She didn't want him to know of the financial hardship they were in.

She rose and smiled at Connor. 'Thank you for everything.'

'You don't have to thank me. I'll go and send my men home and then wait with you until the constable arrives and takes your statements.'

'Thank you.' She felt dreadfully tired.

'Why don't you go and wash, perhaps have a lie down? I'll come and get you when the constable arrives.'

Nodding, she pushed back her tangled hair, eager to be clean and properly dressed. She no doubt resembled a disregarded rag doll. But then, Connor had seen her in such a disorder before on the day she walked into Albany with Jarrah and Akala.

With a last look at George, who seemed to not notice the terrible state she was in, she slipped past Connor and hurried to her bedroom.

Closing the door, she leaned against it for a moment. Head bowed, she gazed at her torn dirty nightdress, her snagged shawl and her bloodied feet. After surviving the shipwreck and then living in the bush, she thought she'd never be in such a condition again. How wrong had she been?

CHAPTER 15

'What do you mean they've gone?' Louisa asked Hunt in surprise. 'Who has gone and where have they gone to? Are they coming back?' She stood in the middle of the holding yard after finally tracking down Hunt.

The sheds were deserted, quiet, and she didn't understand why. Usually the business part of the station was heaving with workmen going about their jobs.

Hunt couldn't meet her eyes. Shuffling his boots in the dirt, he tucked his thumbs into his belt. 'I can't rightly say, missus.'

'You can't, or won't?'

He tipped his hat back. 'Perhaps I should talk to Mr Henderson.'

'No. He's not up to it.' Louisa fought to control the urge to scream in frustration. 'Which men have stayed behind?'

'Well… there's me and Carter, some of the blacks… Su Lin of course.'

She stared at him in utter dismay. 'When did this happen?'

'Last night.'

'And no one thought to tell me?'

'It was late. You were all asleep.'

'That's no excuse! You should have woken me to inform me that our entire workforce was abandoning us in the middle of the night!' she shouted at him, angry, disappointed and suddenly very worried. How could they possibly run a station this size with less than five men?

'I'm sorry, missus. But I'm staying, and Carter, and with the blacks we'll manage the flock. Especially now the lambs are sold.'

'But the other men, their wives… Edith and Hattie…' Her mind worked frantically. They'd have no one to work in the dairy, no one to work in the laundry.

'I'll see if some of the black gins, er, women will do it.' Hunt shrugged uncaringly.

'The aboriginal women from the camp aren't trained even if they wanted to do it, which I very much doubt. Not just anyone can make cheese and butter.' Louisa felt slighted, hurt that the stockmen's wives had gone without explanation or goodbyes.

'They got better offers elsewhere, missus. After the shearing shed fire, losing the wool clip, the bushrangers stealing the horses, the selling of the lambs… We can all see that King's Station is struggling at the moment. Everyone was worried they'd not get paid again and they wanted to be settled before Christmas. You can't blame them for going.'

'No, but I don't have to like the underhand way they went about it. Sneaking away like that! Where is their loyalty?' She turned away, wondering how she was going to break the news to George.

She dragged her feet walking back to the house, not wanting to face George, whose spirits were already low. This news would be another blow and she wasn't certain he could cope with any more.

The months since the gang of bushrangers had held them up and ransacked the house and barns and stolen the horses had been the stuff of nightmares. They'd sold the lambs early to bring in some cash. Old ewes were sold, too. Louisa's money that David had given her the night the ship went down and the extra she had found in the portmanteau was all gone now. She'd used it to pay the bills and wages and still they needed more money. She didn't know what to do or how they could get it.

At the kitchen she hesitated, not wanting to go further.

'Missus?' Su Lin appeared from around the corner carrying a basket of herbs and vegetables. 'You want me?'

'No, no. I don't want you.' Louisa gave the briefest of smile to reassure the older woman.

'Tea?' Su Lin didn't wait for her answer and went into the kitchen.

Louisa leaned against the bench and gazed out over the yard. Today the folding wall panels were fully open to catch any stray breeze. Su Lin liked the kitchen best when the panels, which acted as windows and ventilation were open wide. She rarely closed them as it gave her a panoramic view of the house and garden, yard and sheds.

Su Lin brought over a china teacup and saucer and filled it with tea. 'You no worry.'

'I can't help it.' Louisa stared down into the tea.

'Good times come again. You see.'

'They had better come soon, or we'll not be here to see it.' Louisa sipped the tea.

'Boss not well,' Su Lin spoke as she washed the herbs in a bowl of water. 'He no help you.'

Louisa sighed. 'No.'

'But you,' Su Lin paused to stare at her with unblinking eyes, 'you strong. Missus hold on.'

'How though, Su Lin? We have no money and the men have left. We have no income until the next shear and the new lambs are born.'

'Missus no worry.' Su Lin pointed to the crude calendar on the wall, which was marked with special days, so she could prepare in advance. 'Christmas. Happy day. Boss like Christmas.'

In two days, it would be Christmas Day. Louisa wasn't keen to celebrate it. She felt there was nothing to celebrate. Last Christmas had been spent with David on the ship, eating and drinking, singing carols with fellow passengers, then the ship had gone down…

After marrying George, if she'd been asked, she would have said that this Christmas would be a celebration of new beginnings, but not now. Most of the men were gone, money was short, George dispirited, and it was the anniversary of David's death. There was nothing to rejoice about. 'I would like to cancel Christmas, Su Lin.'

'No, missus, no.' Su Lin began measuring out flour, working at double the pace anyone else would do. 'Christmas make Boss happy. Yes?'

Louisa sighed. 'I don't think anything would make George happy right now.'

'You no worry, missus.'

Taking a last sip of tea, Louisa went along the covered walkway and into the house. She found George in the front sitting room, placing books into boxes. 'What are you doing?'

'Some of these are first editions. I'm going to send them to a friend in Sydney. He can sell them for me.'

She sat on the edge of a chair. 'We need to go to the bank and re-mortgage the property.'

'Not this again, my dear.' George continued packing the books away.

Frustrated, Louisa took a deep breath. They had argued each day about going to the bank since the bushranger gang had robbed them. 'We need money, George, more than what a few books will bring.'

He leaned his hands on the table, head bowed. 'I don't need you to tell me that. I know it all too well.'

'The men have gone.'

His shoulders bowed even further. 'I expected it.'

'Hunt and Carter have stayed.'

'Good men. Loyal. I gave them a job after they finished their sentences when no one else would and now they are showing me I did the right thing to believe in them.' He sat down on a wooden chair by the window.

'And we can't pay them their next month's wages.' Louisa felt ill at the thought.

'They'll stay for bed and board. I'll make it up to them.'

'How will we run this place with so few?'

'The blacks will help. Some of the black lads will shepherd the sheep for tobacco and food, and if they don't work, then the sheep will be fine on their own. Until we get the shearing done next spring, the flocks will have to see to themselves. We don't have the horses spare.'

'I'll have to learn more skills. The few men we have cannot do all the work.'

'No!' He put his hand up in apology for shouting. 'No, my dear. You can't do everything that a dozen men used to do.'

'Very well then, I'll go into town and find a job that I *can* do.' She finally voiced the idea that had been playing on her mind for weeks. 'I could live somewhere cheap. Send money back to you.'

'No, no, no!' George slapped his leg angrily. 'As if I would ever allow that to happen. You are my wife. You belong here. Imagine what people would say!'

'I don't care what people will say. I can earn money.'

'What a few shillings? A station this size cannot run on a few shillings!'

She threw her arms up in frustration. 'Then what do you suggest? We have the bank overdraft to consider, we received the notice to pay only yesterday. That's besides everything else we have to pay.'

He let out a deep breath and stared at the box of books. 'I'll sell some land to Connor. He'll buy it at a good rate.'

'Will that work?'

'With our reduced flock, we can manage on less land.' He looked around the room. 'It just means we'll have to tighten our spending. I'd rather live quietly than be constantly in debt to the bank. I've seen it too many times where before long the bank owns everything and the farmer nothing. Eventually he just walks off his land.'

'That won't happen to us.' Louisa hated to see the sorrow in his eyes.

He sighed deeply. 'You must hate me.'

She jerked her head up in surprise. 'Why would I hate you?'

'You've married a man who has nothing. I should never have gone through with the marriage. I was being ridiculously selfish. You should be free.'

'Not this again! Stop it, George. What is done is done. Don't mention it again, I beg you!' Louisa walked to the window and thought of Connor. He was the one man she wanted and who she could never have. 'I don't need to be free.'

George gave her a half smile. 'You like being married to an old penniless man?'

'I like being married to my best friend.' She went to him and she grasped his weathered hands. 'We'll get through this. And we'll do it *together*.'

'Very well, then. I'll write a letter to Connor and get Hunt to take it over today.'

* * *

CONNOR STOOD on the veranda and read the letter Hunt had just delivered.

'Is it bad news?' Nancy asked, rolling her wheelchair to come beside him.

'I need to see George.' He glanced at Hunt who stood at the bottom of the steps. 'I'll ride back with you. Take your horse to the stables for some water.'

'Yes, sir.'

'What is it?' Nancy snapped. 'Why must you go there again? You're never away from the place!'

'George wants to sell me some land. I have first refusal.'

'Sell land?' She leaned back in her chair with a frown. 'Why would he want to do that?'

Connor sighed sadly, his emotions mixed. 'He's short of money. Nothing has gone right for him this year.'

'Not since he married the stranger from the shipwreck. The blacks would say she had bad spirits.' A smugness entered her voice.

'Don't talk utter rubbish!'

Her eyes narrowed. 'People will think she is cursed.'

He looked at her, the woman he had thought was his best friend and realised that they had both changed so much recently. She had become bitter, nasty, and he hated to see it. 'I'll stay the night there and have a good talk to George.'

'Stay the night?'

He paused as he went to walk away. 'I'll see you tomorrow.'

'Don't go, Connor. I need you here. Go and see George in the morning. He won't be expecting you to drop everything and go over there this afternoon.'

'He needs a friend to talk to.'

'As do I!' she barked. 'He has his wife!'

'Who isn't a man or a farmer.'

'You need to remain here and look after your own station, your own wife, not someone else's.'

He stiffened at the barb. 'I'll not listen to you when you're like this.'

'No, God forbid you would ever listen to me, Connor Munro!'

He walked down the veranda to the French doors leading into his bedroom. Their constant bickering was driving him insane.

He'd just finished packing clean clothes into a leather bag when Nancy rolled into his bedroom.

196

'I'm asking you not to go.'

He fastened the clasps on the bag. 'Our friend needs my help. Why are you always against me helping George? He is your friend, too.'

'You don't care about George. You only care about *her!*'

He wasn't often angry, but at that moment a white-hot rage filled him and he could easily have throttled Nancy. 'What a disgusting thing to say to me. I've been George's friend since I arrived in Albany years ago. I would do anything for him, as he would for me.' He grabbed the bag and his hat and stepped to the door where he paused and turned back to her. 'I won't live like this any longer. We are continually snapping at each other like dogs. I want a divorce.'

He quietly left the room, the anger leaving him as quickly as it came. Instead he felt dead inside, cold and sad.

He heard Nancy scream in rage and something smashed against his bedroom door, likely his porcelain water jug. He kept walking.

* * *

LOUISA POURED MORE wine into the glasses on the table and sat down. In the golden candle light, she watched the emotions play on George's face as he and Connor discussed the land sale. She could see how hard it was for him to admit his problems to Connor, and equally she saw how difficult it was for Connor to watch his friend be in such dire straits.

George sighed as Su Lin came in to clear away the dinner plates. 'As I see it, selling land will keep us out of the bank's clutches for a while, hopefully until the next lambing season. It's either that or we sell the whole property and move away.'

'It won't come to that.' Connor ran his finger around the edge of his wine glass. 'I'll buy your land at the going rate, not the knock down price you offered.'

'I want us to do a good deal, Connor, you're my friend.'

'And as your friend, I'll not rob you.' Connor smiled his thanks to Su Lin as she removed his plate and with a loaded tray left the rom.

'You're a good man.' George raised his glass in acknowledgment to Connor.

'At least *you* think so.' Connor sipped his wine, his eyes hooded.

Louisa watched him. Something was wrong with him tonight. He wasn't a talkative man at the best of times, but tonight he seemed edgy.

'What do you mean?' George asked.

'I asked Nancy for a divorce today.'

George jerked forward nearly spilling his wine. 'You did *what*? Why?'

'Because all we do is argue now. We aren't good for each other. I do not love her, and she hates me. I seem to bring out the worst in her.'

Louisa sat very still, heart pounding. Connor could be free. Yet, she was not.

'When did this all start to happen?' George frowned. 'Though to be fair, you probably shouldn't have married her. Pity is not a reason to marry someone.'

'We were close at the time.' Connor shrugged. 'I thought it was the right thing to do.'

'It was noble of you, yes, but not the correct thing for either of you.'

Connor snorted. 'I remember you telling me that the night before we went to the church.'

'And *you* thought you *knew* better.' George shook his head. 'I am sad though.'

Connor sighed heavily. 'It has to be done for we can't live the rest of our lives at each other's throats.'

'No, it is no way to live. Shall we shift ourselves to more comfortable chairs?' George grunted as he rose from the table.

Louisa went to help knowing his ankle was paining him today. They went into the sitting room where George sat in his chair by the unlit fire and she and Connor sat at opposite ends of the sofa.

She couldn't look at Connor. She couldn't afford for him to see her desperate hope, but then she chastised herself. Who was she kidding? Even if Connor could get a divorce, she was married. Besides that, lately Connor had given her no reason to think he'd want her as a wife instead. They kept themselves distant from each other, and that was the best way to be.

'After this wine, let's open a bottle of whisky.' George stretched out his legs. 'It is a night for drinking I feel. You don't mind do you, my dear?'

She summoned a smile from somewhere. 'No, of course not. I may join you I think, would that be allowed?'

George laughed. 'It's not very ladylike, but you're in your own home, so I see no harm in it.'

Louisa went to the cupboard and brought out a bottle of George's expensive whisky imported from Scotland. He had two bottles left from his last shipment and there would be no more orders for it once they were gone. She poured out three tumblers and handed them around. She held up her glass. 'What shall we toast to?'

'Getting out of debt!' George yelled.

All three of them cheered and tipped the liquid down their throats. Louisa gasped and choked but smiled through watery eyes.

'Pour another, dear girl.' George grinned.

Once more glasses were filled and raised.

'To the future, whatever it may bring!' Connor cried.

They drank, and coughing, Louisa filled up the next round.

'Your turn, my dear.' George nodded to her.

Louisa raised her glass. 'To us,' she said quietly.

The two men repeated her words and the whisky disappeared once more.

Hours later, both bottles of whisky were empty as was a bottle of port and they were into the brandy.

Eyes nearly closed, George lounged sideways in his chair. 'You two are my... my favourite people... in the whole world.' He waved his empty glass in their direction.

'I couldn't imagine my life without you both now.' Smiling sleepily, Louisa looked at her glass of brandy and felt the need to be sick.

'You've lost colour... in your face.' Connor peered at her. 'Are you going to be sick?' He swayed slightly but was in better shape than George.

'There is a possibility, yes.' Louisa blinked to clear her fuddled head. She put the glass on the table by the sofa and pushed it further away from her. 'Must go to bed.'

'Me too.' Groaning, George heaved himself up only to fall back into the chair. He started to sing, which made Connor and Louisa laugh.

George wrapped his arms around them as they heaved him up. '*and she was as sweet as a rose...*'

Connor laughed. 'Help me get him to bed, Lou.'

Feeling light-headed, Louisa turned out the lamps, except one which she carried. Holding on to each other, they swayed and stumbled into the hallway.

In George's bedroom they eased him onto his bed and Louisa pulled off his shoes, nearly falling over herself. George started snoring loudly, flat on his back, fast asleep.

Connor grinned, threw a blanket over him and turned out the lamp.

In the hallway once more, Louisa hesitated in going into her room. She looked up at Connor in the dim light. He was so close she could smell the brandy on his breath. They stared at each other and Louisa felt herself lean forward as if pulled by an invisible force.

'If I touch you that will be the end of me,' Connor whispered a warning.

'I don't care.' A thrill of excitement ran down her back. 'I wish you would…'

He groaned as he took her in his arms and kissed her hard. She gripped his shoulders relishing the feel of his lips on hers. She wanted this more than air.

He lifted his head and gazed at her. 'We should stop. It's not right.'

'I don't want to.' And she didn't. At that moment she didn't care about anyone or anything but having this man touch and kiss her. She wanted to be held and wanted and loved. Couldn't she have that just for a short time?

She pulled his head down for another kiss and he crushed her into his body.

'We must stop, Lou,' he spoke against her mouth.

'No, please, no.' She kissed him again trying to show him how much she needed him to stay with her. She was tired of wanting him and not having him.

Without releasing hold of each other they went into the bedroom and his kisses grew more demanding, more eager as he traced the line of her neck with his lips to where it reached her lace collar.

A driving urge guided her hands to his clothes. She didn't know what she wanted or needed but it was something only he could give her. Her hand strayed over the bulge in his trousers. She'd grown up on a farm, she knew what mating was and wasn't frightened at the idea. In fact, her body pulsed with a desperate need. She wanted to see him naked, ache for him to be hers. Their clothes were a barrier and she was quickly undressing him while they kissed.

'Lou …'

'Yes, yes …' A button came off her bodice, but she didn't care. Nothing mattered but the feel of his skin on hers. Her corset was peeled away, and he lifted her chemise over her head making her shiver.

Connor backed her against the bed and she lay down, pulling him with her. He was all hard muscle and demanding mouth. She revelled in his attention. Her skin tingled as he kissed her breasts, her stomach, while his hands were gentle and caressing.

When he looked up at her, he smiled. 'You are so beautiful, Lou.'

At that moment she *felt* beautiful and desirable.

He touched her lips with a fingertip, desire and longing in his eyes. 'You're mine now, Lou.'

'I've been yours since the first moment I saw you.' She reached for him. 'I like that you call me Lou.'

'Because Lou is who you are to me now.'

They made love until tiredness lolled them to sleep. Satisfied and in awe of the whole experience, Louisa lay snuggled in Connor's arms and had never been happier in her life.

The cockerel crowed his morning call before the sun had even crept over the horizon. Louisa stirred, unused to having a body beside her. She woke to find Connor's face next to hers on the pillow.

His hands began to create a lazy pattern over her skin. He played with her jet necklace, the only thing she wore, a smile on his lips. 'Ready for round two?'

She smothered a giggle with the blankets, delighted he wanted her again. Her head was pounding, but she wasn't going to turn him away. Who knew when she'd ever get this chance again?

An hour later as a pink light spread across the room from the dawn sun, Connor dressed quickly. He paused to kiss her. 'Happy Christmas Eve.'

'And to you.' She cupped his cheek. 'I'll see you soon?'

'Yes, I'll send a note.' With a last kiss, he went to his room to mess up his bed to look as though it had been slept in.

Louisa stayed in bed, not wanting to get up and face the day or let the world in on her yet. The thought of breakfast didn't sound appealing and she knew Connor would be riding home soon after and didn't think she could face seeing him ride away. She'd let George see him off and remain in her room.

She yawned and sleepily went to the water jug and poured a glass of water which she took back to bed. She lay looking up at the mosquito netting replaying the night, the hours of lovemaking, the touches, the kisses, the caresses, the blinding need for fulfilment. She couldn't help but smile. Now she knew what all the fuss was about. She knew why affectionate poems were written, why songs of adoration were sung and why people would do anything for the one they loved.

Connor had made her into a woman. She was his, and he was hers, at least in their hearts.

A moment of unease entered her head, but she pushed it away. Tomorrow she'd think of the future, but not today.

CHAPTER 16

onnor slapped the dust from himself as he left the stables and headed for the house. He'd been riding the property boundaries for nearly two weeks. He'd left straight after Christmas Day, which had been a painful tense day spent with Nancy who refused to speak to him. They'd put on a good show though in front of the workers and house staff. When neighbouring farmers had arrived to wish them season greetings he'd smiled and laughed, and Nancy had done the same. They'd both shown the world a false happiness.

The sunny hot days riding with his men to check the sheep and the water levels in the creeks had soothed him somewhat. He thought constantly of Louisa, of the situation he was in. To divorce Nancy would set him free, but not Louisa. Neither of them could hurt George. They were in a mess and he didn't know how to fix it.

He entered the house through the back door and found Mrs Mac counting sheets in the linen press.

The housekeeper turned to him. 'You're home then, sir.'

'For a short time. I'm travelling to Perth tomorrow. Can you see I have a bag packed, please?'

Mrs Mac's expression dropped. 'Tomorrow?'

Connor's step checked. 'Is that a problem, Mrs Mac?'

'Aye, well, you see, sir, Mrs Munro… she's not been herself.'

Connor frowned. 'In what way?'

'Nay I think it's just a phase. The wee mistress has been missing you.' When agitated Mrs Mac's Scottish accent became more pronounced.

'What's happened? Where is your mistress?'

'I think in her room, but—'

Connor walked away ignoring the rest of her words. He strode down the hallway to the bedrooms and after a slight knock entered Nancy's. He stopped and stared. Nancy still wore her nightgown even though it was the afternoon. Her long dark hair hung in tangles. She held a glass of whisky in one hand and the stare she gave him was of pure hatred.

'Drinking in the afternoon, Nancy?'

'Whys not?' she slurred. 'Why shh… should I care… what time… it is?'

'This is no way to behave.'

'How sh-should I behave? Like you?' She hiccupped. 'You and your-your whore?'

'Don't!' he snapped. 'Don't make this someone else's fault.'

'You married *me*!' She waved the drink towards him, splashing some over the side of the glass. 'Me! Till death do us part…'

He flinched. 'I know.'

'But you-you don't want to be married to me anymore, do you?' She blinked slowly.

'I'm sorry. I thought I could make it work and that you and I running this place would be enough. Creating Munro Downs into the best sheep station in the country was all that I was focused on.'

'And my father's money helped you…' She swayed in her chair. 'You wanted the-the money.'

'No.'

'Yes. Marry the cripple and f-father will pay you well.' She laughed like someone demented.

'You were my best friend.' His heart broke at the sight of her. This wasn't the Nancy he used to know. Five years of being in the wheelchair and hating her life had changed her. 'Please stop drinking and let us talk sensibly.'

She shook her head and took another drink. 'You had... had your chance at Chris-Christmas, but you went off. Always riding away...'

'Nancy, please.'

'What, Connor? Please what? Forgive you for not *loving* me enough?' She poured more whisky into her glass from the bottle on her dressing table.

He raised his hands up in surrender. 'What do you want me to do?'

'There is nothing-nothing you can do. You can't love me as I want to be loved.' She shrugged resignedly.

'I do love you, you know I do.'

'As a friend, like a sis-sister. Huh! It's always been like a sister. I don't want you as my *brother*, I want you as my husband, a man!' She threw the glass at the wall, where it shattered into hundreds of pieces. 'Not once... Not once have you ever thought to touch me with desire or passion. *Not once!*'

He blinked, horrified that she would even think that. 'We married as friends, you know that.'

She suddenly looked completely sober. 'You are a stupid, *stupid* man! I didn't want to be your *friend*. I *want* to be your wife, your lover, the mother of your children!'

He took a step back, confused and at a loss. 'When? When did you start to feel like that? We are mates. That's all we've ever been.'

'I've always felt like this, Connor. You were just too blind to see it.'

'That's not fair. You could have said something years ago.'

'Would it have made any difference?' she scoffed and turned her head away.

He ran a hand through his hair. He felt like the air had been knocked from him. 'I don't know.' But he did know, in his soul, that he hadn't desired Nancy the whole time he'd known her.

She laughed scornfully. 'No, I don't think it would have. You've always seen me as a mate. Even before my accident you didn't want to marry me. Then after the accident you felt guilty. I became the mate you married to save her from a life of being alone. Well, I hate to break it to you, Connor, but I've still been alone in this sham of a marriage.' She gripped the edge of her chair, her knuckles white. 'You spend every day out there, building your empire, and I've been stuck in this house, trapped, trying to keep busy, but slowly going mad with boredom.'

'I take you into Albany,' he defended and immediately realised how ineffective that sounded.

'You take me when it suits you. When you're not too busy and when you can drop me off at my father's house and forget about me for a day or two.'

'Am I such a terrible person?' He felt like one. He felt as though he was the biggest cad in all of the colony.

She sighed a long sad sigh, tears filling her eyes. 'No. You are simply self-centred like most men. I wish we hadn't married. I would have been happier with my father in Albany and not living with anticipations that never amount to anything.'

Never had he expected her to feel like this. 'I wish you had told me this before now.'

'Why? Would you see me in a different light? Would I suddenly become the woman you desire? I don't think so.' She wheeled to the French windows. A light breeze drifted up the lace curtains. 'My father will not allow you to divorce me.' She stared out through the open doors to the land beyond. 'He's too proud to have a divorced daughter back living with him. Besides, he gave us a lot of money for this station.'

Connor stiffened. He hated Nancy's father, the man thought he was some kind of God just because he was wealthy and a descendant from some lord back in England. 'I'll pay it all back to your father. I can give him a third of it right now.'

'Buying your freedom,' she said softly, tiredly.

'I'm sorry, Nancy.' And he was. He was so very sorry that he hadn't been able to make them both happy.

'I am, too.'

* * *

WITH HER HEAD against the warm flank of Daisy, the cow, Louisa pulled gently at the teats and squirted milk into the bucket. The easy rhythm was soothing to her troubled thoughts. Connor was constantly on her mind as was the lack of money to keep the station going. Both were concerns she couldn't control. Connor was married to Nancy as she was married to George. In the eyes of the law she was an adulteress, but in her heart, she was in love. In the two weeks since Christmas she'd not heard from Connor. She tried not to doubt his feelings for her, but it hurt that no note had come from him. Was he regretting their night of passion? She shook her head, making Daisy stamp her leg. No. He felt the same as she did. She was sure of it.

Aside from Connor there was the problem of money, or lack of it. She and George had talked until they were exhausted about how to gain more income. Selling land to Connor would ease some of the burden, but only temporarily. George alternated between wanting to sell the station to being dead against the idea of leaving. She didn't want to leave the station and argued the breeding of sheep could still keep them going, albeit as a much smaller concern. George's grand days of owning land as far as he could see, and living the high life of a rich gentleman, were now over.

'There you are, my dear.' George hobbled into the cow barn,

leaning heavily on his cane. His ankle could barely support him now and he walked with a limp and in constant pain.

She looked up at him. 'You need me?'

'Yes, in the kitchen.'

'Kitchen? Can it wait until I've finished here?'

'No. It's important otherwise I wouldn't disturb you. Leave that.' He waved towards the cow and bucket.

Untying the rope that held Daisy in the stall, Louisa pulled her around and sent her out of a side door into the field beyond. Picking up the bucket, Louisa glanced at George. 'What is this about?'

'You'll see. Don't wait for me, I'll catch up.'

Quickening her steps, Louisa headed for the kitchen. George's vagueness annoyed her. Surely anything to do with the kitchen was Su Lin's domain? She had no time for guessing games. Since the majority of staff had left the station she was doing so many jobs that each night she fell asleep before the moon had barely risen.

Su Lin wasn't in the vegetable garden so she skirted around to the front of the building and went inside the dim interior. 'Su Lin?'

'Here, missus.' Su Lin came out of the storeroom, a worried look on her old face.

'Mr Henderson says I'm needed.' Louisa placed the milk bucket into the stone sink.

'In there.' Su Lin pointed to the storeroom.

'For heaven's sake! What is this all about? I don't have the time for this.' Louisa stormed into the storeroom and jerked to a halt. 'Akala?'

The girl raised her head and peered through one eye not swollen shut from the beating she'd endured. 'Loo… sa.'

'Oh, my goodness!' Louisa fell to her knees beside the girl where she was curled up under the shelving. 'What happened to you?'

'Mother…'

Louisa blinked in confusion. 'Kiah? She is back? She did this to you?'

Akala shook her head. 'No, not Kiah.'

'You said mother?'

'Mrs Mother… Mrs Casey mother.' The girl began to shake. Talking had made the spilt in her lip widen and start to bleed again.

Louisa stared in astonishment, trying to make sense of it all. 'Mrs Casey thrashed you? She did this to you? She hurt you?'

'Yes.' The girl nodded but didn't cry.

'Why?'

Akala shrugged. 'No likey. Ses Akala bad girl. Akala never be whitefella. Never daughter.'

A blinding rage filled Louisa. She wanted to take a horsewhip to Mrs Casey.

'Missus.' Su Lin stood in the doorway. She held bandages and a bowl of water.

Swallowing the anger, Louisa forced a tender smile at Akala. 'Let's get you into the house and see to those cuts, shall we?'

Akala's big eyes widened. 'I no go back!'

'No, no. You're staying here. I promise you. This is your home now.'

'Stay with Loo… sa?'

'Yes.'

The strength seemed to leave the girl and she flopped against the wall. 'I stay with Loo… sa.'

Louisa's chest tightened with emotion. 'Come.' She took the girl's hand and led her out of the storeroom. Outside in the sunlight, Louisa hid her shock at how badly Akala had been beaten. The girl was all skin and bones, the thin smock dress she wore was filthy and torn.

In the spare bedroom, Louisa sat Akala on the bed and she and Su Lin tended to her cuts. The tenderness and bruising they could do nothing about, but when Louisa lifted the dress off Akala and saw the marks on her back she stifled a cry. She glanced at Su Lin, who shook her head sadly.

'Salve.' Su Lin left the room to gather the array of Chinese medical cures she had in a special red box.

'Why did Mrs Casey beat you?' Louisa asked Akala as she dabbed away the dried blood on the girl's back from what looked like whip marks. 'Did you do something very bad? You can tell me.'

'Mrs Mother wanted a daughter. Me be daughter.' Akala shrugged. 'I good. I clean. I stay quiet when doctor home. Mrs Mother angry I can't read books.'

'She was teaching you to read?'

'I no good.'

'Surely it must have been more than not being able to read?'

'Mrs Mother angry all the time. I burn food. I drop plates. I can't walk in shoes. Ribbons fall out. No daughter.'

A loud bang made them jump. Akala scuttled off the bed and to the corner of the room where she huddled into a ball. Louisa swung around as doors being thrown open and footsteps sounded. She stiffened in fright as a black warrior in full war paint stood in the doorway, a spear in his hands.

'What do you want!' She nearly screamed in terror, backing away and putting herself between him and Akala.

The warrior pointed. 'Akala!'

'Jarrah?' Akala scrambled out from behind Louisa's skirts. She spoke quickly in their language.

Louisa relaxed. Looking through the war paint she could see it was Jarrah. The native who led her through the bush to Albany and who she'd not seen since. He would not harm them.

Akala looked at Louisa. 'Jarrah angry.'

'Why?'

'Woman die.' Jarrah spat, the whites of his eyes showing his fury.

Scared, Louisa's stomach clenched. Her throat went dry and her heart raced. 'You're going to kill me?'

'No, not Loo… sa,' Akala said. She spoke again to Jarrah in their language and he replied. Then as quickly as he arrived he was gone.

Hand on her heart, Louisa felt the need to sit down on the bed for her knees were shaking badly. 'What was that all about? He looked terrifying.'

Akala sat back on the bed next to her. 'Mrs Mother. She will die.'

Louisa stared at Akala. 'No! No, Jarrah mustn't kill her. He will hang.'

'Jarrah not kill her. Spirits will.'

Su Lin poked her head around the door. 'Missus all right?'

'Yes. I'm fine.'

'Blackfella gone now.' Su Lin hurried into the room, long pigtail swinging. 'Mr Henderson watch him go.'

'Jarrah is family to Akala,' Louisa explained, feeling calmer. 'He wasn't here to harm us.'

She helped Su Lin to smooth the salve over the cuts and then dressed Akala in one of her nightgowns which was far too big but was better than nothing. With Akala tucked up in bed and eating Su Lin's food from a tray, Louisa left her to find George.

He smiled as she came out onto the veranda. 'Is the girl settled?'

'Yes.' Louisa sighed as she sat down. 'Jarrah has gone?'

'Yes. I watched him until he merged with the horizon. There was a pack of black fellas waiting for him at the end of the drive. I could just make them out.'

'Heavens, he scared the life out of me covered in all that war paint.'

'The blacks do look striking and fierce when they are all done up, I'll give them that. John and I once attended a corroberee of the tribe down by the river. They invited us as sort of elders or leaders. Black men only, you understand, so we were very privi-leged to attend being white. Very impressive.'

'I don't want Jarrah getting into trouble.'

'He won't if he's clever. There's fresh tea in the pot.' George indicated the tea setting on the table between them. 'Though I'd not like to be in Mrs Casey's shoes right now. She'll never know a peaceful day again.'

'Nor should she for doing such a thing.' Louisa poured out tea and then sat staring out at the expanse of fields. 'I feel so guilty.'

'You didn't beat the child.'

'No, but I left her there. I should have made her come with us when I left Albany.'

'We weren't to know that Mrs Casey would lose her mind like that and beat the child. Did Akala say why she did it?'

'From what I can gather, Mrs Casey wanted Akala to be a daughter to her of some kind. Only Akala is a native child, not a white child. She couldn't live up to Mrs Casey's expectations.'

'Like I thought.' George nodded wisely. 'Of course, the girl couldn't be as a white child. Silly of the woman to think she would.'

'But to beat her so badly, George?' Louisa felt angry and ill at the same time. 'I can't let this be. I'll have to confront her about it.'

'What good would that do though?'

'She can't get away with it!'

'No, you are right, she can't, but I think that warrior Jarrah might have his say first, and it might be enough.'

'I'll go into town tomorrow.'

'I'll come with you.'

'Is that wise with your ankle? You should stay here with Akala. I'll take Su Lin, we can do some shopping and get what we need. Akala needs dresses.'

'Well you might as well go to the bank and speak to Philip MacLeod, see how much is left in the account. I'll write a letter of instruction to him and stop by the solicitors and see Tom Andrews. I'll write down my directions regarding the sale of the land to Connor. Andrews will draw up the agreement. Invite him out for a visit, he's not been out here since our wedding.' George sipped his tea thoughtfully. 'I can't take care of Akala by myself, she needs a woman. Su Lin will have to stay. Hunt can drive you in the cart and he can get anything we need from the merchants.'

'Yes, I suppose that makes sense. I'll ask Su Lin for her list. We've not been into Albany for some time. We will need a great deal I should think. Can we afford everything we need?'

'Tell Philip MacLeod that Connor is buying some of our land. Show him my letter to Andrews. MacLeod should give you an advancement. I'll go speak to Hunt now. You'll need to spend the night in town.' With a grunt, George rose from his chair. He paused beside Louisa. 'The girl will recover. She has a home here with us and you'll be able to take care of her. Do not worry.'

She touched his hand briefly. 'I am pleased she is here with us at last.'

He patted her shoulder and left the veranda.

Louisa spent the afternoon with Akala, trying to make the girl feel at ease but nothing would take the haunted look from her eyes. She jumped at every sound and cowered easily. Louisa didn't know what to do to make her less anxious.

'You'll like living here,' Louisa told her as they sat on the grass under the large tree near the house. 'I'll teach you to milk the cows. Do you like milk?'

Akala shrugged and plucked at a grass stem.

'We used to have a nanny goat, but she was taken by some bad men.'

Akala jerked. 'Bad men?'

'Oh, don't worry. They are long gone now. You're safe here, I promise.' Louisa wondered if she could promise such a thing. Could she protect Akala from every bad thing in the world?

Akala looked lost and out of place wearing a huge white

nightgown which billowed in the breeze. She kept looking over the fields towards the bush on the horizon. Did she want to be out in the wild? Did she miss her mother?

Louisa sighed helplessly. 'There's a native camp down by the creek, do you wish to visit it?'

Akala shook her head.

The sound of wood being chopped came from the farm buildings. Akala whipped around, staring wildly.

'It's just Carter or Hunt chopping firewood,' Louisa soothed. 'You are safe here.'

'Mrs Mother come and find me.'

Louisa held Akala's hand. 'No, she won't. She will never come here. Trust me. She won't take you back, and you can stop calling her that. She's not your mother. Her name is Mrs Casey and you will never see her again.'

'No.' Akala again stared into the distance. 'Akala black fella.'

CHAPTER 17

A strong wind blew as Louisa left the haberdashery. Small whirlwinds danced along the street whipping up dust and leaves. She held onto her straw hat with one hand and her parcels in the other. Hunt had driven her into Albany the day before just as the sun was going down. She'd spent a restless night in a hotel overlooking the bay, hoping the bank would give her an advancement on the sale of the land.

This morning she'd gone straight to see Mrs Casey, intent on giving her a piece of her mind, but no one had answered the door. Frustrated she'd gone on to the bank where Mr MacLeod had reluctantly given her twenty pounds to buy what she needed. His dire warnings about the overdue amounts on the mortgage and overdraft left her so low in spirits she wanted to go straight home. However, her meeting with Tom Andrews had been more positive and he promised to have the paperwork regarding the sale done as soon as possible. With a warm smile he assured her he'd come out to King's Station in a week's time when signatures were needed.

Now, as she battled the wind, her eyes squinting against the dirt blowing in her face, she headed for the hotel. She was in two minds to ask Hunt to take her home right now, but that would mean travelling the last part of the journey in the dark, and a small part of her was happy to be away from the problems at the station.

The tearoom she had gone to the first time she met George was on her right and impulsively she went in as a group of women came out. Taking a table in the corner, she ordered tea and cake and remembered the day she was last here with George and Connor. How George had been so full of life and Connor so mysterious. So much had happened in just a year.

'Louisa.'

Louisa turned in her chair, a smile freezing on her face. 'Nancy. How nice to see you?'

Nancy wheeled closer. 'I did wave to you as you came in, but you didn't see me. Would you care to join me?' She indicated her table on the other side of the room.

Louisa balked, wanting to be on her own and not converse with Nancy of all people, but politeness made her say yes.

After settling in at Nancy's table and the waitress bringing over their orders, Louisa struggled to find something to say. She loved this woman's husband. She had the pleasure of him for a full night. Something his own wife had never had. Her pulse raced with guilt.

'So, George is selling land to Connor,' Nancy spoke as she poured out the tea.

'Yes. That is why I'm in town, to arrange it.' She glanced at Nancy, noticing her pale skin, the darkness under her eyes. She looked even thinner than the last time Louisa had seen her.

'George is not with you?' Nancy asked.

'No. His ankle pains him a great deal and he struggles to walk far.' Louisa forked a piece of lemon cake but couldn't eat it.

'Connor did mention it.'

'Is Connor not with you?' It was hard to speak his name.

'No, he's gone to Perth on business. To buy a new ram or

something. I thought to come and see my father while he was away. My father is not in the best of health.'

'I'm sorry to hear it.'

'I've come to buy a few things for him and treat myself to tea and cake, while he has a nap.'

'Are you staying in Albany long?'

'I'm not sure. It depends on my father's health.' Nancy pushed away her plate of uneaten sandwiches and stared at Louisa. 'You are looking very well, despite your problems. Married life seems to agree with you.'

Louisa smoothed down the white lace ruffle of her navy bodice. She had worn her best outfit today to impress the men she had to deal with. 'George and I have our struggles with the station, but we are a team. We work together in all things.'

'With Connor's help.'

'Connor has been the greatest friend to us.'

'You must be so grateful to have met him that first day you stumbled into town with the blacks.'

'I was, yes, but I would have been grateful to whomever helped me that day.'

'Yet it was my husband who came to your rescue and has been doing so ever since.' Nancy's tone grew bitter.

'As I said, he has been a great friend.'

'Do you have any regrets?'

'About what?' Louisa sipped her tea, not liking this encounter.

'Marrying George, a man old enough to be your father.'

'None at all.'

'Not when you could have been free to marry someone else? Perhaps a handsome younger man of wealth?'

Louisa stiffened. 'There is no man of my acquaintance that you describe.'

'Really? Did you even try to find someone else? You were so quick to accept George's proposal.'

'I proposed to George.'

'You did?' Nancy's eyes widened in shock. 'How unconventional.'

'No other man had offered to marry me, and we were causing talk by my staying with George. It seemed a logical thing to do.'

'Logical or calculating?'

'Calculating?'

'Did you think marrying an old man would leave you a rich widow soon after?'

'I never once thought that, not once!' Fury built in Louisa's chest. She wished she could tell Nancy the true nature of George's so-called wealth.

'Many people think that was your plan.' Nancy grimaced as though she'd tasted something sour. 'But if you'd gone to Sydney like you had planned, you'd have married someone there.'

'All that is irrelevant now.' She was hurt and offended by Nancy's stinging accusation. Why was she bringing all this up now?

'Is it?' Nancy's direct stare never left Louisa's face. 'Perhaps you and George should sell up and move away? Start again, far from here and the memories it holds. George is getting old. I'm sure you could both benefit from selling King's Station. You'd be able to live a good life somewhere else.'

Louisa felt as though she was being verbally attacked in a subtle, false-friend way. 'It's a consideration, certainly. But not one I think we will act on. We'll fight to hold on to the station for as long as we can. King's Station is our home.'

'King's Station is in dire circumstances, is it?' Nancy couldn't hide her smugness. 'And you *need* the land sale to Connor to help you out.'

Louisa eyed her suspiciously. This wasn't the normal conversation two women had over tea. Was Nancy needling her for information of some kind, or just being plain nasty? 'Are you not in agreement with Connor on buying our land?' Louisa asked. Was that the woman's problem?

Nancy shrugged. 'We don't need that land. That money could be used elsewhere on the property. I think he is thinking with his heart and not his head.'

Louisa's hand faltered as she reached for her teacup. 'A farmer always needs more land.'

'*We* don't.' Nancy lifted her chin, her expression cold.

'I must be going. I've much to do before I go home.' She'd had enough of Nancy for one day.

'Stay away from my husband.'

Half out of her chair, Louisa stared at her, not sure if she had heard her correctly. 'Pardon?'

'I will not make a scene here. However, if you don't stay away from Connor then I'll make life so hard for you that you'll have to move away. I have contacts. I'm a local person, well respected, and my father is a wealthy important man in this town. I will ruin you and George and King's Station will be worth nothing and no one will buy it.' Nancy pushed back her wheelchair from the table. 'Connor will *never* be yours.'

Louisa's heart thumped in anger. Nancy was a wolf in sheep's clothing. 'And you believe he is yours? Even though he doesn't love you?'

What colour Nancy had left her face. 'How dare you!'

Louisa leaned in close to whisper harshly, 'I dare! I won't be treated like a fool. You invited me to this table pretending to be a friend when in fact you only belittle and threaten me!'

'I am not your friend in the slightest.' Nancy's lip curled in disgust. 'You'll never have him!'

Louisa gathered her parcels. 'And you never did.'

Leaving the tearoom, Louisa pounded along the streets, raging at the useless feeling burning inside her. How could this complicated situation ever be rectified? She loved George like a friend and Connor felt the same with Nancy. How would they ever be together without causing a great deal of hurt? She groaned in anguish, not knowing what to do.

The sound of dragging chains and harsh commands halted her as she went to cross the street. Lost in her own thoughts she'd not seen the policeman on his horse, and trudging beside him a line of five men, chained to one another. The hounded men looked shattered, slumped as they shuffled along.

'Hang 'em, I say.' A man standing a few yards from Louisa waved his fist in the air. 'Robbing bastards!'

Shocked at his language, Louisa stepped away, but her gaze caught the eyes of the captured man first in the line.

Geoffrey Porter.

The bushrangers had been caught.

Geoffrey's stare narrowed as he recognised her, then he gave her a cold smile. Her stomach clenched in fear, but as the policeman flicked a whip and told them to hurry along, her sense of panic faded. They were caught and would surely hang. They were no threat to her or George or King's Station any more. The gang's hold up had nearly broken them, but once more she had survived another setback.

Louisa lifted her head and stiffened her back, she walked along the street and didn't look back.

'Missus?' Hunt nearly barrelled into her as she rounded a corner.

'Oh, Hunt. Good. I want to go home. Can we travel it in the dark?'

'Yes, we'll take it steady and light the lamp. Are you sure you don't want to wait for morning?'

'If you think it's unsafe then I'll wait, but I'd like to sleep in my own bed tonight.'

'Fair enough then, missus. The cart's all loaded at Paddy O'Leary's.' He took her parcels from her. 'It'll only be the last part of the journey will be in the dark. We should be fine.'

'Let us go then.' She walked with him towards the stabling yard. 'We can call at the hotel to collect my bag on the way.'

'Mrs Henderson!'

Sighing deeply at being hailed to a stop, Louisa glanced across the street and with dismay watched Doctor Jamieson hurry towards her.

'I'm so pleased to see you in town. I was going to come out to King's Station.'

'Why?'

'Mrs Casey is concerned over Akala. She'd like her to come back. We assume she has gone to you, unless she's gone walkabout?'

Louisa blinked in surprise. 'That woman wants her back? You cannot be serious, doctor? Do you honestly think I'd let her go back after the state she arrived in at the station?'

'The girl shouldn't have run away!'

'Run away! She is lucky to be alive after the beating she received!'

'Beating? What beating?' Jamieson looked baffled.

'Mrs Casey's treatment of Akala, a *child* in her care, is deplorable! I've a mind to go to the authorities over it, but the horrid woman would only deny it, and after all she is only a *black* child, isn't she?' Louisa said scathingly.

'I am not aware of any of this. Perhaps the child is lying?'

'Come to King's Station, doctor, and see her injuries for your-self. Mrs Casey treated Akala with no more thought than if she was a wild animal. I went to your cottage this morning to speak with your housekeeper about it, but she didn't answer the door.'

'Mrs Casey is unwell. She says a black warrior came to the cottage and frightened her half to death. He has put a spell on her apparently. She's taken to her bed and won't come out of her room. That's why she wants Akala back, to undo the spell. It's all nonsense, of course, as a man of science I cannot agree that a spell is effective. However, she is adamant, and she has become ill with the stress of it.'

'The woman is an idiot. She deserves everything she gets.' Louisa went to walk away, but the doctor's words forestalled her.

'Mrs Henderson, I was not aware of Akala being beaten, I hope you believe me. I would not condone that in my own home. True, I didn't want the child with us, but she stayed out of my way and I believed she was a help to Mrs Casey, so I allowed her to stay. This goes to show that the natives should not mingle with white people, it's not natural.'

She stared at him for several moments. 'No matter what colour a person's skin is, doctor, we all feel pain the same.' She gave him a look of loathing and walked away.

Hours later, Louisa regretted asking Hunt to take her home. A gale howled as dark rain clouds chased them along the dirt road towards home. The inclement weather brought darkness early and although Hunt had lit the lamp and hung it from the side of the cart, they had to keep stopping to relight it as the wind repeatedly blew it out.

They were halfway home and out in the open countryside when the hail hit them. The horse, called Pepper, shied, neighing in fright as ice balls the size of a child's fist pummelled them.

'There's nowhere to get out of this!' Hunt yelled at her above the noise of the hail hitting the cart. He had to work hard to keep Pepper under control. The wind whipped Hunt's hat from his head and sent it flying into the air. Hunt swore.

'What can we do?' Louisa held onto her own hat, the pins not strong enough to keep it on her head.

'We can't stop out here.'

The hail changed to a heavy downpour that fell so hard it blotted out the landscape. Within moments they were drenched and cold.

'Do you want to ride in the back, missus? You can get under the canvas.'

'No, I'm wet now. I can't get any wetter.'

A flash of lightning lit the pewter grey sky and thunder cracked overhead making them cringe at its loudness. Night descended quickly, and the lamp was ineffective against the wild weather. They trudged on, heads bent against the onslaught. Pepper snorted in fear every time thunder rolled overhead. With the storm not abating, Hunt climbed down to take the horse's bridle to lead him and his presence beside him settled the gelding somewhat.

After a few more hours they saw the distant twinkling lights of King's Station. Hunt jumped up beside her again and Pepper knowing he was close to home and a good feed, picked up the pace.

'We made it, missus.' Hunt gave her a grim smile, his hair plastered to his head.

'Yes. Thank you. I'll buy you a new hat, too.'

He gave a rare chuckle. 'It'll take me five years to break it in.'

They rounded the back of the house and Hunt slowed Pepper to a halt near the kitchen. Cold, wet and shivery, Louisa gratefully climbed down from the cart as Akala ran out from the kitchen.

'Loo… sa!' She thumped into Louisa, hugging her around the waist.

'I'm wet.' Louisa smiled. 'Let me get inside.'

Su Lin came out of the kitchen, holding up a lamp. 'Missus! You came through the storm.' She shook her head at the crazy notion. 'Mister George he not well. Glad you home.'

'Not well? What is wrong with him.'

'Old body, missus.' Su Lin's eyes were anxious. 'I'll make a hot bath and food, yes?'

'That would be heaven, Su Lin. Thank you. There are parcels in the cart. Everything you asked for.'

Su Lin mumbled something Chinese and hurried away as Louisa and Akala went into the house.

Louisa found George by the fire, dozing. 'George, I'm home,' she said softly so as not to startle him.

He opened his eyes and smiled. Sitting straighter in the chair, he frowned at the state of her. 'Look at you, girl. You'll catch your death. What possessed you travel so late? Come by the fire. I only lit it because of the storm. It's been a scorcher today. We were glad of the rain. I thought you'd be staying another night in town once you weren't home by sundown.'

'It was a late decision and one I regret!' She pulled at her wet skirts, staring at him. George looked dreadful. His eyes were sunken in his head, his skin pale, starkly showing the brown sun spots on his face. 'Su Lin said you don't feel too good?'

'It's nothing and you're home now.' He patted her hand. 'That always makes me feel better.'

Much later, after a wonderful hot bath, where Akala sat on the floor beside the tin bath in silence, Louisa ate a plate of cold ham and fried potatoes while telling George everything about the trip.

'Tom Andrews is coming here then for the signatures?' George nodded happily. 'That saves another trip for us then doesn't it? Good man is Tom Andrews. I must get my will changed while he's here. It's long overdue.'

They chatted for a little while longer about household matters, before Louisa yawned. 'I'd best go to bed. I'm worn out.'

George waved a hand towards Akala who slept beside Louisa on the sofa. 'She's barely said a word the whole time you've been gone. She's as quiet as a mouse, always hiding and jumping at shadows.'

Louisa looked down at the sleeping girl. 'Mrs Casey has done so much damage.'

'Well, from what you say after seeing Doctor Jamieson, the woman is suffering herself now. Akala will forget in time.' George eased himself up from his chair. 'I'm away to bed, too.'

Louisa rose slowly, not wanting to wake the child. 'I'll let her sleep here tonight. If she wakes she'll come into my bed.' She placed a thick shawl over Akala and then kissed George on the cheek. 'Goodnight. Call me if you need me.'

* * *

A WEEK LATER, Louisa was hanging clothes on the line strung between two trees at the side of the house. Su Lin usually did the job but she was busy preparing food for Tom Andrews's visit as they were expecting him any day.

Collecting the empty laundry basket, she looked around for Akala as she headed back to the kitchen. The girl had started a habit of disappearing during the day and only returning at sunset. She grew quieter every day and Louisa was worried the damage caused by Mrs Casey would never heal.

Rounding the kitchen wall, her heart leapt as Connor rode in. 'I thought you were coming tomorrow?' She greeted him with a smile.

'I arrived back from Perth last night and saw George's message. I thought to come straight over in case Andrews was already here.' Connor dismounted and led his horse into the stable block where Hunt took the reins.

'Mr Andrews isn't here yet,' she told him as they walked back to the house slowly.

Connor took his hat off and ran his fingers through his hair. 'Damn, that means I'll have to come back.'

'But you'll get another chance to see me,' she laughingly teased.

'I've not got time.' He sounded irritated.

She glanced away, hurt. 'We barely see each other as it is.'

'I can't help it. I have a station to run.' He paused and gave her a soft smile. 'Sorry, that was rude. I have missed you.'

'And I you.' She longed to reach out and kiss him. 'I understand how difficult this situation is.'

Connor slapped his hat against his leg. 'I don't see a way to fix this.'

'I know. I saw Nancy in town last week. She warned me off you.'

Connor stopped walking and stared at her. 'She did what?'

'She believes there is something between us.'

'I hope you denied it!'

Louisa stepped back, angry at his manner. 'What is there to deny? What could I possibly say?'

'You don't know her, or her family's reach in this district. She could ruin us both.'

'Is that all you care about?'

'You don't understand. I'm not going to lose all that I've worked so hard for over... over—'

'Over what?' Rage burned in Louisa's chest. 'Over *me*? Is that what you're saying? That I'm not *worth* it?'

Connor grabbed her arm. 'You are married to George. We have nothing at the moment. I can't see a way around this. It's driven me mad while I've been away trying to think of a solution.'

'What are you saying?' Fear replaced the fury. 'Do you not want me anymore?'

'Yes, of course I do...' His shoulders slumped. 'I love you, I know that much, but the whole situation is impossible.'

Her stomach clenched at the desolation in his eyes. He had said he loved her. Her heart flipped in response. 'Yes. It's difficult for us both.'

'We'll hurt George and Nancy if we continue this... this...'

'Nancy was nasty to me, but I understand that. She is losing the man she loves. I would feel the same if I was in her shoes.'

Connor groaned and looked up at the clear blue sky. 'We'll have to stay apart from each other.'

She nodded, unable to speak. One night that's all she'd had with him. One night to feel what it was like to be properly loved. She swallowed down the lump in her throat. She had no one to blame but herself. She had agreed to marry George knowing he was an old man, knowing that Connor wasn't hers. She hadn't waited to find someone else. No, she'd jumped straight into marriage with George thinking it was what she needed because she was alone in a strange country and was scared of remaining alone.

'I'll stay away. I can't see you…' Connor choked, tears in his eyes. He coughed and turned away. 'I'd consider it a favour if you'd encourage George and Mr Andrews to come to me to sign the papers. I don't want to come back here.' He stalked back to the stables to collect his horse.

'Connor,' she called to his retreating back, but he ignored her. In moments he was thundering out of the yard.

A range of emotions swirled through her head. Why was it all so hard? She was so tired. She felt as though she was constantly fighting for happiness. Whenever she thought she could be content, something happened to alter her life, first it had been her parents' death, then the shipwreck, the death of David, surviving living in the bush, then meeting Connor and George. How much more could she take?

Louisa walked away from the house, away from everyone and headed for the creek at the bottom of the paddocks. Her heart ached like she'd been stabbed. How foolish was she to fall for a man she couldn't have?

She walked uncaring of where she went. At that moment she wasn't concerned about anything and if she could walk until she died so much the better.

She heard the laughing long before she saw the children. She realised she'd ambled as far as the aboriginal camp which sat on the banks of the creek. Children were jumping into the water from an overhanging tree. Older boys, their black bodies shiny and wet, were daring each other to climb to higher branches and with whoops and screeches they jumped off into the water below.

Louisa watched them for a while and then realised that Akala was on the opposite bank, a part from the other children. She stood leaning against a thin tree, one finger in her mouth, watching the others. A group of girls played in the shallows, but she didn't join them.

Movement from further along the bank caught Louisa's attention. Several native women came down to the water, talking to the children. One woman, who Louisa believed was called Nia and who sometimes worked up at the house, called to Akala, but the girl shook her head and hid behind the tree. After that she was left alone.

Louisa sighed, feeling sorry for Akala. The girl was between two worlds. Not a white person but no longer a complete native either. Turning back for the homestead, Louisa felt weighed down by sadness and responsibility.

When she entered the house, she found George entertaining Mr Andrews in the front room.

'Ah, my dear, there you are. I couldn't find you.' George held out his hand to her which she took and stood by his side.

'It's lovely to see you again, Mr Andrews.' She smiled, forcing herself to act normally. 'Was your journey tolerable?'

'Dusty.' He returned her smile. 'But I have the delights of King's Station to compensate me.'

Louisa turned to George. 'Connor was here earlier. He extends an invitation to you and Mr Andrews to Munro Downs for the signing of the papers. Would that be agreeable?'

'Munro Downs?' Mr Andrews tapped his finger against his mouth. 'I would like to visit there, if that's acceptable to you, George?'

'Of course, of course. Splendid idea. Shall we go in the morning? I'll send a note tonight to Connor, so he knows to expect us.'

'I won't join you,' Louisa quickly added.

'No, my dear?' George frowned.

'I don't want to leave Akala again. You understand, don't you?' She knew he wouldn't question her further about that.

'Yes, indeed.' George patted her arm. 'Well, Andrews it looks like you and I are having a night at Munro Downs. We'll leave in the morning, but for now, let us take refreshments out on the veranda.'

They settled onto chairs and Louisa poured out tea that Su Lin brought on a tray.

Mr Andrews selected a piece of apple pie. 'What are your plans, George, with the money?'

'Firstly, we must pay our bills, which will give us some security until the next wool clip and lambing season. This money will keep the wolf from the door.'

'You must feel some loss at losing land you worked so hard to obtain years ago?'

George let out a long sigh. 'It is what it is, dear fellow. I am not of the age where I can start again and build. As long as we have enough to keep us going each year, then that is all I need.' He gave a warm smile to Louisa. 'We don't need much do we, my dear?'

'No. We live very simply here.' Louisa handed him a slice of pie. But he pushed it away. Surprised because George never refused food, she watched him as Mr Andrews talked of farming. Since the start of their money worries, George had grown older before her eyes. The lively talkative gentleman she had met when first arriving in Albany had been replaced by a worn-out old man who had lost his fight.

The following morning, Louisa sat at the table eating breakfast, her thoughts on Connor and his revelation that he loved her. How could she live without him?

'Good morning, Mrs Henderson.' Mr Andrews walked into the room, clean-shaven and smelling of soap.

'Good morning. Please help yourself to breakfast.'

Andrews poured fresh coffee from the pot and sat down. 'George not up yet?'

'It takes him a little longer to get ready in the mornings now.' She buttered a slice of toast. 'Have you been to Munro Downs before?'

'No, I haven't and I've been eager to see it for a while now. Munro Downs is the largest station in the region and I'm told it's like a small town.'

'Yes, I suppose it is.' She thought about Connor's home and realised she'd never seen much of the homestead or the working buildings. Her visits there had been contained to the house, making polite talk to Nancy. She would like to see the whole station and learn from Connor the skills it takes to run a big station, but then, what was the point for King's Station would never be as it once was. The reduced land and work force altered the dimensions of the place. The worker's cottages remained empty, the shearing shed was still a black burnt out ruin. Perhaps they could rebuild it with the land sale money.

'I thought George wanted to get on the road early?' Mr Andrews spoke breaking into her thoughts.

Louisa wiped her mouth with a napkin. 'I'll go see what he's doing. He's probably cut himself shaving.' She smiled at him. 'Help yourself to some more eggs.'

She left the room and went along the hallway. Usually she could hear George humming a tune while he got ready in the morning, but there was no noise coming from his bedroom. She knocked on his door and poked her head around. George lay fast asleep.

'Really!' She laughed and entered the room. 'George wake up. You've overslept, and we have a guest!' She shook his shoulder. There was no movement. She shook it harder. 'George! Wake up! Mr Andrews is waiting.'

A tingle of fear trickled along her skin. Hesitantly she touched his skin and jerked back at the coldness of it. 'George!' she yelled, shaking him. 'Wake up.'

She heard movement behind and turned as Mr Andrews came in.

'I heard you yell.'

'George,' his name came out on a whimper.

231

'Oh, dear God.' Andrews hurried to the bed and felt for a pulse on George's neck.

Louisa stared, realising that George's skin held a yellowy tinge.

'He's gone.' Mr Andrews stepped back. 'Good Lord, what a tragedy. I'm so very sorry, Mrs Henderson.'

Louisa couldn't take her gaze off the one man who had stood by her and given her the security she craved after the shipwreck. He was her best friend.

She was vaguely aware of Su Lin coming in and leaving again, filling the air with Chinese words. Mr Andrews took Louisa's elbow and led her out onto the veranda where she sat and gazed out over the paddocks, her mind blank. Moments later, a horseman rode fast down the drive, she thought it to be Hunt, but wasn't sure nor really cared.

George.

George was dead.

Mr Andrews joined her and placed a glass of brandy in her hands. 'It'll make you feel better.'

She held it but didn't drink. Brandy wouldn't make her feel better. She was alone. Again. She wanted George to wake up and smile at her. She needed him to come out onto the veranda and tell her he had another hole in one of his socks, or that he'd dreamt of being in India again. She wanted to hear his chuckle, his voice, listen to his stories and see his smile that he always had for her.

A hard knot of emotion seemed lodged in her chest.

She rose from the chair and slowly walked inside to her bedroom. She gently placed the glass beside her bed and then climbed under the blankets. She hoped she would never wake up.

CHAPTER 18

*I*n the days that followed, Louisa remained emotionally detached. George was buried under a large tree and next to John, his former business partner, in the small cemetery beyond the farm buildings. Louisa had visited John's grave before with George, and noted a few other graves surrounding the tree which belonged to King's Station workers who had died over the years. Mostly George had visited John's grave alone, for she had found it difficult after losing her brother, that David had no grave for her to visit, and so the little cemetery was one place on the whole station she didn't like to go near.

As at their wedding, many of George's friends from Albany and neighbouring farms came to see him laid to rest. Hunt had made the coffin himself as a tribute to his respected employer. A select group of the aboriginal elders stood a distance away to show their esteem to the Boss Man, as they called him.

Mr Andrews and Connor had organised everything and left Louisa to her silence and grief. She'd stayed in the bedroom and only came out on the day of the funeral. Once the mourners had departed, she'd thanked Mr Andrews for his support, ignored

Connor and Nancy altogether and then returned to her room and locked the door.

'Missus! Missus you must come out!' Su Lin's banging on the door disturbed Louisa from the half-daze she lingered in.

Disorientated, she scrambled out of bed and without thinking opened the bedroom door. 'What is it, Su Lin?'

Su Lin, despite being barely five-feet-tall, marched into the room and opened the curtains. 'No more sleeping, missus. You get up!' She flung the window wide, letting in the fresh air and sunlight.

'What are you doing?' Louisa snapped. She felt light-headed and annoyed.

'I bring in bath!' Su Lin gave Louisa a disparaging look. 'Mr Andrews, he come back. You make ready.'

Louisa blinked, not understanding. 'What are you talking about?'

'I bring in bath.' Su Lin snatched the key from the bedroom door lock and triumphantly popped it in her pocket. 'No locky!'

Left in peace, Louisa stood in the middle of the floor and tried to make sense of the old Chinese woman's jabbering. Mr Andrews? He was back? Why? She scratched her head and felt the greasiness of her hair. She'd not left the bedroom since the funeral and when was that, yesterday, the day before? She couldn't remember. She'd spent her days sleeping and her nights grieving for George. It was a pattern she wasn't ready to break yet.

She went to climb into bed but caught sight of herself in the mirror. Wearing only her nightgown, she looked like a pale ghostly figure of someone she used to be. Her hair, long unwashed hung untidily and she had dark shadows under her eyes. Her cheeks looked sunken, gaunt. When had she last eaten properly?

Su Lin returned carrying the tin bath. It took her several trips to fill it up with hot water. 'You get in, missus. I wash.'

'No... I don't...'

'Get in!' Su Lin demanded adding another bucket of water. 'Mr Andrews here.'

Slowly Louisa stripped off her nightgown which Su Lin seized upon immediately and bundled away.

'Why is Mr Andrews coming? And why must I see him?' Louisa knew she sounded like a petulant child, but she couldn't help it.

'Business, missus.' Su Lin pour a jug of warm water over Louisa's head making her gasp at the suddenness of it.

'I have no business with Mr Andrews.' Louisa grabbed a cloth and the soap and lethargically began to wash her body while Su Lin scrubbed her hair.

'I not know, missus. Rider came with message yesterday.'

'Yesterday? At the funeral?'

'Funeral last week!' Another jug of warm water was poured over Louisa's head to rinse the soap from her hair.

Louisa blinked, rubbing the water from her eyes. 'The funeral was last week?'

'You abed long time.'

A week? She'd locked herself in her room for a week! She couldn't believe it. Suddenly, her stomach grumbled loudly.

Su Lin tutted. 'You eat now.'

'Yes, I will,' Louisa promised, remembering the untouched trays of food that Su Lin left outside the door morning and night.

While Louisa dried herself, the little old woman hurriedly stripped the sheets from the bed, tutting and complaining in Chinese.

From her wardrobe, Louisa pulled out a black crepe skirt and bodice. King's Station had seen two deaths in just over a year and she didn't think she could handle it. She thought fleetingly of kind Edward, he too had died too soon.

She had not expected George to leave her so quickly. She

thought he'd have years left. A sob rose in her throat, but she fought the urge to cry.

Quickly she donned her undergarments and then the skirt and bodice. Her hair she brushed out and then still damp she twisted it into a knot at the back of her head and secured it with tortoiseshell combs.

Her reflection in the mirror looked washed out and pale, but she didn't have the energy to dab a bit of rouge powder to give colour to her cheeks. What did it matter how she looked?

Taking a deep breath, she lightly touched the deckchair in silent acknowledgment and left the bedroom, her sanctuary.

George's bedroom door was closed, and she was thankful for it. She walked to the front room. Her chest tightened at the thought of seeing George's things in the drawing room, so she averted her gaze and went straight out onto the veranda.

The fresh summer heat hit her like a physical force, even the slight breeze was hot.

Her legs felt weak and she leaned against the rail. A kookaburra laughed loudly from a tree branch, the noise making her flinch. She'd been in a silent world and didn't want to leave it.

'Missus, you eat now.' Su Lin carried a tray containing soup, bread and a bowl of strawberries. She set it on the table as Louisa took a seat. 'I make you tea.'

'Where is Akala?'

'Gone to creek. Swim.'

'Swim?'

'Swim. She play with children.'

'Oh, she is?' The knowledge that Akala was playing with the other children pleased Louisa.

'You eat. Make baby grow.' Su Lin suddenly pointed to Louisa's belly.

'Pardon?' Louisa frowned, sometimes she misheard the old woman.

'You make baby grow.'

'What baby?'

Su Lin indicated to Louisa's stomach again and gave her a look as though Louisa was a simpleton before scuttling back inside the house.

Gradually, and rather tiredly, Louisa ate the soup and nibbled at the bread. A baby? She tried to think rationally, but her head was fuggy. A baby. *She* was having a baby? What nonsense. The old Chinese woman was losing her mind.

The sweet taste of strawberries stirred her taste buds and she relaxed back and ate more of them. She thought of nothing, not trusting her emotions if her mind strayed to George. On the brown parched lawn, a magpie hopped about pecking at insects. She watched it for a while until the sight of a horse and gig coming up the drive made her sigh. She didn't want to see anyone or talk or be a hostess. She just wanted to be left alone.

Mr Andrews climbed down from the gig and took off his hat. 'Mrs Henderson. I'm so pleased to see you looking more yourself.'

She stood and shook his hand. 'Please have a seat, Mr Andrews, while I ask Su Lin for a fresh pot of tea.'

'Mrs Henderson…' He stood nervously twisting his hat in his hands. 'I am on my way to Munro Downs.'

'Oh, I see. I do apologise, I had believed you were visiting me.'

'I am… that is… I must speak with you and Mr Munro.' He was sweating and appeared ill at ease.

'Whatever is the matter, Mr Andrews?' Her stomach clenched at the thought of something else bad happening. 'Are you unwell?'

'No, that is—dear me. I have news, about the will. George's will and I must speak to Mr Munro.'

'Then why have you come here?'

'I thought… I thought to speak to you first, but I should wait. I'm not being professional, you see.' He took out a handkerchief and wiped his forehead.

Louisa abruptly sat down. George's will. Her mind whirled and her stomach rebelled.

'Mrs Henderson, will you not accompany me to Munro Downs?'

She recoiled as though he'd slapped her. Go to Connor, see him and Nancy! 'No, I can't!'

'Of course, of course, forgive me.'

'Tell me what you have to say,' she spoke harshly, frightened.

'Madam, I can't pretend this isn't happening. I'm sorry, but it can't be helped. I don't know what George was thinking, not changing his will after your marriage.'

'He… we… never got around to it…'

Mr Andrews pulled a chair closer to hers, his eyes anxious and worried. 'George's will was years old, over ten at least.'

She nodded already understanding what he was about to say. 'It's not mine, is it?'

Mr Andrews shook his head. 'I'm sorry, but King's Station now belongs to Connor Munro. George left him everything.'

She looked away, her gaze focusing on the magpie. Peck. Peck. Peck. Connor. Connor. Connor.

Mr Andrews cleared his throat. 'I'm sure Mr Munro will be generous indeed. He and George were such close friends, were they not? He was willing to buy your land to help you. I'm sure he wouldn't see you go without, as George's wife.'

Louisa summed up whatever courage she had left and gave Mr Andrews a fleeting smile. 'Please give my regards to the Munros. Good day to you.' She rose and left the veranda, not inviting him in.

Not wanting to return to her room, or see George's belongings about her, she walked straight through the house and out of the back door. Su Lin was busy in the kitchen, so Louisa skirted around it and headed towards the paddocks beyond.

Her feet kept moving, she had no idea where she needed to be or where she wanted to go. The sun blazed down and wearing mourning black she was soon lathered in sweat. She'd come out without a hat, so stupid of her.

She kept walking until the creek stopped her. For several minutes she stood watching the water gently flow by. Impulsively she stripped off her bodice, corset and skirt. Wearing her bloomers and chemise she stepped into the shallows and waded out into the middle of the creek. The water was low, being summer, but there was enough to cover her as she sat down. The coolness eased her over-heated body.

Tears filled her eyes, blurring the sky and clouds as she floated on her back. King's Station, her home, was no longer hers. She loved this place. She felt a sense of belonging here. How could she leave it? To walk away from George's memory seemed unbearable.

It all belonged to Connor, and he belonged to Nancy.

She glanced at her flat stomach and Su Lin's words banged into her brain. A baby. Su Lin thought she was having a baby. Why would she think that? Had she seen her and Connor in bed together at Christmas?

Her mind froze. Had that night created a baby? She blinked rapidly, trying to remember when she last had a monthly show. She couldn't recall.

She sat up abruptly in the water.

When? When was it? She had to think.

She'd didn't know when it was.

* * *

CONNOR STOOD by the window in his study gathering his wits about him. Andrews arrival was imminent, and he imagined that he would have Louisa with him for the reading of the will. Or would he? Why the man had wanted to do it here and not at King's Station he didn't know. Perhaps because Louisa had not left her room since the funeral? Maybe she hadn't left her room

239

today either. Should they have the reading of the will without her? He was desperate to see her.

Despite the need to stay away from her, for his own sanity, he couldn't do it. He'd ridden over every day since the funeral and asked Su Lin if she'd come out of her room. Each day he had ridden home more wretched that she refused to see anyone. He ached to hold her, ached to tell her that he would make everything all right again, but he couldn't do that. Nothing would ever be the same again.

He grieved for George keenly. The old man was his dearest friend and they had spent so many happy years building their stations side by side. Now he was gone, and the hole he left couldn't be filled.

Mrs Mac knocked on the open door. 'Mr Andrews has arrived, sir.'

'Thank you.' He sucked in a deep breath and left the room.

Nancy and Mr Andrews were talking in the drawing room as he entered, and he shook the solicitor's hand.

'Louisa is not well enough to attend,' Nancy said, her tone hard.

Connor nodded, unable to comment for the crushing disappointment.

'I called in to see her before coming here. She is suffering greatly.'

'And so she should be,' Nancy scoffed. 'George was such a good and decent man, who will be much missed by many. Maybe now she is only just learning what she took for granted and has lost.'

Connor clenched his jaw, fighting the urge to shout at the shrew which his wife had become. He stared at Andrews. 'You saw her? She has left her room?'

'How dramatic!' Nancy butted in.

Andrews eyed Nancy before giving a nervous look to Connor. 'Yes, I briefly spoke with Mrs Henderson.'

Frustrated, Connor took a seat by the unlit fireplace. 'Shall we get started? I'm at a loss as to why you wanted to read the will here. Surely King's Station is the more natural choice with Mrs Henderson in attendance when she is well enough? Shall we not postpone the reading? However, coming here won't be a waste of your time as I have other business I wish to discuss with you later. You are staying the night?'

Flustered, Andrews nodded. 'Yes. I'd be grateful to stay, thank you. Having Mrs Henderson here for the reading would be the correct thing to do. However, with Mrs Henderson being so indisposed and the contents of the will concerning you—'

'Me?' Connor blinked in confusion. 'Surely if George has left me a little something to honour our friendship, then you could have simply written to that effect?'

'But he hasn't just left you a *little* something.'

'I don't understand.' Connor jerked to his feet unable to sit still. 'Perhaps we should go to King's Station and speak with Louisa… Mrs Henderson. She may need our guidance.'

Nancy tutted. 'She is a grown woman and doesn't need *you!*' she snapped at him.

Connor glared at her, resisting the urge to walk from the house and ride straight to Louisa. He needed to hold her, talk to her.

Andrews opened a leather satchel and withdrew several papers. 'The will is fairly simple and straight forward, Mr Munro, and since I am here—'

'It is?' Connor frowned, switching his attention back to the other man.

'Oh, just let him get on with it, will you!' Nancy demanded harshly.

Quietly and efficiently, Andrews read out the will and with each sentence Connor grew more and more astonished. 'Surely there must be some mistake? George has left nothing for Louisa?'

Nancy laughed. 'Oh, what an exceedingly satisfying result.'

'Be quiet!' Connor grated between clenched teeth.

Andrews sighed sadly. 'George didn't change his will after his marriage. He intended to do it for he spoke to me of doing it the day he died. I was to write it up the following morning before we came here to get the land sale papers signed.'

'He would never want to see Louisa go without,' Connor could barely speak. His heart hammered in his chest. King's Station was his – all that extra land, another homestead, more water for bigger flocks, or even run a cattle herd instead of sheep. All of that was his, but at the expense of not only losing George, but robbing Louisa of everything she had.

'I will need you to come into town, Mr Connor, as there are papers to sign at the bank and the deeds for King's Station will be put into your name, and so on.'

Nancy grinned. 'We shall travel into town at your convenience, Mr Andrews. We have much to think about how we will manage a whole other station.'

'Yes, of course.' He looked worriedly at Connor. 'And Mrs Henderson?'

Nancy wheeled her chair closer to where Andrews sat. 'Mrs Henderson will soon be vacating King's Station, but she can take whatever will fit into a cart. I don't want her leftovers, and we are generous people, aren't we, Connor?' Her smug face made him murderous.

Without another word Connor stormed from the house.

CHAPTER 19

*C*oming out onto the veranda, Louisa took the note from the Munro Down's rider. 'Thank you.'

'No reply is needed, missus.' The rider doffed his hat, remounted his horse and headed back down the drive.

Opening the note, her heart fluttered expecting it to be from Connor. Instead she read the word, Nancy, at the bottom of the page and her stomach dipped.

Louisa,

As you are aware King's Station is now ours. Connor and I have a great many plans concerning King's Station and I'm sure you must be eager to start a new life of your own elsewhere away from such memories.

You have permission to take whatever you wish that will fit onto a cart, but you must vacate the premises by tomorrow morning.

Nancy.

P.S. Don't think to call Albany home, for you are not welcome there either.

. . .

LOUISA LOOKED up as another rider came down the drive. He passed the first rider, halting to talk to him for a moment before riding on towards the house. She waited for Connor to dismount and come up the stairs.

'Louisa.' He glanced at the note she held.

Silently she handed it to him and waited for him to read it.

'You're not leaving,' he said, screwing the paper up and throwing it onto the floor. 'She's not in control.'

'This is your home now.'

'No, it's not. It's yours. If George had changed his will in time, all this would be yours.'

'But he didn't, did he? And I can't stay now.'

'You must. I won't lose you.'

'The choice isn't yours to make, but mine. I won't stay here.'

'No, Louisa!'

'We know we did wrong. We broke the rules and now we are paying for it.'

'I won't let you go. I'll come with you.'

She smiled sadly, loving him so much she thought she would burst. 'We both know that is impossible. You can't simply walk away from Munro Downs.'

'It is nothing if you are not in my life.'

She cupped his cheek tenderly. 'I will never forget you.'

'No!' He crushed her to him, kissing her hard in desperation. 'You're mine,' he whispered against her mouth.

She sobbed against his chest, an unbearable pain in her heart. 'I have to go.'

'Just wait.' He held her by her shoulders and peered into her face, his eyes wet with tears. 'Listen to me. I'll leave Munro Downs, I'll put it up for sale, and this place. We'll start again somewhere else.'

'But Munro Downs is everything you've built. How can you leave it?'

'How can I stay there without you?' He kissed her softly. 'I can buy more land, more stock. You mean more to me than a station.'

'And Nancy?' Louisa wiped her eyes, getting control of herself once more. 'What of her?'

'I don't care. I don't love her.'

Walking away, Louisa leant on the veranda rail. 'I must go from here, Connor. I can't stand being in this house without George. I miss him too much.'

He came to stand beside her. 'Then go to Albany. Wait for me there. I'll speak to the land agent and the bank. Sort out my finances.'

'Then what?'

'We'll sail to Melbourne.'

A flicker of hope fluttered in her chest. 'Are you sure?''

'Do you love me, Louisa?' His earnest gaze, those beautiful blue eyes reached into her soul.

'You know I do!' She smiled. 'With all of my being.'

'That's all I needed to hear.' He kissed her again. 'Pack what you want to take. Take a room at Fiona's boarding house, by the water. Do you know it?'

'Yes, I had lunch there with George once.' Excitement grew inside her. 'I'll leave first thing in the morning.'

'I'll be only a day or two behind you. I'll just need to arrange everything, so Munro Downs continues without my presence. Tell Hunt, Su Lin and the others to carry on as normal. I'll pay their wages before I leave.'

'Yes, they'll need reassuring.'

'Go down to the docks and secure us a passage on a steamer to Melbourne. I think Paddy Jones sails to Melbourne every Friday. Book a cabin with him, mention my name. We are good friends.'

'I will.'

'I'd best go. There is a lot for me to do.' He pulled her in close for another long kiss. 'Safe journey tomorrow. I'll see you on Wednesday, Thursday at the latest.'

She held him tight. 'I'll be waiting.'

Once Connor had ridden away, Louisa went to her bedroom and began packing all her clothes. When her wardrobe and drawers were bare, she left the room in search of Su Lin and Akala.

She found Su Lin first weeding the kitchen herb garden. 'Su Lin. I have some news.'

The old woman straightened and faced her. 'Yes, missus?'

'I'm leaving in the morning. Going to Melbourne. King's Station doesn't belong to me anymore, it belongs to Mr Munro. He wants you to continue working here as normal and he'll pay your wages. Do you understand?'

'Yes, missus. I stay. Work for Mr Munro.'

'Yes, that's right.' Louisa hesitated. 'Thank you for everything, Su Lin.'

Su Lin bowed and mumbled something in Chinese. 'You be happy, missus. Baby make you happy.'

'You must stop talking about a baby! There is no baby.'

Su Lin gave one of her rare smiles and bowed. 'Su Lin no wrong.' She hurried away into the kitchen.

Louisa tossed her head, believing the old woman to be a little crazy. After speaking with Hunt and the other stockmen, Louisa headed for the creek to find Akala. The girl was barely at the homestead now, preferring to live at the aboriginal camp.

Akala was playing in the shallows with a group of young girls but on seeing Louisa she scrambled up the bank. 'You swim, Loo... sa?'

'No, dearest. I must speak with you though.'

One of the girls slipped and fell into the water making the others all laugh. Akala spoke in her language to the group and they laughed even more. It did Louisa good to see Akala accepted now.

'Listen to me, Akala.' She squatted down so she had the girl's full attention. 'I'm leaving tomorrow. Not coming back. Do you want to come with me?'

'Where you go?'

'To Albany first and then on to Melbourne.'

'Albanee?' Akala's eyes widened in alarm. 'Me no go to Albanee.'

'I'm going to Melbourne and will live there on another station eventually.'

'You go to big smoke?'

'Yes. Big smoke. Do you wish to go, too, with me?'

Akala shook her head. She glanced back at the girls who were splashing and playing. 'Akala stay. Akala not whitefella.'

'Of course. This is your home now.' From around her neck, Louisa unclasped the gold chain with the Whitby jet pendant she always wore and fastened it around Akala's neck. 'This is yours. To remember me by.'

Akala fingered the necklace. 'Loo… sa come back soon?'

Shaking her head, she felt the tears well. 'No, Akala. I'm not coming back.'

Impulsively the girl hugged her around the waist and then ran off down the bank to the water's edge. She stopped and turned to Louisa. Her smile was wide as she waved farewell.

'Goodbye!' Louisa waved, blinking back tears, and then lifting her skirts she hurried towards the homestead and to finish her packing.

* * *

CONNOR WORKED LIKE SOMEONE DEMENTED. He spent hours talking to his station manager, telling him of his plans in the strictest confidence, for he wasn't ready to confront Nancy with his news just yet.

At night, he stayed in his study, sorting out his financial

records, and updating the stock records ready for the sale. He wrote many letters, dispatching riders on the hour to the bank, the land agent, his solicitor and many other places of business in Albany.

By Wednesday he was deep in ledgers and paperwork. He'd not washed and only eaten bits from the trays Mrs Mac brought to him. He was counting out the money he kept in his safe when Nancy wheeled in.

'What is driving you so earnestly that you're cooped up in here all the time?' she asked.

'I've much to do.' He paused and stared at her. She wore the riding habit she always wore when she drove her small gig. 'Have you been out for a drive somewhere?'

'Yes. I needed some fresh air.' Her sharp gaze never left his. 'What is keeping you so consumed in this study?' she asked, eyeing the mess on his desk. 'Is it to do with King's Station?'

'Partly, yes.' He slipped a pile of money into a leather wallet and then started counting the next pile.

'What are your plans for it. George clearly let it run down to near ruin.'

'I'm selling it.'

Her eyes widened in surprise. 'Selling it, really? I hadn't expected that. I thought the extra land and the creek would be beneficial to Munro Downs?'

'Well, the new owner can buy this place as well, and have the whole lot for the right price.' He stood and closed the safe before putting another load of money in a separate wallet.

'What do you mean, buy this place?'

'I'm selling up.'

She gasped. 'No!'

'Yes.' He flashed her a cold smile. 'I'm leaving.'

'You can't. You live and breathe Munro Downs. It's all you ever wanted!'

'I want something more now.'

'Something more?' She scowled. 'I don't understand. What more could you want?'

He ignored the question. 'I'll see that you are cared for. You can go live with your father or once this place is sold I'll buy you a cottage of your own in Albany at your choosing.'

'What? No! I mean, what are you saying?'

'I'm going to Melbourne. I'm done here. I'm selling everything.' He stashed the wallets into a satchel and added some papers.

She was deathly pale and then her eyes narrowed with hate. 'You're going away with her, aren't you?'

'I told you I wanted a divorce weeks ago. I'm going to Melbourne where my family is.'

'With *her*.' Nancy grounded out between clenched teeth. 'You are, aren't you? Answer me!'

'I don't know what Louisa is doing,' he lied.

'Do you think I'm stupid?'

'I'll be leaving in the morning, Nancy. You can stay here until the place is sold.' He turned his back on her to tidy up some of the ledgers.

'She won't have you. I won't let her!'

Sighing, Connor swung around to speak, but froze on seeing the gun pointed at him. She had another pistol laid on her lap. 'What are you doing? Put that away!' Fear clawed at his innards. 'Nancy!'

The pistol blast shattered the quietness.

A searing pain exploded in his stomach. He fell back, clutching at the desk to stop himself falling. The room spun. He tried to stay upright, but his knees buckled. As he went down, he watched in horror as Nancy struck matches to his papers, their edges curling, going brown and then sparking flames.

His focus wavered as the pain ripped through his body. 'Nancy...'

She laughed dementedly as she lit more papers and scattered

them about the room. She knocked the lamp over and it broke, spilling oil across the floor. A lit paper lay in its path and with a sudden hiss the oil went up in a blaze, catching alight the curtains.

'Nanc...' Blackness was creeping over his senses. He tried to get up, to call out as Nancy laughed and put the other pistol to her head and pulled the trigger.

* * *

OUT IN THE BAY, boats plied their trades and an occasional horn sounded carried on a cool breeze drifting off the water. Louisa walked the veranda of Fiona MacDonald's Boarding and Tea Rooms. She reached the end of the veranda and walked back again. Pacing was the only thing that was stopping her from running out onto the street to keep checking for Connor. It was Friday and he still hadn't shown up. When he didn't arrive on Wednesday she didn't mind, knowing he had so much to do that he would turn up on Thursday. Yesterday, she had waited in all day, pacing the veranda, waiting for him, but again she'd gone to bed disappointed. Now it was Friday afternoon and still no sign or note from Connor. Their passage was booked on a steamer which was departing on evening tide at eight o'clock tonight.

'Mrs Henderson, I swear you'll tread a path on my floorboards with all your pacing.' Fiona came out with a tea tray.

'Sorry.' Louisa stood still, twisting her hands instead.

'Whatever is the matter?'

'I'm waiting for someone. We are to leave tonight for Melbourne.'

'And they are running late, I gather?'

Louisa nodded.

'I'm sure they will show up soon.' Fiona smiled reassuringly. 'Now, I'm away to the bakers to collect my bread supply.'

Left alone, Louisa continued her pacing, wishing with all her heart that Connor would walk onto the veranda at any moment. She made herself sit down and drink the tea Fiona had brought out, but she ignored the dainty cakes on the plate for her appetite was gone. Lately, she had felt queasy on first waking in the morning.

'Mrs Henderson!' Fiona's frantic calling made her jump.

'What is it?' she asked as Fiona hurried out to her.

'I've just been up the road to the bakers and many people were gathered about gossiping, at first I didn't take any notice until I heard the mention of Munro Downs, which is out near your home.'

'Munro Downs?' Louisa frowned, worried. 'What were they saying?'

'It's been burnt to the ground! Imagine!'

Louisa gasped. 'No. That can't be. Are you sure?'

'I went straight up to Mrs Fletcher, whose son works as a stockman at Munro Downs, and asked if it was true. She said her son, Robbie, had visited her yesterday after fetching the police.'

Sadness overwhelmed Louisa and she sat back down on the chair. That is what had delayed Connor then. His house had gone up in flames. 'I can barely believe it, such a beautiful house it was, too. Was anyone hurt in the blaze?'

Fiona unpinned her hat. 'Well, that is not all the news.'

'Oh?'

'Tragic happenings. I don't know what to make of it all, for the news will shatter this town.'

'What news?' Suddenly Louisa wasn't sure she wanted to hear it.

'As I said, Robbie was here fetching the police. You'll never guess why.' Fiona shook her head, a shocked expression on her face. 'Nancy Munro is dead.'

Louisa's stomach flipped. 'Nancy Munro? Are you sure?'

'I am.'

'How can she be dead? Was she unable to escape the fire?'

Louisa blinked rapidly in surprise. Nancy dead? She couldn't take it in.

'I don't know all the details, Robbie was in a tearing hurry and had to go and only managed to see his mother for a few minutes.'

'Are you sure she is dead?' Louisa felt it was too unbelievable.

'Apparently, she shot herself and her husband too!'

Louisa felt herself go light-headed, she gripped the edge of the table and fought the faint.

No, he couldn't be. Not now. Not Connor. It was all silly gossip, which spreads faster than bushfire and fuelled on half-truths. She slapped a hand over her mouth to stifle a moan of anguish from escaping.

'Connor Munro was one of the nicest men I have ever met. Such a gentleman,' Fiona said sadly. 'And one of George's best friends. To lose two wonderful men in the district in such a short time, I can barely believe it, really I can't.'

Louisa wanted her to stop talking. 'Connor is not dead. I would know somehow,' she whispered, her mind not accepting what she was hearing.

'No, he *is* alive, well *barely* alive from what Robbie said. There's not much hope for him.'

Her head snapped up and she glared at the other woman. 'You said Nancy shot him,' she snapped.

'She did, but he survived though, apparently. He's in a bad way. They had to pull him from the fire. He's probably burnt as well… poor man.'

'Stop! Stop saying such things. I must go…' She stumbled to the door on legs like jelly. 'I need to see Connor.'

'Go? My dear, you must wait until morning.' Fiona rushed after her.

'No! I must leave now. Please, will help me?'

'How? I don't have a pony and trap.' Fiona held onto her. 'No one will take you to Munro Downs at this late hour.'

'Then I'll walk. I must get to Connor!' Crying, Louisa couldn't think straight. Her thoughts were frantic and scattered. Connor shot, burnt, close to death. She couldn't bare it. Her stomach heaved.

'Wait here.' Fiona raised her hands as though in surrender. 'I'll go up to Taylor's Timber Yard and see if one of his men will take you. I can't promise you they will though. I'm sure they'll be wanting to go to their homes for their dinner.'

'Please try. I'll pay whatever it takes, but I must leave immediately.'

CHAPTER 20

*L*ouisa thought she'd never arrive at Munro Downs. The journey throughout the night proved slow and frustrating. A driver from Taylor's Timber Yard, a thin unwashed man called Spike, had offered to take her and she'd climbed on board his rickety old cart and set off as the sun was descending.

They hadn't got far when Spike pulled out a flagon of rum from under the seat and began drinking. At first, Louisa had tried to make conversation with him, anything to keep her mind off the disaster that happened at Munro Downs, but with every mile Spike grew drunker and less inclined to talk.

Before long, Spike was slouched on the seat, the reins drooping from his fingers. Taking control, Louisa drove the old nag onwards through the night while Spike snored beside her.

They rumbled past the gates of King's Station as dawn broke. She was surprised the nag had survived the journey for it was all skin and bones. Louisa couldn't see much from the road, but she longed for Su Lin's calming presence and her old age wisdom. Emotion clogged her throat as she thought of George. She missed him terribly.

At last as the sun broke over the horizon, flooding the countryside in golden-pink light, and setting the birds into chorus, Louisa set the horse through the gates of Munro Downs and up the long drive towards the smoking ruins of the house.

A dog barking woke Spike and he scratched his chin as he came fully awake. He looked at Louisa for a long moment as if trying to remember what happened.

'You all good, missus?'

'I'm fine.' She halted the horse at the end of the drive where it circled around the lawn and stared at the blackened remains of the once lovely homestead.

All that was left were brick chimneys, standing like scorched soldiers at attention. Through the odd wisp of smoke, Louisa saw several men standing at the back of the house, holding tin cups, talking quietly. The smell of burning wood was strong.

She handed the reins to Spike, climbed down and took her bag out of the back of the cart. Quickly she counted out some money and handed it to him. 'Here's your money.'

'Right you are, missus.' He touched the brim of his hat with a forefinger and turned the horse around.

'Go down that lane there to the stables. Someone will give you and the horse food and water.'

'Thanks, missus.'

Louisa picked up her skirts and hurried around the destruction towards the men, her heart in her mouth.

'You need some help, missus?' one man asked.

'Oh, it's you, Mrs Henderson,' another man said, breaking away from the group.

Louisa couldn't remember his name. 'Mr Munro is he… where is he?'

'He's been put in the gardener's cottage.' The man pointed further behind him, towards the outbuildings hidden behind extensive gardens and mature trees.

'Thank you.' She dropped her bag and ran as fast as she could, not caring that workers stared open-mouthed at her. Rounding

255

the corner, she saw a gravelled path which wound through the lush rose beds and nearly bumped into Mrs Mac.

'Mrs Henderson!' Surprise widened the housekeeper's eyes.

'How is he?' she croaked, bracing for bad news.

Mrs Mac's face softened. 'Nay, not so good. The doctor is with him now. How he survived the night we don't know. He's a fierce fever and has lost a lot of blood.'

'Take me to him, please.'

'Of course. Come this way.'

Louisa followed her down the path to a white wattle and daub cottage, which was tucked away behind a little orchard. Inside the cottage a woman stirred a pot over an open fire, she bobbed her head to Louisa. One door led off from the room into a bedroom. The room stank of blood, though it was spotlessly clean.

A tall man rose from a chair at the little desk by the window. He held out his hand to her. 'I'm Doctor Hanson, Munro Down's resident doctor.'

'How do you do? I'm Mrs Henderson, a friend of Connor's.' She let go of the man's hand and went to Connor's beside.

Lying still, face wan and sweating, Connor looked dreadfully ill. She glanced at Doctor Hanson. 'How is he?'

'I won't lie, Mrs Henderson, it's touch and go, but it has been since he was shot.'

'He will wake up though, won't he?' She turned to stare at him. 'He will recover?'

'I certainly hope so.'

She could tell he held something back. 'But?'

'The bullet went into his stomach and out through his back.'

She swallowed, tears filling her eyes and dripping over her lashes.

'If he survives his wounds, I am almost certain he will be paralysed. The bullet went very close to his spine.'

She jerked as if she'd been punched.

'I'm sorry to give such devastating news.' Hanson sighed.

Stifling a cry, Louisa sat on the chair next to the bed and took Connor's hand.

The doctor came closer to the bed. 'He has a strong constitution, which puts him in good stead. A lesser man might have succumbed by now.'

'Is there anything I can do?'

Hanson shook his head. 'Not really. Talk to him. I'd like him to wake up, so I can assess him better, but while he sleeps, his body is healing, or trying to at least.'

'I'll get you some tea, Mrs Henderson,' Mrs Mac said, making for the door.

'And I'll check my other patients. I run a small clinic once a week to check the aboriginal children from the camp.' Hanson gave Louisa a fleeting smile. 'That's where I'll be should you need me, but I'll be back soon.'

Once they had left her, she turned her attention fully to the man she loved. She carefully stroked his forehead, peering keenly into his face for any sign of him waking.

'Connor, it's me, Louisa.' She kissed his fingers. 'Open your eyes for me, please!' she begged him.

Through the day, Louisa sat beside Connor's bed, refusing to leave him. She helped the doctor sponge him down as a fever raged his body. Mrs Mac brought in numerous trays of tea and sandwiches for them both as the afternoon drew into evening.

Lamps were lit and outside the sounds of a busy station grew quiet and were replaced with the old night call of a bird and the bellow of one of the cows.

When Louisa woke, a pain shot down her neck where she had slept awkwardly in the chair all night. Doctor Hanson had gone to his own cottage, but she had wanted to stay with Connor.

Quietly, she leaned forward and kissed Connor softly on the forehead. 'Dearest, it's me, Louisa. You're going to be fine, but you need to open your eyes. I'm here for you, and will help you recover, and Mrs Mac wants to feed you lots of good food. Connor, please wake up. Doctor Hanson says—'

'How can I sleep with you talking to me?' he whispered.

She jumped as though he had shouted. 'Oh, my darling. You're awake!'

Connor moved and then winced in pain. He groaned and sweat broke out on his forehead.

'Don't move, my love.' She held his arms down by his side.

'What's happened. What's wrong with me. I hurt everywhere.'

'I'll go and fetch Doctor Hanson.' She started to rise but he touched her hand.

'No, stay. What's happened?' he asked on an intake of breath.

'You were shot a few days ago.'

'Shot?' he quizzed, then as he remembered his eyes clouded. 'Nancy.'

'Yes.'

'She shot herself too.'

'Yes.'

'She's dead?'

'Yes.' She tried to think of something else to say instead of yes.

'Poor Nancy. I made her unhappy. I should have tried harder to be a better man.'

'Connor—'

'There was flames.'

'The house is gone. Burnt to the ground. I'm sorry.'

'It's just a house.' His voice was dull, laden with sorrow.

'I must fetch Doctor Hanson.'

Connor nodded and stared up at the ceiling.

While Hanson examined Connor, Louisa paced in the other room which had been vacated by the gardener and his quiet wife. Finding a bucket of water, she had a rushed wash and tidied her hair. At the doctor's call, she entered the bedroom again.

'How is he?' she asked, sitting down. Connor was asleep again.

'His temperature is down, thankfully. I've redressed his

wounds. He refuses to believe he might be paralysed.' Hanson put away his tools of trade. 'Time will tell, of course, and I hope I am wrong, but he had no feeling in his toes when I pinched them just now. However, that could be down to the swelling near his spine where the bullet exited.'

Louisa's heart seemed to somersault in her chest. 'We must try to help him. The feeling might come back?'

'Perhaps. All we can do is let nature take its course and allow his body to heal.'

'He looks like he has some colour in his cheeks,' she said brightly.

Hanson patted her shoulder. 'The worst could be over. I'll return again in a little while. In the meantime, you must eat something. You must keep your strength up if you want to help me nurse him.'

'Yes, I will,' she promised, suddenly hungry.

Mrs Mac brought in breakfast, which Louisa surprisingly enjoyed as she sat by the fireside.

'Shall I make a tray for Mr Munro?' Mrs Mac asked, tidying the neat and sparse cottage.

'Yes, he may like something when he next awakens.' Louisa had a thought. 'Could you get a message to King's Station, Mrs Mac, and ask Su Lin to come here with her medicines? She is very good with them, George swore by her healing capabilities.'

'I don't know what Doctor Hanson would say.'

'He seems to be a busy man, perhaps he would like his duties shared?'

'Yes, well, He is a dedicated man, even attending to the blacks. And there is a large workforce here, injuries and sickness happen, and some of the men suffered burns when they ran into the house to save Mr Munro, though of course Mrs Munro was beyond saving...' Mrs Mac sniffed. 'What a business. She was a troubled soul.'

Louisa remained silent and rose to return to Connor. 'If you could have someone fetch Su Lin, I'd be grateful.'

Back in the bedroom, she rushed to Connor's side when she saw he was awake.

'Can I get you anything?' She held his hand. 'Are you hungry or thirsty?'

'Water, please,' he said weakly. 'I don't like you seeing me like this. I feel as feeble as a kitten.'

'You've been shot, Connor, of course you're going to feel frail.' She held his head up so he could sip from a cup, but even that movement made him moan in pain.

'Hanson believes I won't walk again.' Connor stared at her. 'If that's true then I won't want to live as Nancy did, stuck in a wheelchair for the rest of my life until I'm twisted with bitterness as she was.'

'Don't talk this way, please. Your body will heal, and you will walk again.'

'But if I don't,' he gripped her hands tightly. 'I'll put a gun to my head too.'

She reared back. 'No! Stop it.' She walked to the window and stared blindly out of it, then suddenly she turned and gripped the bottom bedrail. 'How dare you speak of such things to me,' she said harshly. 'Do you think I've not suffered enough? I've survived a shipwreck, my brother being struck down before my eyes, George dying, you being shot! And now you say you'll easily take your own life just because you can't walk? What about me? Do you want to leave me to be on my own again?'

'Louisa…'

Tears filled her eyes. 'I can't take much more.'

'I'm sorry.'

'You have much to live for, Connor.' She swallowed and took a shuddering breath.

'Do I?'

'Yes! Me! There is nothing stopping us from marrying when you have fully recovered.'

Anger blazed in his blue eyes. 'I won't marry you if I can't walk.'

She raised her trembling chin in defiance. 'If I was in a wheelchair would you reject me?'

'But you're not.'

'But if I was? Do you love me enough to marry me no matter what?'

'Yes, but this is different.'

'How is it?'

'I have a station to run!'

'Then I'll run it for you, or with you. We'll do it together.'

'No.'

'Then we'll sell up and move to Melbourne.'

'And do what there. I'm useless now. What can I do as a cripple? No, I won't do it. I won't tie you down to me like this. We have to learn from past mistakes.'

Louisa gave him a haughty glare. 'You can stop feeling sorry for yourself for a start.'

'You don't *understand*.' He laughed suddenly, but it was a mocking laugh without humour. 'Nancy got her revenge, didn't she? Now I know how she felt. I guess I deserved it.'

Compassion quickly filled Louisa. 'You and Nancy should never have married, not when you didn't love her.'

'But I should have handled you and I better. I don't know…'

'You can't help falling in love, Connor.'

'I'm tired.' He turned his head away from her and closed his eyes.

Distraught, Louisa left the bedroom.

'Mrs Henderson?' Mrs Mac touched her arm. 'Is everything all right? Come with me. I think you need a lie down.'

Mrs Mac led her into the other room, where a cot bed had

261

been made up for her. 'I've made this up for you as you can't spend another night sleeping in a chair.'

'Thank you.' Louisa dithered, head down, fighting tears.

'I know how much he cares for you. I've known him for a long time, and I've witnessed many things. Mrs Munro was never good for him. Don't get me wrong, I admired that woman greatly, but towards the end, she started acting odd and took to drinking. I'm sorry she burned down that beautiful house. I loved that house as though it was my own.'

Louisa's head snapped up. 'It was Nancy that set fire to the house?'

'Yes. So, you see, her mind wasn't right at the end. She wanted to kill Mr Munro and herself. Thank God she only succeeded in doing herself in.'

Louisa couldn't stop the tears falling.

Mrs Mac came and put her arms around her and Louisa was grateful to feel the arms of another person around her. 'There now, a good cry will set you right.'

'I'm sorry.'

'For what? I know you and Mr Munro have affection for one another. I've known him too long, he's like a son to me. Mrs Munro didn't bring him the happiness she should have, and I was sorry for him and for her, and I'm sorry for you, too. You've been through it in the last year or two, haven't you, pet?'

She nodded, feeling wretched. 'We never wanted to hurt anyone.'

'Sometimes, you don't get a say in who gets hurt.'

Helping her into bed, Mrs Mac unbuttoned Louisa's boots and then put the blankets over her. 'Sleep now. I'll sit with Mr Munro.'

Louisa hiccupped and wiped her eyes, surprised by the compassion in the housekeeper who George had always said was a hard woman. Yet, perhaps, to survive out here in this country you had to be hard, and perhaps Louisa was going to have to be just as fierce if she was to last as long as Mrs Mac.

* * *

LOUISA WOKE the next morning to sunlight flooding the room.

'Morning, missus. Did you sleep well?' The gardener's wife brought in a bucket of water, her happy freckled face was a welcome sight.

'I did, yes, surprisingly. Is Mr Munro awake?'

'He was earlier, Doctor Hanson was with him. What a kind man the doctor is. He's not been here long, you know. We needed a doctor at Munro Downs though. Stupid stockmen are always getting gored by bulls or cut by barbed wire and the like.'

'I'm afraid I don't know your name, and I should since I'm staying in your cottage.'

'I'm Mrs Elton, and don't you worry about me and Mr Elton, we're fine enough in the shearers' quarters. They lie empty most of the year, you see, so we're fine up there. Besides, it's not forever, is it? Once Mr Munro is back on his feet, he'll rebuild the house as soon as he can.'

At that moment Mrs Mac came in carrying a breakfast tray. 'Good morning, Mrs Henderson, Lydia.'

Still smiling, Lydia Elton collected a few bits of clothes for her and her husband and left them alone.

Mrs Mac took the lids off the plates of food, but the smell of bacon made Louisa's stomach churn.

She dashed to the chamber pot and heaved into it repeatedly.

'Oh my!' Mrs Mac was beside her instantly, holding her hair up and patting her on the back. 'Goodness me.'

'I'm so sorry,' Louisa panted, wiping her mouth.

'Nay, you have no need to apologise. But it can't have been something you ate, you didn't have any dinner last night.' Mrs

Mac frowned. 'Are you in the family way, Mrs Henderson, if you don't mind me asking?'

Louisa closed her eyes and swayed. Heavens she truly must be.

'Never mind, my dear, many a widow has brought a child into the world.'

'Oh, it's not Geor—' She clamped a hand over her mouth.

Mrs Mac's eyebrows rose to nearly touch her hairline. 'Well, I say. That answers a lot of questions then, doesn't it?'

'It does?'

'Aye, why else would you rush through the night to be by his bedside? It's as I said yesterday, you love Mr Munro, don't you?'

Louisa nodded, feeling wretched under Mrs Mac's scrutiny.

Mrs Mac took a big breath and let it out slowly. 'Well, you two will have to get wed, that's all there is to it. It'll be the talk of the town, mind you, but you're used to that, aren't you?'

Later, after Louisa has washed and changed her undergarments, she donned the black gown of mourning again and headed for Connor's bedroom.

Connor was staring up at the ceiling, a white blanket over him. The little window was open allowing the soft morning breeze to freshen the room.

'Good morning.' She smiled coming to his side, her head in a whirl as much as her stomach.

He glanced at her. 'Is it?'

'Yes. For you are alive.'

'Apparently.'

'Connor! You promised me,' she warned him.

'I can't feel my feet, Louisa! What have I got to look forward to? Answer me that!'

'Our baby.'

His head jerked to stare at her. 'What did you just say?'

'I said, *our baby*.' She challenged him to look away.

He stared at her for several long minutes. 'Are you sure?'

'Yes.' She suddenly had to sit down now she had finally accepted the truth of it.

'From that one night at Christmas?' he whispered.

She nodded, her throat thick with emotion. 'I'm so scared…'

He reached out a hand and took hers in a tight grip. 'Don't be scared, for you have me, always.'

'You promise me?'

'I do.' His smile was full of love. 'A baby?' His voice was wondrous.

'So,' she straightened her back, trying to be brave, 'is that enough to get better and marry me? Or am I to have this baby alone and raise him as George's child far away from here?'

He blinked rapidly for a moment and she could tell he was thinking of her proposal. 'What if I'm a cripple?' he choked out.

'We'll adapt. You'll still be Connor Munro, the man I love.' She kissed him, showing him the deepness of her love and devotion.

For a long time, Connor lay silent. 'Help me.'

'To do what?'

'I want to sit up.' He started to push his hands under his hips and heave himself up.'

'Connor, no, your stitches. Let me get Doctor Hanson.' Full of concern, Louisa didn't know whether to run for the doctor or push Connor back down on the bed.

'Woman,' Connor gave a grimace that passed for a smile, 'I need to sit up.'

'Do you need the chamber pot?'

'No, I need to start getting better.'

'Darling, please, just relax and keep still. You're lucky to be alive. You are too weak to—'

'Lou.' He stopped her protest mid-flow. 'My love, I have to get better as soon as possible.'

'Connor, please, there is plenty of time.'

He tenderly placed his hand on her stomach. 'Not really. We need to get married and—'

Her eyes widened. 'Is that a proposal of marriage?'

'Of course, what a silly thing to say. You're the love of my life.' He frowned at her as though she was a little simple and continued, 'and we need to rebuild the homestead before this little one makes his appearance. You can design the house, if you like?'

Her heart melted at his gentle touch on her stomach. She never thought she would be anyone's love of their life. 'It might be a girl, you know.'

'And if she is, then we'll call her Georgiana, after George.'

Tears filled her eyes and she nodded. 'That would be a fitting tribute to a wonderful man. But if he's a boy?'

'David.'

She gasped back a sob. At that moment she couldn't have loved him much more if she'd tried.

Connor cupped her face, his gaze loving. 'I am determined to walk again. I won't let this incident affect my life with you. Somehow, I'll be the man you need and want. Do you believe me?'

'Yes.'

'You and I will build the best damn station the west country has ever seen, yes?' His expression was full of hope.

Louisa smiled tremulously. 'I look forward to doing that.'

'We'll unite King's Station and Munro Downs and raise our children to love the land. That's worth fighting for, isn't it?'

'I truly believe that is the reason why I survived the shipwreck.'

'Kiss me, my brave woman.'

And she did.

AFTERWORD

Author's Note

Through researching the complex world of Aboriginal regional languages, I've tried to use authentic aboriginal words for that small area of Western Australia, and I'm hoping I have got it right (I did my best). Any mistakes are mine alone.

ACKNOWLEDGMENTS

Thank you to my wonderful fellow authors in my various online groups who are always encouraging; there are too many to name!

To my editor, Jane Eastgate, thank you for finding my mistakes.

To my talented cover designer, Evelyn Labelle, you always give me what I want, thank you!

Thank you to my family and friends. Your support means the world to me, especially my husband.

Finally, the biggest thank you goes to my readers. Over the years I have received the most wonderful messages from readers who have told me how much they've enjoyed my stories. Each and every message and review encourages me to write the next book.

Most authors go through times when they think the story they are writing is no good and I am no exception. The times when we struggle with the plot, when the characters don't behave as we wish them to, when 'normal' life interferes with the writing process and we feel we haven't got enough time in the day to do all we have to do those messages make us smile!

A few words from a stranger on social media saying they

loved my story dispels my doubts over my ability to be an author. I can't express enough how much those lovely messages mean to me. So, thank you!

If you'd like to receive my email newsletter or find out more about me and all my books, please go to my website where you can join the mailing list.

http://www.annemariebrear.com

Printed in Great Britain
by Amazon

21989503R00158